WALKING
with
ghosts

WALKING
with
ghosts

BRIAN JAMES FREEMAN

Published in September 2018 by PS Publishing Ltd. by arrangement with the author. All rights reserved by the author. The rights of Brian James Freeman to be identified as Author of their Work has been asserted by him in accordance with the Copyright, Designs and Patents Act 1988

FIRST EDITION

ISBN
978-1-786363-23-7
978-1-786363-24-4 (Signed Edition)

Design & Layout by Michael Smith
Printed and bound in England by TJ International

PS Publishing Ltd
Grosvenor House
1 New Road
Hornsea, HU18 1PG
England

editor@pspublishing.co.uk
www.pspublishing.co.uk

Contents

Part One: Weak and Wounded

Part Two: More Than Midnight

Part Three: Dreamlike States

Part Four: Lost and Lonely

Acknowledgements

For my parents and for Kathryn, who lived through each of these tales with me, often more than once...

With special thanks to Peter Crowther and the entire team at PS Publishing for laboring over this beautiful edition; to Robert Mingee for dragging the best versions of these stories out of me with a chain-fall; to Vicki Liebowitz, Richard Chizmar, Mindy Jarusek, Norman Prentiss, Rick Lederman, Robert Brouhard, Tabitha Brouhard, Dan Reilly, Serenity Richards, and Brad Saenz for the technical support; to William Peter Blatty for the humbling introduction and all the kindness over the years; and to the editors who published the original versions of many of these stories. Without all of you, this collection would not exist.

"Running Rain" originally appeared in *Corpse Blossoms* edited by Julia Sevin and R.J. Sevin, published by Creeping Hemlock Press, October 2005.

"Mama's Sleeping" is original to this collection.

"An Instant Eternity" originally appeared in *Turn Down the Lights* edited by Richard Chizmar, published by Cemetery Dance Publications, December 2013.

"Where Sunlight Sleeps" originally published on *Horror Drive-In* edited by Mark Sieber, April 2009.

ACKNOWLEDGEMENTS

"Marking the Passage of Time" originally appeared in *Shivers II* edited by Richard Chizmar, published by Cemetery Dance Publications, August 2003.

"Walking With the Ghosts of Pier 13" originally appeared in *Shivers* edited by Richard Chizmar, published by Cemetery Dance Publications, August 2002.

"A Mother's Love" originally appeared in *Shining In the Dark* edited by Hans-Åke Lilja, published by Cemetery Dance Publications, February 2018.

"Pop-Pop" is original to this collection.

"Answering the Call" originally appeared in *Borderlands 5* edited by Elizabeth E. Monteleone & Thomas F. Monteleone, published by Borderlands Press, November 2003.

"The Final Lesson" originally published as "Bigger and Better" on Horrorfind.com edited by Brian Keene (2001) and as "One Last Lesson" in *4 Fear of...*, published by Borderlands Press, August 2006.

"Loving Roger" originally appeared in *In Laymon's Terms* edited by Richard Chizmar, Kelly Laymon, and Steve Gerlach, published by Cemetery Dance Publications, June 2011.

"Among Us" originally appeared in *Inhuman #5* edited by Allen Koszowski, November 2011.

"Not Without Regrets" originally published as "Pulled Into Darkness," a Limited Edition chapbook by Cemetery Dance Publications, 2004.

"What They Left Behind" originally appeared in *Shivers III* edited by Richard Chizmar, published by Cemetery Dance Publications, August 2004.

"The Temperament of an Artist" originally appeared as "Art Work" in *Writers' Workshop*, July 1995.

"The Gorman Gig" originally published as the Featured Short Story of the Month on HorrorWorld.org. Fiction edited by Nanci Kalanta, June 2006.

"One Way Flight" originally appeared in *4 Fear of. . .* published by Borderlands Press, August 2006, as "Passenger 36-B."

"Monster Night" originally published as an eBook original for Cemetery Dance's "13 Days of Halloween" celebration, October 2012.

"Tomorrow Could Be Even Better" is original to this collection.

"One More Day" originally appeared in *Shivers V* edited by Richard Chizmar, published by Cemetery Dance Publications, January 2009.

"The Christmas Spirit" originally published by the author as an eBook single and chapbook, December 2016.

"Silent Attic (Amy Walker)" was originally published as an eBook exclusive short story in July 2010.

"Danny Dreams (Daniel Walker)" originally appeared in a very different form as "A Dreamlike State," as an eBook exclusive short story in July 2010.

"Ice Cold Dan the Ice Cream Man" is original to this collection.

"Losing Everything Defines You" originally published as "Something to Be Said for the Waiting" in *Shivers IV* edited by Richard Chizmar, published by Cemetery Dance Publications, May 2006.

"As She Lay There Dying" originally appeared in *Shivers VII* edited by Richard Chizmar, published by Cemetery Dance Publications, October 2013.

"How the Wind Lies" originally published as a chapbook by White Noise Press, April 2016.

"Perfect Little Snowflakes" is original to this collection.

"The Plague of Sadness" originally appeared in *Shroud #11*, May 2011.

"The Last Beautiful Day" originally appeared in *Shivers VI* edited by Richard Chizmar, published by Cemetery Dance Publications, December 2010.

"Story Notes" copyright © 2018 by Brian James Freeman

Introduction

BY WILLIAM PETER BLATTY

In recent years, many critics and readers have claimed the short story is dead, but I believe they haven't been looking in the right places.

Take Brian James Freeman for example. Since he was fourteen years old, his stories have been published in anthologies and magazines where they have achieved positive reviews, acclaim, and nominations for awards—yet his most popular stories have been published on the Internet, particularly as eBook singles and small collections.

Some of these e-stories have been read by tens of thousands of readers, but because novels are the prized currency of modern publishing and he isn't a novelist producing books for the mass market, Freeman's work often goes overlooked.

That is about to change with the publication of this collection.

Within this volume are short stories featuring haunted men and women who are trapped by demons of their own creation. Many of these demons are figurative, but when you least expect it, there are a few literal demons as well.

In each of these stories you'll discover someone who might not be all that different from yourself, and you'll find yourself thinking about these characters for days, or even weeks, after you've closed this book. Do not be surprised if you return to the bookshelf to read one or more of the stories a second time.

Freeman's prose is clean and lovely, painting the canvas of the printed page so unobtrusively yet with such pronounced effect. These are evocative tales written with a clear mind that has focused in like a laser on a hidden truth about the human condition. Most of all, Freeman writes like someone who has seen the darkness lurking within the human heart and is compelled to shine a light on our deepest fears. His writing will leave you both chilled and deeply moved.

Now it's time to turn the page and begin your journey. Don't look over your shoulder and do not fear the darkness ahead. Freeman has lit a path into your heart of hearts, and he will guide you past the demons waiting there.

Just don't wander too far from the light or, like many of Freeman's characters, you might not find your way back home.

Foreword

BRIAN JAMES FREEMAN

This is probably a mistake.

There's a desire to use these pages as a crutch to prop up the works that follow, but stories should stand all on their own without any help from the author after the fact.

That said, this *is* probably a good time to address the most frequently asked question that arrives in my inbox. More than a few readers have been puzzled by why I only write short stories or novellas these days. They seem to believe I have a choice in the matter, but I really don't. As far as I can tell, my brain arrived from the factory wired to write short fiction. That's just fine with me. I *love* short stories.

My favorites dive into some fairly unpleasant subject matter. Why do these dark tales appeal to me so much? No clue. I don't even know where the stories I write come from, not really.

Ideas tend to arrive in a burst of unexpected inspiration, usually from a combination of things I notice in the course of my day. Occasionally, though, I'll just be sitting around, minding my own business, when an entire story forms from out of nowhere. It's like watching a short film unspool in my brain.

The biggest obstacle is whether I'll be able to translate what I see in my head into words on the page. This is much harder than you might think. I usually fail, but sometimes I capture enough of the power behind the original idea for the story to work. I'm not a natural at writing, words do not just glide out of my fingers and through the keyboard and onto the screen, but I try my best and I keep working at it anyway. What else am I going to do? The stories keep coming, demanding to be written.

My writing "process," such as it is, is to try to get *something* down on paper and then, once that part is done, spend as much time as I can editing that *something* into a readable story, if possible. This could be dozens of drafts. It could be more. Like I said, I am not a natural who gets things right easily or on the first try.

In the end, no matter how many drafts I complete, the stories are rarely ever finished. Yes, I do reach a point where I send the story out on submission, but every story in this collection has been revised or even rewritten for this book. Why? Because I know, deep down, I didn't do the story justice before. I *believed* I had at the time, but it turns out there were better words to use if only I had thought of them sooner; scenes that could have added texture if only I had realized they needed to be written; and other sections that never should have been written in the first place, what was I thinking anyway?

When I'm between projects, I'll often find myself drifting toward my "finished stories" folder—a poorly selected moniker if there ever was one—where I'll open manuscripts and tinker here and there until it's time to give up on them again.

That's where the title of this volume comes from. It's how I would describe my life with these short stories. In my head, I walked among these events, transcribing them to the best of my ability and then rewriting in an attempt to convey the realness of what I first experienced, but even after I typed The End, they never left me alone. Not really. These characters are still waiting for me to walk with them again. And I do. Often.

But it *is* better to have gotten the stories down on paper as best I can, that much is true. The ghosts aren't nearly as boisterous once the story is written and published. But still, they wait. They often have more to say.

Collected here are twenty-nine ghosts that have haunted me at one point or another since I was thirteen years old. I'm ready to visit with them again.

Shall we walk together?

WALKING
with
ghosts

Ghosts are always hungry.

— R. D. Jameson

One need not be a Chamber to be Haunted.

— Emily Dickinson

Monsters are real, and ghosts are real too. They live inside us, and sometimes, they win.

— Stephen King

PART ONE

WEAK AND WOUNDED

"The waters of our heart are deeper and faster than they look . . . "

Running Rain

THIS IS ONE OF THOSE PERFECT NIGHTS when he doesn't even need the streetlights.

The world is bathed in the beautiful glow of the full moon, enough light to see for miles in every direction when he tops the hills.

The trees along the sidewalks sway in the winter wind and a dog howls somewhere in the distance, setting off the other dogs in the neighborhood like dominos toppling.

Tonight, he runs.

Running frees him from the pain of life, from the memories, from the nightmares.

Even with the bitter air nipping at his exposed skin, he runs.

He runs and he whispers the names: *Benjamin, Amanda, Susan, Michael, Andy, Beth, Lauren, David.*

He crosses back and forth from one side of the neighborhood to the other, and he doesn't stop when he reaches the place where the blacktop road ends and the woods begin.

He continues onto the dirt trail the kids keep clear every summer, the winding path along the river.

He runs and he memorizes the way the moonlight shimmers across the icy water.

The way the moonlight dances.

The first time he saw this river, he thought: *Those waters are deeper and faster than they look.*

That thought has troubled him ever since.

When he returns home, he is out of breath and his hands are shaking and his lungs are burning, but he's free.

He's been cleansed for another day.

He stands on the porch in the moonlight, bent over, his hands on his knees, and he gulps in the winter air.

He consumes the coldness, but a fire still rages inside of him.

"How was your run?" his wife asks from the kitchen as he locks the front door.

She's making hot chocolate. He can hear the water boiling on the stove.

This is their routine.

This is all they can talk about.

He stands in the living room, his heart still racing.

"Not bad. I took the path along the river," he says.

There's a sigh in the kitchen.

He knows what his wife is thinking, what she'll say, so why'd he tell her where he went? Why didn't he lie? Why *can't* he lie about this anymore?

He has deceived his wife before, but he can't stop himself from telling her this particular truth over and over again.

She may as well just say what she's going to say. Then they can get on with the fighting. It's the only time they even talk to each other these days.

Each night they argue about him running near the river, but deep down, they're arguing about everything else.

Every secret. Every truth. Every lie. Every loss they share.

While he waits, he strips off his sweatshirt and unties his shoes.

Finally, with a trembling voice, his wife says: "Why don't you take a shower and have some hot chocolate?"

He doesn't respond.

Tonight, she's holding in the words she needs to release, but he can hear the tears well enough.

He stands in the shower, under the steady spray of water, and the pipes behind the walls whine like the pressure is so great they might burst.

The mirror fogs and the heat thaws his frozen flesh.

Goosebumps explode all over his body.

When the hot water hits his skin, he feels the night chill again.

It's deep inside of him; it's everywhere.

It's a coldness that will last for ages.

It's a coldness that devours him.

He imagines a block of ice inside his chest slowly melting, sending rivers of glacial water to the furthest reach of each of his limbs.

This thought reminds him of his father trying to explain to him the nature of a parent's love for their children.

He was merely a child then and his father had said: *The waters of our heart are deeper and faster than they look.*

His father was an educated man, but he wasn't good with children and the statement was meaningless to his son at the time.

Now those words mean everything and he wishes his father were alive to discuss them. Yet time only moves in one direction and not one second can be called back, no matter how badly we want it.

The squeak of the bathroom door interrupts his nightly meditation on the duality of love and loss.

He stands motionless, surrounded by the rising mist like a man lost in the fog, waiting for something to happen.

A moment later, the door closes again.

He turns off the water, grabs a towel from the rack. He steps out of the shower.

He's drying his hair when he notices the fogged mirror.

I love you, his wife has written in the condensation.

He wonders if something happened in her session with the therapist he refuses to see.

Maybe there was a breakthrough.

Maybe things are getting better.

Maybe they'll be able to move on with their lives soon.

Or maybe she's just desperate to feel like there's some kind of hope left for them.

When he enters the room, his wife is in bed, under the covers, facing away from him.

He is very quiet and does not turn on the light.

He dresses for bed, slips under the covers, and listens to his wife's deep, troubled breathing.

Eventually, he falls asleep, but only because he ran and repeated the names.

If he hadn't, he'd be up all night.

Not that his sleep will be easy.

There are still the nightmares.

There are still the memories.

These ghosts live in his mind and in his heart, speaking to him, telling him every lie and every truth he doesn't want to hear.

Sometime after midnight, he opens his eyes from a sleep so shallow it is worthless.

His wife is not next to him.

He crawls out from under the covers, muttering as his feet touch the cold wooden floor.

He puts on his slippers and robe.

He moves through the dark house, each step soft, as quiet as can be. He knows where every loose floorboard awaits and he avoids them with ease.

He stops at the end of the hallway, across from the kitchen where his wife is sitting on a barstool at the island.

She holds a photograph, clutching it to her chest.

She has lit a candle but otherwise there is no light.

His cup of hot chocolate is on the counter, forgotten.

He watches his wife cry and he considers his options.

A moment passes.

He returns to bed.

She doesn't need to hear his excuses and he couldn't find the words even if she did.

In the morning, the daylight sneaks past the curtains and burns his eyelids. He rolls over.

His wife is gone.

The school where she teaches is a forty-minute drive and she leaves before he even knows a new day has arrived.

She'll be back.

She always comes back, although most days she doesn't want to return to the house, to the neighborhood, to the town.

He knows this because he knows her.

She wants to sell the house, but he won't hear of it.

Why does he insist they stay in a place so alive with so many painful memories?

Maybe because their neighbors understand the pain.

They understand the grief.

They understand the anger.

Even if they don't truly *understand*.

Everyone in this neighborhood has lost someone: a son or daughter or close friend.

They've all memorized the names of the dead.

Benjamin, Amanda, Susan, Michael, Andy, Beth, Lauren, David.

That's why he needs to stay.

If they were to leave, he and his wife would be alone with their demons.

Here they can be haunted with everyone else.

As he lies in bed watching the sun slash a path across the room, he thinks about their only son.

Benjamin was the first to vanish into the woods, but he would not be the last.

11

In the months prior to Benjamin's death there had been a great deal of tension in the house.

When he wasn't with his girlfriend, he was depressed and locked in his room, playing music much too loudly, as if to provoke yet another argument with his parents.

He hadn't been accepted into any of the colleges he had reluctantly applied to, and he refused to see a therapist to examine the causes of his wild mood swings.

Anger to suicidal depression to irrational outbursts became the norm.

When gently pressed about his plans for after high school, Benjamin declared that taking more worthless classes wasn't his next step in life.

He wanted to be a rock star.

Or a movie star.

Or an Internet sensation with millions of followers.

Someone *famous.*

Benjamin said if he had to, he'd run away and make a name for himself all on his own.

But Benjamin was never going anywhere.

Benjamin was missing for nearly four hours before his father had any idea something was wrong.

His father had been out drinking with some coworkers, a relatively new habit that might have grown into a real problem eventually, and he thought that might be why his wife was still awake when he arrived home long after her usual bedtime.

But instead she told him she didn't know where Benjamin could be, his phone was going straight to voicemail, and she didn't know what to do.

He was really angry again and he said we were going to regret not supporting him after he was dead ... I thought he was just pissed because we wouldn't help him buy that car until he came up with a plan for the fall, but you know how he's been lately . . . *He said he was headed to the river with his friends, but it's so late . . . You don't think he . . . He couldn't have . . . right?*

He feared the same thing his wife couldn't put into words, and he thought of the river.

Something about that river had always bothered him.

Those waters are deeper and faster than they look.

He had warned Benjamin to be careful there, even when his son was just a toddler who thought the neighbor's shaggy dog was the most wonderful of all of God's creations.

He asked his wife to call Benjamin's friends, even though it was the middle of the night.

Some of them would be awake. Drunk or high, maybe, but able to answer the phone.

He sat slumped at the island in the kitchen with his chin against his chest as if waiting for a jury to return their verdict.

It came swiftly.

Benjamin's friends had last seen him by the river around sunset, but they didn't know where he went after that.

He had been in a foul mood, and he hadn't wanted to leave with them, and they had finally left him there alone.

They hadn't heard from him since, but they did know his girlfriend had dumped him earlier in the day.

She was headed to college in the fall. She said it was time for a clean break for both of them.

And now Benjamin was missing.

Running to the river that night was the first time he had run in years.

His legs shrieked in pain and he had to slow to a shuddering walk.

The heat of a million suns beat down on him even though it was night. His skin pulsated.

The humid summer air saturated his lungs as he limped and dragged himself forward, huffing and puffing with every step.

When he reached the trail at the end of the road, the path cloaked in darkness, he hesitated.

The swaying shadows seemed alive with his worst thoughts and fears.

But he pushed on, his heart hammering inside his chest, and when he reached the river, he noticed the way the moonlight lit the water.

The way the light danced.

He searched for his son, but found no one.

There was a rope hanging from a low-lying tree branch, though, dragging in the water. The swift current tugged on it with invisible hands.

He would think of that rope when the nightmares came.

When he returned home, his wife was hysterical.

He asked her to call the police, but he told her not to mention what Benjamin had said before he left to meet his friends.

He didn't want anyone thinking their boy might have killed himself.

There had to be more.

He was right.

Two police officers arrived and they said not to worry.

Teens stay out too late all the time.

Most runaways get tired and lonely and hungry and come back within days.

Benjamin was probably fine.

Don't worry folks, one officer said. *We'll find your boy.*

The police never did.

Three days later, the first body turned up, but it wasn't Benjamin.

Those waters are deeper and faster than they look.

He wanted to believe his son was alive.

Hope and faith were all he and his wife had left.

They hoped for the best, and they prayed Benjamin had run off to pursue his dreams, but once the first body was discovered, hope and faith were fleeting.

The Riverside Killer had come to town.

Each victim was found hanging from a tree branch over the river, their mutilated corpse bobbing in the fast-moving current like a bloated apple.

A rope was used to lift them into place.

Piecing together the little information they had, the townspeople realized the killer must not have secured Benjamin's body well enough and the water had dragged him downstream.

A rookie mistake on the killer's part.

That was everyone's best guess, and his mind would not stop churning over the facts of the matter on the night his running ritual began.

He started running after the third funeral, but he left the house not actually knowing what he meant to do.

He walked a few blocks before his legs switched gears into a slow jog.

His legs remembered what it meant to pound your energy, your rage, your restlessness into the pavement.

His legs remembered the sense of freedom running could unleash within a person.

Soon he was running every night, and when he was called to the path and the river by some force he barely acknowledged, he answered that call without hesitation.

It was his secret route.

It was his secret place.

Yet one night, when his wife asked how his run had gone, he couldn't stop the words from spilling out of his mouth.

He couldn't stop himself from telling her the truth of where he went every night, telling her every truth he had been hiding from her.

And now he still can't stop telling her those things, over and over again, even though that truth is slowly killing her.

———————

Eight teenagers died over the course of the summer.

Benjamin, Amanda, Susan, Michael, Andy, Beth, Lauren, David.

Then six months passed and no more names were added to the list.

Everyone asked who the murderer could have been, but all they had to hold onto was the moniker given by the media.

The Riverside Killer: another name no one in town would ever forget.

He remembers all of this and more as he lies in bed, wasting the day away while his wife is teaching her sixth-grade students.

He quit his job last fall after an ugly confrontation with his boss. No one has asked him to come back.

Instead, he spends his day drifting in and out of consciousness, reliving every decision, every mistake, every regret.

In the early evening he hears the front door open and close.

He opens his eyes.

His wife stands in the bedroom doorway, her blurry form almost shimmering in the setting sunlight.

His vision clears and his wife's beauty is stunning, and the lust that springs from within him surprises him.

She says she'd like to talk.

"We need to talk" are her exact words, a phrase that has never meant anything good, not once in his entire life.

She says she wants their marriage to work, but she needs his help.

He nods, but he's thinking: *If you had called the police right away, our son might be alive. All those other kids might be alive. Maybe the police could have stopped the killing before it began.*

Once again he refuses to see the therapist—he refuses without words, he refuses with a strong shake of his head—but his rejection of the idea doesn't seem to bother his wife the way it normally does.

She says she understands his reluctance, but at the very least he has to start talking to *her.*

They have to talk about something other than his nights spent running along the river.

She needs the marriage to work.

Their marriage is all she has left.

He agrees with everything she says, but he doesn't reply.

Later, when he leaves for his nightly run, his wife is sobbing as the door closes behind him.

Benjamin is dead.

He knows he has to accept this, has to move on with his life, but for now all he can do is run and remember.

Benjamin, Amanda, Susan, Michael, Andy, Beth, Lauren, David.

Maybe tomorrow will be the day he and his wife discuss where their lives are headed and whether they fit into each other's plans for the future.

But for now he runs.

Tonight, storm clouds are unleashing their cold rain in heavy waves.

He runs like the rain, free of the memories and the pain.

He runs along the muddy path in the woods and he watches the rain strike the river like a hailstorm of bullets.

He runs harder and he thinks: *Those waters are deeper and faster than they look*.

He runs and his legs burn and he wonders, not for the first time, if maybe there should be no tomorrow.

If he dies, he'll never again have to remember the memories he has sunk into the deepest waters of his heart.

Every night, he wants to run so fast that he leaves the memories behind for good, leaves them to drown in the river, but he's never fast enough to escape the knowledge of what he has seen and done.

He runs even harder, his legs nearly tripping over themselves in his frantic urgency, and he repeats the names of the dead.

He runs and he tries to forget what his son said the day he disappeared.

He tries to forget that his son had wanted to be famous.

He tries to ignore all the ways, both good and bad, a person can become a household name in the modern world.

Sometimes a moniker given by the media is enough.

His son's body was never found.

He repeats the names of the dead, and the rain and the river whisper them back.

The river calls to him.

If he dies tonight, he'll never again dream of why the Riverside Killer vanished without a trace.

Why the Riverside Killer will never return.

If he responds to the river's call, he'll never have to remember why the killing really ended...

And why he has the nightmares...

And why he must repeat the names of the dead...

And what *really* happened to his son...

The waters of our heart are deeper and faster than they look.

Mama's Sleeping

SOMEONE HAD SHOVELED the crumbling sidewalk and Jacob *was* grateful for that small favor as he made his way toward the brick apartment building, but he was also fairly certain he should have called off sick like most of his coworkers apparently had. Temperatures in the teens, wind chill less than zero, and most of his stops so far had required him to trudge through two feet of snow from the previous week's storm.

He wondered again what he was doing with his life. This was no way to make a living. Not only was the pay significantly less than the vo-tech program had promised, but people genuinely seemed to hate him. Sometimes kids threw snowballs or chunks of ice at his distinctive red and white work van with the VeriNet logo on the side. Adults yelled things he couldn't hear over the drone of the engine, although he was surprisingly good at reading lips when it came to the nasty names he was called.

Jacob had spent time in the joint and he never would have guessed that "cable repair technician" might end up being the most despised thing he could be known for. Some days he felt like public enemy number one, as if people thought he was personally responsible for the lies the flashy VeriNet advertisements used to get suckers locked in for two years of substandard service.

That said, he had a job to do—a job he *did* appreciate having, given his record—so here he was, making his way past the battered cars sleeping in the snow valleys their owners had excavated. There were also dozens of vehicles still cocooned in dirty mountains of ice, either because they were abandoned or because no one cared enough to liberate them. This had once been a nice part of town, maybe fifty years ago, but now you wouldn't want to be caught walking these streets after dark.

Jacob entered the lobby of the apartment building. Three of the overhead lights were busted and a fourth flickered as if taking a few last gasps of breath before dying. The green tile floor was wet with melted snow. A trashcan overflowed with junk mail. There was a dark puddle that Jacob slowly realized was blood no one had bothered to clean up.

"Jesus," he muttered. He checked the work order one more time — J Smith, Apartment 6B — and he groaned when he saw the date the troubleshooting call was logged. Four days ago. *Christ.* Folks were usually plenty pissed if one day had passed before someone arrived to fix their cable, let alone four.

He started up the stairs to the sixth floor, taking care not to slip and fall on the narrow steps. His health insurance plan was useless and he couldn't afford a trip to the emergency room. Hell, he wouldn't even be able to pay his *regular* bills if he had to take time off to go to the hospital.

As he passed the door to the second floor, he heard Mexican rock music blaring. Thanks to his time in prison, he *habla un poco de Español*, just enough to get by, but not enough to follow anyone speaking too quickly or a singer screaming over heavy guitars and drums. The song was probably about chasing *señoritas* anyway; most of that music was in his experience. Nothing wrong with that. He loved the *señoritas* very much. Who didn't?

The door to the third floor did nothing to block the noise of kids running and shouting in the hallway in a mix of English and Spanish and Spanglish. There were wails and piercing shrieks, the likes of which only children could produce, sounds that might be blissful happiness or profound anger or both. Jacob shook his head, wondering how the neighbors tolerated the commotion.

By the time Jacob reached the sixth floor, he was sweating. He located apartment 6B, knocked on the door twice, and announced his presence and his company's name, as was standard operating procedure. Then he waited to discover how bad his day might get. Sometimes he was greeted with a stream of profanities about how late he was, how long the customer had been without service, and everything else that was apparently his responsibility and burden. That said, sometimes the customers were gracious and appreciative of his work. There was no way to guess which way the service call might go. Nice part of town, bad part of town, it didn't matter. You met angels and assholes in both places.

After a minute, Jacob knocked again. The scheduled appointment window was huge, 11 AM to 4 PM in this case, so it was possible the customer wasn't home, which would absolutely suck given the stairs. He would have to make his way back to his van, report to dispatch, and wait fifteen minutes before trying to contact the customer again. If there was still no answer at the door, he could log the appointment as a no-show and let this be someone else's problem on a different shift. Or perhaps he would be back tomorrow. You never knew how the cards of customer service might be dealt.

As Jacob prepared to knock for the third and final time, he heard the click of a deadbolt unlocking. The door opened a crack and a metal chain sagged in the opening. At first Jacob thought no one was there, but then he spotted the eye peering out at him, halfway down the door, nearly at his waist. The eye of a child.

"Hello, I'm Jacob from VeriNet." He tilted the ID badge pinned to his parka toward that watching eyeball. "I was sent to check on a problem with your cable."

The door opened further, enough so Jacob could determine he was speaking to a little girl. Her yellow dress was dirty and there was a smudge of peanut butter on her face. Her hair was in a ponytail, but it hadn't been washed in a while.

"Mama's sleeping," the little girl whispered, raising one finger to her lips.

This wasn't an entirely surprising statement, not on this side of the tracks where half the kids had no fathers—immaculate conception babies some people called them—and their moms lived on food stamps and state assistance. Sleeping in until noon was probably pretty common in this building, in fact. Yet Jacob was shocked by the size of the televisions he saw in some of the most dilapidated apartments in town. Between what those luxuries cost to purchase—or more likely rent—and the price of the services VeriNet sold these people, he wondered why they needed so much help from his taxes.

The little girl stared at Jacob and he began to feel uncomfortable, as if she had somehow heard what he was thinking. Those eyes were both beautiful and haunting, and they were not trusting.

Jacob forced the thought from his mind and returned to his standard script for these situations. "There's a service fee if VeriNet has to send someone else again for the same problem. When does your mother usually get out of bed?"

"I don't know." The little girl sniffled and Jacob realized her eyes were wet with tears. "She hasn't woken up in days."

Oh ʃhit. Everything clicked. He had heard stories of technicians finding customers dead, sometimes in bed and sometimes on the toilet and sometimes in the garage with the car still running, but it hadn't happened to him. Not yet, at least. He took a deep breath.

"How many days?" he asked, keeping his voice calm and casual.

"Three. I think."

"It's okay," Jacob replied when he couldn't think of anything else to say. "Maybe she's just real tired, right?"

The little girl closed the door without another word. Jacob wasn't sure of his next move. He doubted anyone was home in the other apartments on this floor. They were too quiet compared to the rest of the building. His cell phone was locked in the glove compartment of his work truck, per company policy. And that little girl was in there, all alone, with her almost certainly dead mother.

Jacob was still debating what to do when the door swung open. He stepped inside and the little girl closed the door behind him. The living room was neatly decorated with shelves of books, several potted plants, two side tables with reading lamps, and a couch. There wasn't any clutter and the apartment smelled clean. The furniture wasn't fancy but it was well cared for. Maybe he had misjudged the people who lived here.

"Where's the television?" Jacob asked out of habit.

"Mama's room," the little girl whispered. "She has the television. I got the radio."

"Okay, just stay here. I'll check on her."

Jacob forced his best smile, set his workbag next to the couch, removed his heavy winter gloves, and entered the apartment's lone hallway. There were three doors. To the right was a bathroom and to the left was a bedroom where he could hear the local pop station counting down this week's hits. Straight ahead was the master bedroom.

Jacob's heart accelerated as he approached the bedroom door. He was almost certain of what he would find and he didn't know what he would do then. He certainly hadn't expected to be put in this situation when he left his apartment this morning.

Jacob knocked on the door. No answer. He struggled to remember the name of the customer on the work order, which he had left in his bag in the living room. A common name . . .

"Hello, Ms. Smith? This is Jacob from VeriNet. I'm here about the problem with your cable."

No answer. He knocked and spoke louder. Still, no answer.

Jacob turned the doorknob, stepped into the room. The curtains were drawn and he walked toward them, keeping his eye on the figure under the comforter on the bed. The sheets did not rise and fall. He didn't attempt to muffle the impact of his work boots, but the person in the bed did not react.

Jacob pulled the curtains open, allowing the blinding winter sun to flood the room, and as the light illuminated the bed, he was convinced the woman was dead. He didn't need to examine her any closer to be sure. Her skin looked like wax and she wasn't breathing.

Oh shit, Jacob thought, stepping out of the bedroom and closing the door. As he made his way down the hallway he did his best to keep his expression neutral, but he had no idea if he was successful. The little girl stood by the couch.

"What's your name?" he asked.

"Elizabeth. How's my mama?"

"You were right, your mother's sleeping." The words were a spur-of-the-moment decision. He saw a telephone in the kitchen. There hadn't been one in the master bedroom. He knew what he needed to do next. "Did I hear the radio in your room?"

"Mama says it's okay so long as I don't bother the neighbors."

"That's very smart of your mother. Can you show me your radio?"

"Okay, I guess."

Elizabeth opened the door on the left side of the hallway and Jacob followed her into the small pink and white bedroom. The radio perched on the petite dresser was a little bit louder now, but the music was still so soft the girl didn't have to worry about any neighbors complaining. Some teenage pop star Jacob couldn't name if his life depended on it was belting out a tune that sounded like every other song on the radio these days. Even the soft parts of the music were loud.

"Are you sure my mama's okay?" Elizabeth asked, her voice conveying suspicions that all was not well in her world.

Jacob knelt before her, wiping a tear from her cheek. He took her small hands into his much larger hands. He squeezed in what he hoped was an encouraging manner, and the sensation of her tender flesh touching his callused skin sent an electric jolt through his body. He released her hands and his face flushed.

"Everything will be okay if you're a *good girl* and don't make a fuss," Jacob said as he reached under her yellow dress.

Elizabeth's eyes grew wide in horror as Jacob's fingers looped into her cotton underwear and yanked them toward the floor. She squirmed backwards, but he grabbed onto her arm and squeezed hard. The struggle set his entire body on fire, sending more electric thunderbolts through every muscle. This was the burning hunger that had landed him in prison, keeping him away from temptation for several very long years—and yet his time in the concrete cellblock suddenly felt like it was so very long ago.

"Mama!" the little girl yelled. "Mama!"

Jacob slapped her across the face and shoved her hard to the floor. She landed with a grunt.

"I said to be *good*," he growled as he fell upon her. She gazed up at him in fear. Blood trickled from her nose.

The radio on the dresser beeped and a broadcaster interrupted the music for the first time Jacob could remember since 9/11. The voice on the radio was nearly frantic. Something major had happened, a catastrophe of some kind, but Jacob barely heard what the man was saying. He was too focused on seizing this opportunity.

"Be a *good* girl," he whispered, caressing the girl's face, smearing the blood across her cheek as she struggled.

Instead, she cried: "Mama!"

Jacob grinned. "Honey, your mama is *dead*. She's not coming to help you."

The radio broadcaster was speaking even more urgently, and this time some part of Jacob's brain heard the words, but he still didn't understand them. They made no sense.

Then a cold, dead hand gripped Jacob's shoulder and began to squeeze.

An Instant Eternity

"In life there is not time to grieve long
But this, this is out of life, this is out of time,
An instant eternity of evil and wrong."

— T.S. Eliot, *Murder in the Cathedral*

N O ONE WAS SUPPOSED TO BE in the abandoned town. The escorted group of reporters, photographers, and cameramen wore paper masks provided by the U.N.'s media liaison team and they wouldn't be here for more than half an hour. There had been no sign of any civilians when the four CH-47 Chinook helicopters circled the region on the way in and they didn't expect to see anyone on the way out. Only the insane and the sick would still be living here.

Stephen carried his camera close and he walked alongside Rick McDuff, a reporter whose career dated clear back to Vietnam. Nothing fazed him anymore. Stephen wished he could say the same, but he was merely a self-taught photographer on his first tour of duty outside his hometown and, even after several months of traveling to places like this with Rick, he didn't have the courage or the stomach to process the horrific scenes with a cold, clinical eye the way his much older colleague did.

They were passing a crumbling house when a hesitant movement in the shadows caught Stephen's attention. There was a young girl in there, wearing a dirty and tattered dress draped over her skeletal frame. Her skin was pale and her eyes were very blue.

"Rick, look," Stephen whispered, pointing as the girl ducked deeper into the shadows of the interior.

"The house?"

"No, the little girl."

"I don't see anyone," Rick said. He glanced at Stephen for a moment, as if to confirm he wasn't joking, and then back at the ruins. "They searched to make sure the area was clear, you know."

Stephen didn't reply, but he approached the doorway and peered inside. There was no one there and no other signs of movement or occupation, no indication of life at all. Just debris and the broken remains of a household.

"Guess my imagination got away from me," he said, not believing the words but trying to save face. Rick studied him closely as they hurried to rejoin the group and that made Stephen even more uneasy. He didn't want to feel any crazier than he already felt.

He hadn't expected to witness such horrible things when he took this job, but whenever he closed his eyes, he was greeted by an endless parade of children burned by the bombings, grieving widows digging shallow graves with their bare hands, people missing limbs, and scenes of heartbreaking destruction.

Other people's lives echoed through his thoughts like ghosts. Every burned-out car in the middle of a street told a story. Every buckled building. Every smashed skeleton on a scarred sidewalk. Every mound of dirt by the side of the road where the nameless dead rested. Sometimes, during the worst of the nightmares, he couldn't even tell if he was awake or asleep.

When Stephen was a teenager, his father had once drunkenly told him that death was actually a single moment of eternity and there was nothing you could do in that moment but accept your fate. If your time was up, your time was up. Stephen had thought his father was being melodramatic, as he often was while in his cups, but not anymore.

Terror and death surrounded him, whether his eyes were open or closed, and he just wanted to go home to be with his family, to leave this land of destruction behind forever.

The group of reporters entered the old town square full of wild grasses and bushes badly in need of tending. In the center of the square was a statue of a soldier, but almost no one in the group paid the monument any attention. In the distance was the highlight of their visit to this town. Down the hill from them was a nuclear power plant with four concrete cooling towers on an overgrown island on a narrow river. Everyone murmured excitedly.

Everyone except for Stephen, who was studying the ruins around the town square, searching for anyone else who might be hiding and watching them. Insects buzzed around his head, nipping at him, and the sunlight cooked his exposed flesh like a skillet. He felt disconnected from the world. Everything around him seemed to be shifting one step away from reality.

I need to get out of here, Stephen thought. *Or I might never leave this country.*

At least this visit would be quick. Several times the group had been cautioned about the continuing danger from the radiation. They were also frequently reminded by their guides of how the United Nations had dramatically flown into the Hot Zone after the power plant's meltdown to evacuate the community, losing two helicopters in the process. One had exploded on the ground and the other had been shot down by a rebel's surface-to-air missile stolen from an old military stockpile, but in the end, hundreds of townspeople had been saved.

The anniversary of the heroic rescue was the prepackaged story for this leg of the media field trip. Most of the journalists would run with it. Using the prepared news was easier than digging for something deeper, and in the end, you got paid the same either way.

The reporters stomped forward through the overgrown grasses of the town square to get a better look at the power plant, but this was as far as they could go. The road beyond the square was a live minefield.

An advance team had placed a row of tall red cones adorned with international warning signs at the edge of the square and there were also bright red flags indicating the locations of several mines just beyond the cones. As if to reinforce this message, thirty yards into the danger zone were the burnt and twisted remains of the U.N. helicopter that had exploded when it landed during the town's evacuation. Near the wreckage was also a pick-up truck that had been shredded by an improvised explosive device.

"Think you should take a few photos, Mr. Photographer?" Rick asked, scribbling a few names off the monument into his notebook.

Stephen understood the angle Rick had chosen for his report and he started snapping shots to illustrate it: the tall statue from a low view, the remains of the wooden fence that once surrounded the town square, and the charred framework of the burned buildings. When possible, he included the four concrete towers looming in the distance.

With the camera's zoom lenses, he could actually see the old power plant quite well. The island's native vegetation had already consumed the buildings and the thick vines would camouflage the towers before too long. In a few years, they'd simply appear to be some oddly steep hills on the river.

"Time to return to our rides," the lead media liaison announced in his thick accent. "As we take off, try to imagine what it felt like for all the townspeople who were rescued from certain death in some of these same helicopters."

"You get the shots you wanted?" Rick asked while he packed his notebook for the flight to the Green Zone base where they'd spend the night.

"I have enough." Stephen stood by the monument while everyone else dutifully filed back to the street, which led to the field outside of town where the helicopters waited, their powerful engines still revved and ready to go.

He was the last person in the town square. Something still felt very wrong to him. *Déjà vu*, maybe, as if he had been here before. Yet he never had been. He was certain of that. Then he heard a voice on the breeze. Someone calling for him from the group? No, the sound was behind him.

He looked toward the power plant and there she was again.

The little girl.

She was standing in the middle of the street, her eyes wide with terror. She remained motionless a few feet from the ruined pick-up truck as if his gaze had transformed her into a sculpture.

Stephen turned in the direction of the reporters and U.N. personnel walking briskly away from him. He had expected Rick to be waiting, but everyone was already near the top of the hill. No one had noticed he wasn't with them. Panic washed over Stephen.

"Hey, wait a minute! Hey, you guys! There's someone here!"

No one responded.

"Please help me," the little girl called.

Stephen hurried to the edge of the town square where the red cones and warning signs awaited him. He studied the street and the sidewalks lining it more closely than he had before.

Hundreds of mortar shells had peppered the area during the war and the holes left behind from the explosions had been filled with dirt at some point. Those dirt sections — some large, some small, some nearly the width of the street — seemed to be where the mines had been planted based on the red flags around the town square.

Stephen turned again to the group of people topping the hill.

"Hey!" he screamed, jumping and waving his arms. The group kept moving like they had already forgotten the town, vanishing from his line of sight.

"Please," the little girl whimpered.

There wasn't any time to waste. Stephen took a deep breath and slowly stepped past the cones and the warning signs, making sure his shoes connected with firm pavement. He was terrified he was wrong about the locations of the mines and every step made his heart leap in his chest with panic, but when Stephen reached the little girl, he released the breath he hadn't realized he was holding and he relaxed. He dropped to one knee so they were both about the same height.

"I need help," she said very quietly, as if she were afraid to raise her voice.

"Come here." Stephen took her small hand into his own. Her bright blue eyes were filled with tears. Her skin was tight against her bones. "I'll take you to the helicopters and they'll fly you to safety."

"No!" She yanked her hand free, but she didn't attempt to run away.

"Honey, we need to go right now."

"I *can't.*"

"Why not?"

With a trembling hand, the little girl pointed at her battered tennis shoes, which were speckled with dried blood. She was standing on a slight mound of dirt that had shifted under her weight.

"I heard it click," she whispered.

"Oh shit."

Stephen stood and gazed toward the top of the hill. He saw no one. He could hear the rotors speeding up as the helicopters prepared to leave.

In his panic, he almost started to run, but then he remembered where he was and stopped cold. Between him and safety were all those holes filled with dirt, the red flags near the town square, the cones with their warning signs facing away from him. He was definitely on the wrong side of the safe zone.

"Please don't leave me," the little girl whispered.

"I have to get some help. Don't move, okay? Not one inch. I'll be right back. I promise I won't leave you here."

"Please hurry."

"Just don't move, I'll be right back with help."

Stephen navigated his way past where he believed the mines had been buried. His eyes were locked on the ground and sweat poured off his face.

By the time he reached the town square, the first helicopter had risen above the tree line. If Stephen were lucky, they'd fly his way and someone would spot him. Even if they flew in the other direction, he should still be okay, though. The U.N. media liaisons were supposed to do a head count on each helicopter, just to be safe. When they did that, they would realize they were one person short and they'd count again.

Stephen knew he couldn't depend on Rick to realize his photographer was missing since they had ridden on different helicopters at least twice today and there was no assigned seating, but one of the media liaisons would notice. They'd have to notice. Taking care of the journalists was their job, after all.

Stephen raced across the town square while two more helicopters rose into the sky. They headed south, away from the town.

"Dammit," he whispered, breaking into a sprint, pushing himself as hard as he could, his legs churning under him, his camera swinging around his neck. He had been a track and field star in high school, winning several races at the regional level and even finishing in the top three for the high jump twice, but he hadn't maintained that level of fitness since he married and entered the workforce.

Stephen reached the top of the hill where the town's main street became a winding road that passed by a creek and the U.N.'s improvised landing field before twisting into the woods and continuing to an old highway five miles away. He started down the other side of the hill as the last helicopter lifted off.

"*Hey!* Hey, you idiots! You were supposed to count!" he screamed, running toward the field of overgrown grass and forgotten farm equipment. The helicopter continued up and then turned south, following the first three. Stephen jumped and waved his arms like a madman, but still, no one saw him.

"No, dammit! Down *here!*"

The last helicopter vanished over the hills, the sound of the rotors quickly fading away. Stephen was left standing alone in the field full of muddy boot prints, trampled weeds, and abandoned tractors. A candy wrapper blew past him on the summer breeze.

"Dammit, God dammit," Stephen muttered, rushing back to town. He topped the hill and was relieved to see the little girl hadn't moved. His legs were beginning to ache, but he didn't slow until he reached the memorial in the town square.

There he stopped and lifted his camera, focused on the girl, and snapped a couple of shots. If he didn't make it back, he wanted his photographs to survive and explain what had happened. He placed the camera on the wooden bench near the statue.

"You're going to be okay," Stephen called to the girl as he once again carefully navigated his way to where she stood. "Stay very, very still. I'll get you out of here."

"Please don't leave me again," the little girl whispered.

"I won't." Stephen knelt in front of her, wiped her tears away. "What's your name?"

"Lilly."

"That's a pretty name. Listen to me, Lilly. You can't move. Do you understand?"

She nodded.

"You heard something click when you stepped on the dirt?"

"Yes. The bad click. Like the one that killed Mommy. The one Daddy taught me about."

"How did you get here? Where's your father?"

"Daddy's a soldier."

"Does he wear a uniform?"

"Before Mommy died."

"What about after your mother died?"

"Daddy took me and my brothers to some cabins in the woods with some other soldiers."

Oh shit, Stephen thought. *Her father joined one of the rebel groups.*

"Then they went to fight the bad men and they never came back."

"How long have they been gone?"

"Since winter. I came here to find them."

Stephen thought about the last major offensive against the rebels before the truce, five months ago. That battle wasn't too far from this town, maybe ten miles, just outside the capital city. One last stand on the bloody riverbanks and small islands, a night of gunfire and explosions and bloodshed. He shot a lot of graphic photos afterwards, far too graphic to appear in the legitimate news, but there were plenty of websites that would have bought them if he had been selling. Instead, he had erased his camera's memory card at the hotel that night. He might have photographed her brothers or her father for all he knew.

"Mommy died over there," Lilly said, pointing. "We were walking to the market and a bomb in the ground clicked and she told me to get away real fast."

"I'm sorry," Stephen said. He put his hands on his knees to steady himself against a wave of dizziness. The street was so damn hot. The

34

tar in the pavement's cracks was bubbling and the heat shimmered in the air like dancing phantoms. His armpits were damp and his pulse was racing; he could hear his heart beating in his ears. His fingers shook, just a little.

"Please help me," Lilly whispered. "Daddy told me not to move if I heard a click when I was walking. He said he'd help me."

"It's good you didn't move. Are you sure you heard a click?"

"Yes. Like Mommy's."

"Lilly, you're going to be okay. Trust me."

She nodded, believing him in the way children are trained to believe adults. Then she glanced around, as if she heard a familiar sound, and her body swayed and her eyelids fluttered. Her eyes bulged and rolled. Her legs bent at the knees and she started to collapse.

Stephen reached out, caught the little girl by the arms, and held her so her weight was still pressing down on the ground. Her eyes remained closed and her body shook and for the longest moment of his life, Stephen was certain they were about to die. If her weight shifted too much, the mine would explode and they'd both be killed instantly.

Lilly's body stopped shaking, but her eyes didn't open. Stephen continued to hold the little girl in place, her tiny body surprisingly heavy in the blistering heat. He had enough time to wonder if she would never wake up—a terrifying thought considering he was supporting her weight on top of a high-explosive mine—before she began to blink and her eyes finally opened.

"What happened?" she asked, groggy, like she had been awakened from a deep sleep.

"Are you okay?"

"Sorry," she whispered. "I got dizzy. I'm so thirsty."

"It's okay," he said. "I can get you some water."

But he couldn't. Not here. This whole area was poison. There wasn't any clean water anywhere, and even if there were, he couldn't leave this little girl alone in her condition. Instead he kept holding her and he didn't say anything else until she finally spoke again.

"I'm so tired."

"You need to stay still, but don't worry, you'll be okay."

Stephen's mind was running red hot. He had seen so many people killed by mines since he came to this country. Stepping in the wrong place in the wrong field, driving on the wrong road. Once he had watched from a distance as a U.N. bomb disposal unit attempted to disarm a mine buried in the middle of a playground. The men were blown to pieces. They had been pros. They were dead.

Stephen wiped more sweat and tears away from the little girl's face. Considering how exhausted she was and given the situation, he thought she was holding herself together pretty well. Better than some adults he had seen. Maybe because she truly believed there was a way out of the situation, some means to fix this problem. She didn't know the truth like he did.

"Do you know what kind of bomb it is, Lilly? Did your father ever mention that?"

Her eyes had grown glassy, but Stephen's words seemed to wake her up a bit. She whispered, "It hops."

It hops.

A hopping bomb. Stephen understood. Rick had called them Bouncing Betties. They were quite popular for the rebels in this war thanks to all of the Army depots that had been overrun in the early days of the fighting. There were millions of these things littering the landscape, hibernating under the dirt, just waiting to release their explosive fury.

Stephen remembered sitting with Rick in some hotel bar as the veteran journalist explained that a Bouncing Betty was designed to launch into the air after a soldier activated it, detonating approximately three seconds later so the explosion would rip apart a whole group of soldiers instead of maiming or killing just one.

Stephen felt his heart sink as he held the little girl. There was no way off the mine for her unless he could somehow get the U.N. bomb squad flown to the town—and fast.

He contemplated his options. He could start running out of town immediately and hope to find help. It would take him an hour to reach the old highway, at least, and he had no idea what might be waiting for him there. Certainly not a bomb technician. *Maybe* someone who might be able to call for help if luck was on his side. But they'd need to have a working CB radio, which was hard to come by these days. Cell phones hadn't worked for years and the landlines were all blown to hell. Where were the nearest communities supposed to be again? Ten miles up the highway?

Lilly would never last that long. Not even close. She could barely stand on her own. How could he expect her to stand motionless for hours or even days?

His other option was to hope and pray that someone would just happen to come along, someone with the appropriate knowledge to help, or that the U.N. would realize he had been left behind and hurry back for him. But Stephen knew what hopes and prayers got you in this wasteland.

Besides, the media liaisons hadn't even bothered to do the head count like they were supposed to before taking off, so his absence might not be noticed until tonight. And even then, who would guess he had been left in this godforsaken town? More likely, they'd assume he had flaked out like so many journalists before him when they faced the horrors of this war. Some of his colleagues might check for him in the hotel bar, if they checked anywhere.

It could be days before they understood something terrible had happened and even then they might not guess he had been left behind on this trip. Kidnappings and murders were so common in this country, they'd probably assume he was dead in a ditch somewhere and they'd wait for his headless body to arrive in the morgue.

Stephen thought of his wife and daughter and his life back home. Rebecca and Tracy, waiting for him. Desperate for him to return safely. He thought of everything he could lose by making the wrong decision, right here, right now.

Then another idea took shape, one so crazy that Stephen was sure it was the result of the heat baking his brain. Two competing versions of himself started to debate inside his head:

Could that work? Really? Maybe?

What are the odds, though?

What other choice is there?

You're fucking kidding yourself, Stephen.

Well, I have to do something!

But you don't even know if the kid's right about the type of mine. Or what if Rick was mistaken about the way the Bouncing Betties work? What if the little girl's father was wrong about the type of mines in the first place? What the hell are you doing anyway? You need to get out of here before you die!

I can't leave her, I just can't!

The little girl whispered, "Please . . . I'm falling."

"Lilly, you need to stay steady for a little longer, okay? Can you support yourself for a minute?"

She wiped her eyes and nodded. Stephen released her arms, stood and stretched his legs, which were already stiff from kneeling.

She whispered, "Please don't leave me."

"I have to check something over there," Stephen said, pointing at the crumbling remains of a barbershop on the other side of the street.

"What about me?"

"Stay very still. Everything will be okay," he said, flashing a forced smile. "Don't move. I'll be right back."

She nodded, but Stephen could see how weak she was. Standing like that in the hot sun for even ten minutes had to be tough on her. She obviously hadn't eaten a decent meal in months and the water she'd been drinking was most likely killing her.

Stephen carefully made his way across the street to the ruined barbershop. He avoided any patches of dirt that seemed suspect and he reached his destination without incident. He didn't know for certain, but he thought he was probably outside of the blast radius. He watched the little girl as his mind spun with a million reasons why he should hurry away in the opposite direction instead of risking his life. He thought about his wife and his daughter waiting back home for him to return safely.

Stephen stretched his legs, squatting down, standing back up on his tippy toes, all the time watching Lilly. The movements came naturally enough. He had loosened these muscles thousands of times before high school track and field meets, although he had never imagined his legs could ever feel as old and heavy as they did today.

Stephen thought about his crazy idea again and the other voices in his head fell silent, resigned. He knew his timing had to be perfect. Everything had to be perfect. He also needed a lot of luck.

Lilly was frozen with fear, her eyes locked on him. Her legs were shaking badly and her arms twitched. She was about to lose her balance again, to pass out from the heat and the dehydration, and the mine would kill her where she landed.

She opened her mouth but no sounds emerged. She stared straight at Stephen, her eyes pleading for him to help her, to please do something or she would fall and she knew what that meant and she didn't want to die like her mother. Her eyes bulged and started to roll back into her head.

Before Stephen could have a second thought, before he could say a prayer or think of Rebecca and Tracy and have a change of heart, his legs were moving. He deftly dodged the dirt sections, his shoes hitting the solid patches of pavement he had selected on his way across the street.

Lilly's swaying became more pronounced and her feet were on the verge of shifting when Stephen slammed into her at his top possible speed. In the same movement, he grabbed her under her arms and lifted her off the ground. He bent his legs and his knees coiled like springs and he launched himself into the air toward the back of the pick-up truck, pulling the little girl tight to his chest.

Stephen's legs clipped the side of the truck and he tumbled forward, landing on top of Lilly inside the truck bed.

His life flashed before his eyes and Stephen waited what felt like an eternity for the explosion. Again and again his mind repeated the memory of his father talking about death. Right now, here on this abandoned small-town street, he understood his father has been correct: death was making a decision and no mortal could change the outcome one way or another. Death could claim whoever it wanted. There were no exceptions. Death was eternity and eternity was death and . . .

Time snapped back to normal. The three seconds were long past and there had been no explosion. The ragged photographer and the little girl were still alive.

Stephen rolled onto his side and checked Lilly to make sure she hadn't been injured when they landed. The little girl lay there, stunned, her eyes blinking out of sync. Her dirty legs and arms were scraped and dotted with blood.

Stephen gasped in a breath and pushed himself to his knees, tumbling over the far side of the truck, landing hard on the sidewalk. He lurched to his feet, stretched into the bed of the truck, and lifted Lilly into his arms. He carried her to the town square as quickly as he could, not daring to even glance over his shoulder. He didn't stop until he had passed the war monument.

By then Stephen's entire body was trembling as the adrenaline rush came to a sudden end, and he gently placed Lilly on the bench next to his camera. He leaned against the base of the tall metal soldier and stared down the street. There were metal prongs sticking out of the dirt patch Lilly had been standing on, but nothing had happened.

A dud! The damn thing was a dud! Stephen thought just as the mine was violently propelled into the air and detonated.

Even at this distance, the explosion was louder than anything he had experienced in his entire life. The pick-up truck flipped into the air as if lifted by the hand of God. Shrapnel rocketed through the town square, coming so close to Stephen's head that he could feel the superheated metal passing by his ears. The sound of the explosion echoed across the valley.

"Jesus," he whispered. His legs lost all their strength and he collapsed into the tall grasses. They pricked at his exposed skin like tiny knives, but he didn't notice. He didn't care. He couldn't believe he was still alive.

"Are we safe?" the little girl asked, one arm covering her eyes from the beating rays of the sun, the other arm hanging limply off the edge of the bench.

"We made it, Rebecca, we made it," Stephen said, rolling over and staring up at the monument of the soldier, which blocked the angry gaze of the summer sun from his face. That tiny bit of shade was a relief. Stephen reached out and took the little girl's hand into his own again.

"Who's Rebecca?"

Stephen realized what he had said. "She's my daughter."

He pushed himself to his feet, his entire body aching. He felt like he was a million years old. He retrieved his camera, securing it around his neck. He paused, glanced back at the burning truck. It was a miracle they were alive. In that moment of eternity, for whatever reason, death hadn't claimed them.

When Stephen looked back at Lilly, he saw she was already sound asleep. He could understand why. He was exhausted and the heat was nearly enough to knock him back to the ground, but there was no time to waste.

He wrapped his arms under the little girl and he carried her away from the death and the destruction that was her hometown. He would make his way to the old highway and from there they would search for someone with a radio. It was their best and only option.

While he walked, Stephen thought about his wife and daughter waiting for him in his hometown on the other side of the ocean. He didn't want to consider the long road awaiting the little girl. Her journey was just beginning and she had no family, no community. She was trapped in a nation torn apart by war.

But right now none of that mattered. She needed doctors, she needed medicine, she needed clean water and a safe place to sleep. If she didn't get medical treatment soon, her lack of family and a stable homeland wouldn't be much of a problem for her. The dead didn't really care about such things.

Stephen would shepherd the little girl to safety and then he'd secure a seat on the first flight home, even if it meant quitting his job to depart early. He desperately hoped he could leave his haunted memories among the overgrown fields and burned towns and the rivers that occasionally ran dark red with blood.

Death had given him a second chance and he didn't intend to waste it.

Yet for the rest of his life, whenever Stephen closed his eyes, he would see the little girl standing under the hot afternoon sun in the middle of the street, all alone in the abandoned town on the hill overlooking the nuclear power plant. He would never forget Lilly standing in her tattered white dress, frozen in place, her eyes wide and pleading for his help.

That image would haunt Stephen until the end of his natural life, until the moment when eternity returned to claim what it was owed.

Where Sunlight Sleeps

EVERY SATURDAY, HIS LITTLE BOY awakens with the rising sun. The middle-aged widower is already awake in his own bedroom down the hall. He has barely slept in the six months since his wife's tragic accident ripped her from their lives, breaking his heart and devastating his little boy, but he remains in bed and waits for the day to begin. What else can he do?

He hears his son's bedroom door creak open. He closes his eyes and pretends to be asleep. He hopes his son will not speak the words he always speaks on Saturday mornings, but the man's heart knows better.

"Daddy?" his little boy whispers.

The man blinks his eyes open, as if he's just waking up, and he forces a big smile for his son who stands in the doorway in his pajamas. The August sunlight sneaks around the curtains, washing across his little boy's angelic face. The father smiles even though he's frozen inside. He smiles and he hopes today won't be like every other Saturday for the last six months.

"Good morning, Timothy," he says.

"Mornin', Daddy. Can we go on the Mommy Tour?"

The father wants to sigh, but he holds his smile. This is what their therapist, Dr. Linda Madison, has advised him to do.

"Yes, of course. Give me ten minutes to get ready."

His son's smile widens as the little boy bounds back to his bedroom. The father's smile fades into a grimace. He dresses in silence.

———————

The father carefully pulls over to the side of the road and puts the car in park. His son sits in the booster seat in the back, still smiling and following every word of the narrative his father tells every week. Timothy never loses interest or gets bored.

"I would drop her off there and she would go in through those doors," the man says, pointing across the street toward the black and silver office building.

His son nods.

"Then I would drive across town to my work, but at five o'clock I would return here to pick her up and we'd drive home together to make dinner."

The man continues with the story, but his mind is elsewhere. Sometimes he imagines someone has placed a camera across the road to photograph this spot every Saturday. What would that person think of this same car with the same occupants making the same motions, having the same conversation, every week? The seasons have changed, from late winter to spring to summer, but the car appears to be eternal. Is this an echo of some past event? Are the passengers simply shadowy ghosts?

"Do you want me to show you where I met your mother?" the father asks, as he does every week.

The answer is always the same.

The mall has changed considerably in the ten years since the man and his future wife came here on a blind date. The food court where they shared the first of many frozen yogurts has since been torn down, replaced by teenager specialty boutiques with strange names like Wet Seal and Hollister. The man isn't even sure what those stores sell.

The man walks his son to the new and improved food court, which was built on the site of the old movie theater on the other side of the mall. He's grateful there aren't many people around yet.

"Here is the table where we met after Uncle Henry arranged for us to go on our first date."

This orange and blue table under the wide skylight is not the same table, but it serves the purpose for the story. The table is near the Starbucks kiosk that replaced the frozen yogurt stand from the old food court.

"Why did Uncle Henry do that?" his son asks for the twenty-fourth time.

"Because your mother was a friend of Aunt Alicia, and Aunt Alicia thought your mother and I could be great friends if we met. She was right about that, wasn't she?"

"You and Mommy were best friends, Daddy?"

"After you, she was my best friend in the whole wide world, kiddo."

As if on cue, his son says: "Okay, I want to see where you asked Mommy to marry you."

Dr. Linda said the so-called Mommy Tour would help Timothy heal by allowing him to connect with a side of his mother he didn't know. The doctor never hinted this event could become a weekly obsession for the grieving boy.

When the father questioned her about this development, she replied: "Sometimes kids dig these holes inside themselves and hide their feelings there, often bad feelings they're scared of. A colleague of mine calls this the place where sunlight sleeps. Your son will need your assistance to find that sunlight."

"What does that even mean?" the man asked, confused and tired.

"Well, if your son wants to take the Mommy Tour every week, it's because he's digging at something inside himself. Take your son and let him talk. Eventually, you'll learn something new about him and he'll learn something new about himself, and he will open up and reveal what he's been hiding."

The man didn't understand what the doctor was saying, but he would do anything to help his son, so the Mommy Tour continued like clockwork, every week, even after it began to feel like one of the circles of Dante's Hell for the man.

———————

The man slows the car to a stop near the curve in the dirt road. This state park has 40,000 acres of forest, but there was one trail in particular the man and his future wife liked the best when they hiked together the summer they first met. Being young and in love, they did certain things just out of sight of this trail that are not, for obvious reasons, mentioned on the Mommy Tour.

"Okay, Timothy, watch your step," the father says as he leads his son by the hand.

To get to Lover's Lookout (as the kids referred to the area when the man was a teenager) or to Scenic View Point (as the park guidebooks have always called it), you technically had to hike a three-mile trail from the park's Visitor Center.

That trail is rated for hikers of all ages, but there is also an off-limits park ranger access road that brings you within a hundred yards of the scenic view, saving the extended hike. Most people have no idea the dirt road exists, but it's been a lifesaver for the man these last six months. Making the full three-mile hike each way every Saturday probably would have broken him. He has so many powerful memories locked away everywhere in his life, just waiting for him to step on them like a landmine, but some of the most powerful were formed in this state park.

The boy asks, "Is this how you and Mommy came here?"

"Yes, all the time," the man lies. If he told his son about the real Scenic View Trail, they'd have to hike it every Saturday and he no longer has the heart to do that.

The undergrowth in this area isn't hard to push through and soon the man and his son are traveling along a narrow deer path. The sun slices through openings in the thick tree canopy, sending bright beams of light across the ground.

As far as the man knows, no one else uses this shortcut, which means there's never anyone to bother him and his son. The world is peaceful and calm, and they're all alone with the sounds of the forest.

When they reach the actual trail, they're only a few paces from the area on the map labeled Scenic View Point.

His son smiles widely and yells, "Hooray! We made it!"

The man smiles, too. His son's enthusiasm and laughter are the only things that keep him moving forward these days, and they're easily the best part of this heart-wrenching Saturday ritual.

The sight from the clearing at the top of the trail is stunning. Hikers have an unobstructed view of the treetops in the valley below and the curve of the river off in the distance. A fine mist often fills the valley in the morning and the sunsets are spectacular.

It's no wonder the man and his future wife spent so much time here, drinking and talking and doing the other things they did back in the woods where the man eventually discovered the private shortcut he now shares with his son.

"Did Mommy like coming here?"

"Yes, she did. It was her favorite place in the world."

"Did Mommy come here the day she left?"

"Timothy, your mother didn't leave us," the man says, trying to stay calm, trying not to be irritated. "She didn't leave us. You need to stop saying that. She had an accident and she passed away."

The man takes his son's hand and leads the boy back into the woods. He hates this part of the conversation.

"But she might come home?"

"No, your mother isn't coming home. The sooner we accept that, the better. You know what Dr. Linda says."

The man expects his son to start crying, right on schedule, but even though the little boy's jubilant smile is gone, his eyes are dry.

This is different. This could be a breakthrough. This could be *exactly* what Dr. Linda was trying to explain to him.

"Do you have something you want to talk about?"

His son nods as they walk, hand in hand, finding the deer path and making their way back to the car.

"Go ahead, it's okay."

The boy is still hesitant, but finally he replies: "Daddy, why were you yelling at Mommy the day she went away?"

The father grimaces as they continue to walk. He has worked very hard to forget the day his wife died, the day the rage flowing in his veins over some trivial disagreement made him see the world through a red haze. The screaming, the shouting, the swearing. His wife telling him to calm down or he would wake Timothy. The way his hands seemed to move on their own to shove her down the basement stairs. The thud of her head against the concrete floor. The instant regret, the horror when her pulse wouldn't start again, and the act of self-preservation as he scattered some of his son's Matchbox cars at the top of the steps and called 911.

No, the man doesn't like to think about these things, not one little bit.

For many years he had dug a hole deep inside himself to bury his bad feelings, and there they had festered and grown stronger in the dark until the day when they consumed him in a flash of white-hot fury.

The man hopes his son will do better with his own life, but he doesn't know how to answer this new question, so instead he says nothing and the boy doesn't ask again.

Marking the Passage of Time

Time BEGINS TO CRAWL, moving so slowly that a single tick of the second hand on his watch seems to take a minute.

John stares at the TV screen, unable to believe what he's seeing.

Julie is crying and shaking as she fumbles with the phone, desperately trying to enter her mother's number but failing even though she's called her old home a million times before. Her fingers just smack at the buttons.

The anchorman on the eleven o'clock news is frazzled and he's stumbling over his words.

This isn't right at all.

John can't hear the man's cracking voice anymore. All he can hear is a voice in his head, a voice he hasn't heard in years, a voice that asks: *Have you ever considered how we measure the passage of time?*

Somehow that breaks John's will, makes him want to cry—he knows they're probably going to die. Alone and in the dark. Somehow he knows life always comes to that moment of being alone, trapped in the dark. For everyone, everywhere, when time catches up and claims what it is due.

There are colorful graphics on the television screen, leftovers from just minutes before when their world wasn't ending.

People are running around the studio behind the anchorman and the female co-anchor who is speaking into her cell phone, even though she must know they're still on the air. A spotlight falls from the rafters, sparks fly. The camera pans to the right, as if the cameraman gave it a shove before fleeing, and the television screen shows the production staff scrambling in a frenzy.

Time is moving very quickly in that studio, but for John and Julie in their two-bedroom apartment, time is moving oh so slowly.

"How can it be busy?" Julie screams, dropping the phone. She must have gotten the numbers right after all.

And that scream gets John moving. He knows there's only a matter of minutes and there isn't much they can do, but they have to do what they can. They have to try to survive.

"We need to get this place prepared," he says, rolling out of bed.

"I have to call my mother. I have to . . ." She stutters and cries and it's clear she won't be able to help.

John runs to the hall closet and throws open the door. He grabs the staple gun, duct tape, and sheets of plastic he has stored on the top shelf ever since the night his father gave him a list of supplies to always have on hand for the end of the world. That advice was the ramblings of a crazy man, yet here John is, trapped in the sprinting present, needing these materials just like his father said he would.

John staples the plastic sheets over the windows and the front door of the apartment. He rips long strips of duct tape, the tape screaming, and he uses the strips to secure the edges of the plastic and cover the holes created by the staples.

Outside there is chaos — screeching of tires, cars colliding, sirens, even an occasional gunshot — but John does not stop. Time is moving way too fast for him to waste even a second.

When John is finished sealing the door and the windows, he returns to the bedroom.

"We need to get into the bathroom," he tells his wife.

Julie is still sitting on the bed, holding the phone. There is no dial tone. The television screen has turned into a hissing static. How could things fall apart so quickly? Jimmy Fallon should be on the television, not static.

"What's the point?" Julie asks.

"We have to try."

She reluctantly slides out from under the covers and John leads her by the hand to the guest bathroom across the hall. He turns on the light and closes the door, locks it, as if that will somehow help. The space is smaller than a prison cell, but it's nice enough for what it is.

Within a few minutes John has another plastic sheet stapled and taped over the door and the vent in the ceiling. There are no windows. These are all interior walls. This is as far away from the outside as they can get.

"We might be okay," John whispers.

Julie doesn't say anything. From the look on her face, John knows she has realized the end is really here. The lack of a dial tone and the television cutting to static was enough to convince her. This is where the ride known as humankind stops and everyone gets off.

But he isn't giving up. Not yet.

Maybe there's still a chance that they—*they* being the people who are supposed to be in charge—can stop this madness, can save everyone.

"We just need enough time," Julie whispers.

"My father once asked me a weird question," John replies. He's sitting on the toilet seat. Julie's in the tub, her knees pulled to her chest.

Julie says: "Have you ever considered how we measure the passage of time?"

Of course she knows the question. They've been married long enough that she has heard all of John's stories at least once, many of them twice or more—even the ones he doesn't realize she knows.

Now a memory echoes loud and clear in the front of John's mind: his father speaking on the phone. This conversation took place before his father committed suicide after saying the last semi-coherent things he would ever say, giving the last speech of his life:

Johnny, have you ever considered how we measure the passage of time? Early on in life, it's counting the days until the school year is done so we can run and play all summer. Then we grow and move on to slightly more important transitions: elementary school to middle school, middle school to high school. We note our first kiss, file it away in some part of our brain that'll most likely never forget until we get too old and it can't help forgetting. If we're sober, we can recite all the details of our first time in the backseat of a car with a woman. We clearly remember the thrill of the last week of high school and we compare that to the terror and excitement of the last week of college. These two events sound so similar, yet we remember and experience them differently. And it's all because of time. After college, we work toward promotions or better jobs. We marry. We settle down. We still look forward to summer, but now that escape is only two weeks, sometimes only one; sometimes there is no break. We slip into a routine, like a man in the hospital slipping into a coma. Life becomes regimented and we no longer monitor time through our own experiences and goals, but through the lives of others. Our child's first day of school. His first bike. Her first doll house. His first week at summer camp. Her first day at band camp. His championship baseball game. Her first date. His graduation from high school. Her last day home before leaving for college. Then eventually their new families, young and sweet and beautiful and naive. We mark the passage of time through other lives . . . but what do we do when those lives are gone?

His father rambled like that on the phone for much of the night, the same night he told his son how to prepare for the coming end of the world, and John humored his father because he knew no one else would, not recognizing these were truly desperate words from a desperate man. His father loved giving speeches, he loved his conspiracy theories, and he may have sounded crazy to anyone else, but John understood that his father simply liked to talk. Lecturing. Giving instruction about something *important*.

That night, after saying goodbye to his son and hanging up the phone, John's father shot himself in the head, and he never spoke again.

But his words live on. John can still recite his father's last speech with stunning clarity—although he doesn't realize it. Sometimes John talks in his sleep and his father's last rambling words are what he says. Sometimes his night talking wakes Julie and she's terrified to hear her dead father-in-law speaking with her husband's lips. She never dares tell John in the morning what she's heard him say so many times.

And now John remembers the words oh too well and he wants to know how much time they have left because time is slowing again. It's dragging along, millisecond after millisecond.

The light above the mirror dies without any fanfare.

"How did we let this happen?" Julie whispers.

John can hear his wife quietly sobbing.

Time passes. Nothing is said.

John thinks about everything they will lose in a matter of minutes if the news was correct.

He's terrified and his brain locks. He's frozen on a single thought: *How long will summer last this year?*

There are so many regrets. Too many to count. If only the end would come quicker, at least then he wouldn't have to think so damn much.

But that's all he has time to do, so John sits in the dark and he thinks. He listens to his wife sob. He listens to the noise outside, which has finally grown loud enough to penetrate the walls of the apartment building.

There is screaming outside, and John wonders when it will stop.

"Are we going to be okay?" Julie asks.

John has no idea why she asked the question. She knows the answer.

He sits in the dark and he thinks and he listens to his watch methodically counting down until the end of the world.

He sits and he tries not to dwell on his regrets.

Time continues to crawl, moving so slowly that a single second seems to take an hour.

John wants to say something to his wife as the noise outside gets louder, but the only words he finds are: *It's time to be counting the days until school is done so we can run and play all summer. All summer long with our friends.*

They sit alone in the cold darkness and John gropes for Julie's hand and he says: "If only summer lasted our entire lives."

Then they wait for time to claim whatever it has to claim.

Walking With the Ghosts of Pier 13

*O*N THESE HOT SUMMER DAYS *at the beginning of the New World, we're all walking with the dead.*

The thought repeated in Jeremy's mind as he approached his destination, his tattered sandals smacking against the splintered boardwalk with every step.

It *was* a hot summer day. Sweltering, in fact. The sun filled the sky, bright and scorching, and the blinding light reflected off the sand like a field of broken glass. The wooden walkway formed the boundary between the beach and the town, and the planks were timeworn and weathered. Pieces of litter traveled on the breeze.

There weren't many people around—just a dirty bum here, a dirtier teenager there, along with a few elderly couples who probably had nowhere else they could go.

Most of the shops were closed, their heavy hurricane doors bolted shut. Normally the boardwalk and the beach and the small town of Penny Bay would be packed with people this time of year—couples on holiday, families with kids, retirees parked at Pat's House of Bingo, beautiful singles mixing and mingling on the sand all day before heading to the Bermuda Bar and Grill to party all night—but not today. Not now.

In the distance, Pier 13 floated on top of thick supports like a mirage. The summer microcosm stretched over the beach and the changing tides and the fingertips of the Atlantic Ocean. The wooden roller coaster at the end of the pier soared high above everything else, and although the ride's thirteen cars were racing along the track, there were no people strapped into the bright red seats. The padded safety bars only restrained the humid, sticky air.

Jeremy inhaled the salty sea breeze while the waves continued breaking and foaming and retreating as they had for millions of years. The water was blue and beautiful. The sky was clear, nearly perfect. This day might be the dictionary definition of summer perfection, yet there was barely anyone around.

Jeremy could easily recall what this place had been like years ago: the cascading noise of the crowd and the shopkeepers selling their wares, the drone of the small airplanes pulling advertising banners across the sky, the kids running and playing in the surf, the young couples holding hands, the scent of sunscreen and pizza, the soft-serve ice cream cones, and everything else that had made the beach his summer home as a child, when his family lived in New York City and spent the hottest days of the year relaxing here without a care in the world.

Everything real from those memories was gone, but their ghosts remained.

There was a wooden ticket booth at the entrance to Pier 13 with an old-fashioned painted sign displaying the various rates for the amusement park. Locked inside was a kid Jeremy's age, his attention fully occupied by the cell phone he probably wasn't supposed to have with him while working.

"One please," Jeremy said.

The kid jerked back in surprise and looked up from his phone. His skin was acne-scarred, his arms tanned. His red uniform hadn't been washed in days and the expression on his face was tired and bored and maybe a little scared, too.

"One ticket or one All-Day Pass?" the kid asked. A rusted metal fan blew humid air around the booth and a battered radio sat by the ordering window. From the radio came the voice of a solemn reporter reading something off the newswire. The kid added, "We don't got many rides running. Most everyone quit."

"Why are you still hanging on?"

The kid shrugged. There was a bead of sweat forming on the end of his pimpled nose, near the metal stud protruding from a self-piercing that looked infected. "Don't got nowhere else to go."

"Yeah, ain't that the truth. Just one ticket, please."

Jeremy roamed the pier, passing the empty game booths and the empty rides, with the sound of the ocean forever in the background. When he finally found another human being, it was an older woman dressed not in a park uniform but a grimy Sunday dress. She was running the merry-go-swings every three minutes on schedule. There were no riders.

The woman sat under the direct gaze of summer sun even though there was a bent umbrella on the boards nearby. She looked wired and tired, but Jeremy approached her anyway.

"Nice day, isn't it?" Jeremy said. The woman twitched and recoiled as if she had been struck.

"Is that you, Ralph?" she called, her voice raw and aching, her eyes searching wildly, as if she were blind. She looked right past Jeremy twice before she focused on him, her gaze like red-rimmed razors. "Goddamn you, Ralph! Why'd you bring the kids today! Goddamn you, Ralph!"

Backing away, Jeremy kept his eyes locked on her until he could turn a corner, and then he continued to explore the park, certain he would never say another word to the half-human husks haunting this wounded place.

But soon Jeremy found a man of Middle Eastern descent selling funnel cakes, and again he couldn't help himself. He approached the food cart, feeling sorry for the man standing in the blazing sun, dressed in his neatly-pressed red uniform. He probably had a family to support and couldn't even consider leaving this crappy job. Where else would he find work these days?

"I loved these as a kid," Jeremy said as his funnel cake was prepared. He smiled.

The man didn't reply and Jeremy could see the worry in his eyes. He probably did have a family. Maybe he was thinking about them, wondering if they'd be alive when he got home . . . or if he'd even make it home alive. Those questions were on everyone's mind when they walked out their front door these days, so it was easy for Jeremy to imagine what the man might be thinking.

The man said nothing as he accepted Jeremy's payment and handed over the funnel cake. Jeremy thanked him and dropped his change into the plastic jar with the word TIPS written in blue marker on a piece of masking tape.

As Jeremy continued walking to the real destination he had in mind for his visit today, he took a bite of the funnel cake and grimaced. He had certainly loved them as a child, but the sweetness tasted overwhelming and almost bitter to him.

He dropped the rest of the sugary confection into a blue trash barrel. A flock of seagulls descended in a pack, squawking wildly at each other, tearing the funnel cake apart and then turning on each other, sending feathers and bloody beaks flying. Their caws and screams and squeals pierced the shimmering air.

They had grown dependent on humans for their food, but there had been slim pickings lately and that dependence was leading to madness.

When Jeremy reached the wooden roller coaster known as the Screamin' Demon, he stood and watched it run a few times. Thirteen empty cars, chasing each other in circles, always starting at the same place and ending where they had begun their journey. Jeremy could relate.

The mid-day sun baked the roller coaster's fading paint. The metal cars seemed to sizzle. The peak of the first hill was at the very end of the pier, hanging out over the ocean, and Jeremy thought it was the most beautiful view in the world.

He and his brother Jason had ridden this ride hundreds or maybe even thousands of times when they were kids. They had loved the Screamin' Demon, embracing the fear and the thrill and the rush that hit you directly in the gut as you barreled down the first hill toward the ocean. The next turn of the tracks was just out of view, giving you the momentary sensation of certain doom when all you could see was the water. Then the cars whooshed to the left, back onto the pier and climbing the second hill.

The sign over the entrance to the ride's loading line was blackened and scarred. The railed walkway was twisted and burned. Heavy plywood covered a jagged hole in the wooden planks. Yet the Screamin' Demon was still open for business.

The red cars were painted with bright yellow flames and grinning skulls and they roared by on the tracks, the grinding of metal on metal louder than normal. There was no one around to make any other noise: no shrieking riders, no chatting parents waiting on their kids, no teenage park employees pushing carts filled with ice and bottles of soda shouting about how refreshing an ice-cold Coca-Cola would taste. There were simply the cars on the track and the ocean below and nothing else.

"You want to ride?"

The teenage girl running the Screamin' Demon sat on a three-legged stool under a tattered yellow umbrella that had been patched back together with duct tape. She sounded hesitant and lonely at the same time. She probably felt the need for human contact, Jeremy guessed, just like he did. She was pretty in a simple, girl-at-the-beach kind of way with her blonde hair tied up in a ponytail, her blue eyes, her tanned skin.

She added, "Just two tickets."

"Oh, I only have one. When I was a kid, it only cost one."

"That's fine," the girl said, whispering as if there were someone to overhear them. "I really don't care. I'm not coming back tomorrow."

"Quitting?"

"Why bother? My paycheck is probably gonna bounce."

"I haven't been on this pier in a long time."

"Since you were a kid, right?"

"Yeah, my brother and I loved this place."

"Well, I hate it. My boyfriend and I are running away tonight."

"Where you going?"

"Anywhere but this shitty town. Maybe north."

"That's what Jason and I said."

"You queer?"

"No, Jason was my brother."

"Where's he now?"

"Dead."

"Oh."

"He was here last month, waiting in line."

"Oh." She glanced at the twisted metal. "I'm sorry."

"Yeah," Jeremy said, handing the girl his only ticket. She ripped it in half as he moved to take his seat. "I didn't really think the park would even be open, let alone with the coaster running."

"You heard the President, didn't you?"

"Go on living, right?"

"Like nothing has changed," the girl said. "Like there's nothing to fear."

"You scared?"

"Out of my mind."

At the top of the first hill, the roller coaster paused for just a second, allowing Jeremy to take in the full view.

The sparkling waves of the Atlantic had conquered the world from below his feet to the horizon a hundred miles in the distance where the ocean met the beautiful, clear sky. The dazzling rays of sunlight formed an elongated diamond of fire on the dancing water.

Jeremy's skin tingled in the heat even as the ocean wind whipped past him. He could hear the cries of the seagulls and the crashing of the waves against the supports under the pier. He inhaled the salty sea air, conjuring a million memories of summers long gone, awakening a million ghosts who still lived here, and only here, and only in the summer.

"I miss you, bro," Jeremy whispered, and then his stomach rushed into his throat as the roller coaster roared down the hill, the cars screaming along the tracks like the demons they were named after.

He laughed like a kid.

He laughed to release the pain.

He laughed because he had to laugh or his heart would explode in anger and sadness.

When the ride was over, he was crying, and the laughter had been lost to the waves.

"You okay?" the Screamin' Demon girl asked. "Oh man, you didn't knock your teeth on the safety bar or something, did you?"

"No, I'm all right," Jeremy said, removing his seat belt, pushing the safety bar up quickly so he could exit. He wiped away the tears with his hand.

"You're scared, too, aren't you?"

"Yeah, a little."

"We're probably safe, you know? I mean, they hit Disney in Florida the other day. They're kind of moving away from us. We might be safe."

"What did they do at Disney?"

"Man, don't you watch TV?"

"Not lately."

"Well, yeah, a bunch of them landed in a small plane and started shooting everyone with machine guns. Park security was useless. All of the news channels showed it live, too, from a local traffic helicopter. At least nine hundred people dead, lots of kids. The bastards were dressed in black masks and heavy jackets and when they were finally cornered by the Army, they blew themselves up."

"Makes the bombing here look like small potatoes, doesn't it?" Jeremy asked, considering the scarred sign, the twisted metal, and the plywood covering the hole in the pier.

This was where Jason died.

What had he been thinking right before the bomb went off? Had he been watching the ride following the tracks? The beautiful teenage girls in their bikinis? The seagulls swooping down for pieces of pretzels on the boards?

What had been going through his mind?

Jeremy thought about what it must have been like to be standing in line, enjoying the day even though you were packed in with hundreds of other sweaty summer revelers, waiting for your turn when...

Well, what happened next? It wouldn't be like the movies where the audience knows what's coming thanks to the music cues.

No, not at all like that.

There would be no warning.

If you were really close to the bomb, the force would shred your body instantly. You wouldn't hear or feel anything. One second you'd be alive and smiling or laughing or shading your eyes from the sun or wiping your brow or memorizing the curves of the hot chick in front of you in line, and the next second you'd be dead. You'd never have to worry about how your death would affect your family. You'd never have to think about the things you were going to miss or the things you would never get to do or see.

If you were a few yards away from the blast, maybe you'd hear the thunder a split second before the explosion ripped the life from your body, but there wouldn't be time for you to truly understand what was happening. A loud sound and then darkness. No pain, no thoughts.

But if you were a dozen yards away, you might be one of the unlucky ones who was wounded severely enough to bleed to death. You might hang on for minutes or hours, knowing you were doomed once the confusion settled. You'd be frightened and angry and you'd spend your last moments facing down every regret you ever had while wondering how the people you loved would take the news of your death. There would be a lot of pain and not all of it would be from the shrapnel that tore your flesh apart, severing your limbs or blinding you. Then, slowly, darkness and death.

"Small potatoes?" the girl finally said, studying Jeremy with fierce eyes. "Well, do you see all the reporters and cops? They're gone, right?

We're old news. No one cares about the people slaughtered here because there's already bigger and bloodier stories to report."

"I'm sorry. Did you know anyone who died?"

"A couple of employees. One of my best friends. I think he went instantly. Didn't feel nothing." A tear had trickled past the girl's nose. Jeremy stared at her for a moment, at the tear, at her blue eyes, and he wondered if her eyes were bluer than the sea. "At least I want to believe that. Probably isn't true. I miss him. Sometimes I feel like he's still here."

"Yeah, we're all walking with the dead now, I think," Jeremy said and turned away.

The girl called after him, but he didn't look back.

"Was it worth the trip?" the kid in the ticket booth asked as Jeremy exited Pier 13 and stepped onto the boardwalk.

"Huh?"

"Coming to see what they did."

"Yeah, I guess so. My bro is dead. Died here."

"I'm sorry." The kid with the pierced nose sounded sincere enough. "Don't worry, the Army will get the fuckers."

"Anything new on the news?" Jeremy nodded at the battered radio sitting in the booth where the fan continued to blow warm air around.

"Not really, just that the Prez is pretty sure this has something to do with the Middle East. Some new group of extremists with a crazy name. Makes sense to me. You'd have to be really fucked in the head like those desert-baked bastards to strap bombs to your chest and kill innocent people."

"Fucked in the head, or just really angry."

"Yeah, I guess. But angry about what? What could make someone so pissed they'd do this shit?"

"Maybe they don't think they'll be heard any other way. You never know what angry young men will do. It's a fucked-up world."

Before the kid in the ticket booth could respond, the radio crackled. He adjusted the tuning and turned up the volume.

An earnest reporter stated: "Earlier today, the Department of Homeland Security alerted police in eight major cities about possible threats to theaters. The threat is said to be credible, although no other details were provided and citizens are urged to not change their plans based on this report."

"This shit won't never end, will it?" the kid in the booth asked.

Jeremy shook his head. "No, I don't think so. Not for a long time."

"Where you going now?"

"New York City. I used to live there, with my brother and our parents. It's been a long time since I've been back."

"Just stay away from Broadway, man. You heard the news."

Jeremy didn't reply as he walked away, the boardwalk creaking under his steps. His face was coated in sweat. The sun was cooking him, burning him up, and the heat felt good.

He thought of Jason and the beach and the wooden roller coaster and the ocean and the summers of years past.

He thought about anger, and angry young men who feel they must go to extremes to achieve their goals.

He thought about Jason at Pier 13.

He thought about the explosion and the deaths and the future to come.

He thought about the last thing Jason had said to him the day he died: "On these hot summer days at the beginning of the New World, we're all walking with the dead. Love you, bro. Miss you."

Jeremy thought about all the people who might be attending a Broadway show this weekend, following the President's advice to go on living life like the world was just fine and dandy and not coming to an end all around them.

How could anyone look the other way so easily while the nation's body count rose so quickly?

How could anyone pretend everything hadn't changed forever?

How could they go on living their same old lives when so many people were already dead?

Jeremy walked and he remembered the people he had loved and

lost. He remembered the ghosts haunting him, the ghosts he loved, the ghosts guiding him.

Some of those ghosts still lived on Pier 13, some only lived in his heart, but he could feel them everywhere he went.

He vowed to never forget his brother, no matter what happened.

Jeremy thought about anger and angry young men with a cause, and he walked with the ghosts, and he prepared himself for one last trip to New York.

A Mother's Love

ANDREW STOPPED SHORT of where the hallways on the fourth floor of the Sunny Days Hospice Home crossed. Two nurses were gabbing around the corner and he didn't care for the people who worked here. The employees liked to chat with anyone they spotted, and at first he thought they were trying to be friendly, but soon enough he realized they were just being nosy. Who were you here to see, what was your relationship, were you approved by the family—stupid, invasive questions.

His mother was alone right now, and Andrew hated that he wasn't by her side every minute of every day, but he was doing the best he could. There were times when he had to leave her room and venture out into the world. He worked to pay their bills and keep their lives in some semblance of order, even if hers was coming to an end. He ran errands for her, buying her favorite cigarettes even though the doctor had told her to drop the bad habit while she still could, and undertaking any tasks that simply had to be done.

Andrew despised the smell of Sunny Days more than anything, although he understood his visceral reaction was mostly due to his mother's diminishing condition and not the perfumed hallways. He held his breath as the two nurses began walking away from where the two hallways intersected and he scurried on his way as quietly as he could.

All of these hallways looked the same, but he knew them by heart.

He remembered his first visit to this building, to a clean and well-lit office near the lobby where he begged the admissions lady, Miss Clarence, to please admit his mother to the facility, to please help him move her from his home where he could no longer care for her properly.

Miss Clarence had examined the paperwork Andrew completed, and the first issue raised was whether he would have the money required, of course, but he said he could cover the fees if they let him pay in installments. That had to be possible, right? It was, and he was relieved, but once the financial situation was resolved, there was still an even bigger problem: the lack of available beds at Sunny Days to accept a new patient.

"What do you mean?" Andrew asked, his hands shaking and his tired eyes blinking without comprehension. "Isn't everyone here dying?"

"Well, Mr. Smith," the young woman behind the desk patiently explained, "Our guests reside with us for as long as necessary to complete their life journey. We don't like to use the word *dying*. So final and crude. We like to say, they're *moving on*."

"But how long until a bed opens up?"

"There's no way to know for certain, but if you'll agree to the installment plan we discussed, I'll push your mother to the top of the waiting list and we'll call you as soon as there is a room available. Do you understand, Mr. Smith?"

Andrew had understood all right. He would be spending his entire life's savings and then some for his mother's stay in this place, but the people in charge were going to make him wait for the privilege. Powerful people liked to make the little people wait. They loved to flaunt their control over you. Andrew knew this. His mother had taught him well.

But still, he had signed the financial paperwork and gone home and waited like he was told. What other option was there? He loved his mother, and she loved him, and he would do whatever she needed him to do. He understood there was nothing in the world like a mother's love. No girlfriend, no wife, not even another member of your family could love you the way your mother loved you, and you had to love her back just as much, maybe even more.

Now Andrew was consumed by a different kind of waiting. The time of his mother's death—her *moving on*, to use Miss Clarence's term—was drawing nearer and he hated that he sometimes had to be away from her. He loved his mother so much, and he knew he needed to be there when her last moments on Earth came to pass. Being with his mother as she died, to keep her from being alone in those last moments, was a privilege and a responsibility he could never forsake.

Andrew walked through the bright and cheerful hallway he had come to loathe, wincing whenever his shoes squeaked on the gleaming buffed floor. A television blared *Jeopardy* from one room, but many of the rooms were silent. The almost-dead didn't make much noise, Andrew had learned.

He approached the last doorway on the right, where the hallway terminated with a window overlooking a grove of trees. The sun was setting beyond the mountains in the distance and the sky was red and orange and shades of purple like the air had caught fire.

Andrew stopped outside the door.

Could he really do what he had come here to do?

After all of these years of being his mother's only son, her best friend in the entire world, and the only person who loved her as much as she loved him, could he do what needed to be done?

He had to, of course, he just had to, but self-doubt weighed heavily on his heart. He had decided the best approach would be to think as little as possible once he was in the room. Forget emotions, forget humanity, forget the rules of nature, and become like a machine for a few minutes. Be cold, do what needed to be done, and then go home and try to forget his actions as soon as possible.

Andrew opened the door with those thoughts looping in his mind. The fiery sky bled in through the window and washed across the room in waves of eerie light. He made his way to the hospital-style bed where the old woman slept. Her skin was wrinkled and her teeth were yellowed. Her withered chest rose and fell. He leaned in closer to hear her wheezing. He could smell the cigarettes on her breath. The familiar stench had followed him around all his life, sticking to his clothes and his hair and his flesh, and it was unmistakable.

Andrew stood motionless, just watching, and he realized he had to move now or he would lose his nerve.

He put one shaking hand across her dry mouth. She snorted. He froze again.

It wasn't too late for him to change his mind. Could he *really* do this? *Be cold*, Andrew told himself, *be cold cold cold cold*.

His other hand moved and he squeezed her nose closed with his index finger and a thumb. Her head tilted and her eyes blinked open. She was groggy and confused, and she tried to roll on her side, but he leaned forward to block her.

She struggled to move, and then she reached up and clawed at his face with her brittle nails. The pain was intense. Blood trickled from his pierced skin. He hadn't planned on there being any blood; he hadn't even expected her to wake up. He assumed she would simply go to sleep forever, silent and peaceful.

Andrew doubled the pressure with his hand and fingers, turning his head away and closing his eyes to avoid her wild, perplexed, angry gaze. Her torso bucked and she swatted at the back of his head with those calloused and bony fingers.

Then her body stilled, her jaw slackened, and the fight seemed to empty out of her as quickly as it had arrived. She was silent.

Andrew kept his eyes closed as tears welled up and spilled onto the bed. He had done it. He had really done it.

But he couldn't stand the thought of seeing her face like this. He turned away, slipped out of the room, and headed home.

When Andrew arrived at the tiny house in the aging neighborhood where he had lived his entire life, he didn't bother turning on the lights.

He sat in the darkness at the kitchen table and waited for the phone call. He would need to act surprised at the news. He felt empty inside, as if his mother's cancer had been eating away at him, too, but he was sure his mother would be proud of him. She had always loved him so much, and he had always tried to return the love twice over or even more, doing whatever she needed him to do, going above and beyond to make her happy and comfortable, especially as her health deteriorated and the end grew closer.

When the phone finally rang, Andrew answered with a meek, barely audible: "Hello?"

"Hello? Mr. Smith? This is Miss Clarence from Sunny Days Hospice Home."

"Yes, Miss Clarence. I'm here."

"I'm glad I could reach you personally, Mr. Smith. One of our guests has moved on and we have a bed ready for your mother."

"Well, that's just swell," Andrew said, barely feeling like himself. "I'll go tell her."

He hung up the phone and made his way to the bedroom where his mother slept, where she had lived for the last six months as her body weakened and death waited for her to give up the fight.

Andrew loved his mother so much and he was relieved to finally have some good news to share with her.

PART TWO

MORE THAN MIDNIGHT

"There are the dead, more and more of them every minute, and they remember with sadness and horror what it meant to be alive..."

Pop-Pop

ERIN AND RUSS STAND with their mother in the living room of Gram-Gram's home, surveying their surroundings as if they've never seen this place before. Quite the opposite is true, of course. The twins practically grew up here while their mother worked two jobs to pay the bills. Yet today the house feels different. Somehow it looks different, too, even though nothing obvious has changed.

"She's been having good days and bad days," their mother says for the third time since they left Gram-Gram's cool, sterile room at the Sunny Days Hospice Home. "I'm sorry she had a bad day today."

"Mom, it's okay," Erin says, also for the third time.

"What can we help with?" Russ wants to steer the conversation away from their beloved grandmother's final, confusing weeks. The twins haven't visited with their mother or Gram-Gram very much since they left for college last fall, but now they're home for Easter break and they understand the weight their mother has been carrying all on her own.

"I can't just sit around, waiting for her to . . ." their mother says, trailing off. "I can't just sit and wait. I need to feel useful, so I guess I'd like to start the prep work to sell the house."

The house. Not Gram-Gram's house, not the house where Gram-Gram and Pop-Pop raised her. Just *the house.* Erin and Russ exchange a look. They haven't even taken an intro to psychology class, but they recognize the emotional distancing at play with their mother's choice of words.

She continues, "It'll be tons of work, I mean, but maybe we can start packing a few boxes for Goodwill. What do you kids think?"

"Absolutely, we're game," Erin answers for both of them.

"Great!" Their mother's face lights up a little, just for a second, as if they've decided to plan a surprise party for someone they love instead of preparing her childhood home for sale while an aggressive cancer eats away at her mother.

"We'll start in the attic," Russ says. "There's a lot to sort through."

"Perfect!" their mother replies, once again with too much enthusiasm. "I'll run to the store and get some boxes. Will you kids be okay here by yourselves?"

"Absolutely," Erin and Russ say in unison.

After their mother leaves, the twins make their way up the dusty stairs to the second floor. They both grip the handrail tightly out of habit, not even aware of their actions. This was where Pop-Pop slipped and fell one spring day when they were eight years old, breaking his neck at the bottom. He died instantly.

Their mother and Gram-Gram were devastated, and Russ cried on and off for days after the funeral. Pop-Pop had been his favorite person in the entire world.

Yet Erin wasn't particularly sad about the old man's passing, although even at the tender age of eight she knew to keep those thoughts to herself. She had feared Pop-Pop in a way Russ never did. It wasn't that Pop-Pop raised his voice at her or hit her or threatened her or anything awful like that; there was just something off about the way he sometimes looked at her, causing her a sense of unease she couldn't exactly explain or even describe. This is not something Erin has ever shared with anyone. What would have been the point once he was gone?

Gram-Gram's decline began right around her husband's death, a connection the twins made as they grew older. First her mobility decreased, then there were serious health scares including a possible stroke, then the memory loss appeared with frightening stealth, and finally the cancer arrived in the night like a thief. It's been a difficult decade for the graceful woman they love so very much.

When the twins reach the second floor, they stop under the familiar attic access. As kids, they discovered they could reach the knotted pull-down cord with the assistance of a chair borrowed from Gram-Gram's sewing room, and over time they turned the attic into their own little clubhouse. Russ grabs that cord and tugs it toward the floor. The compact ladder unfolds with a shrill screech and darkness greets them from the opening in the ceiling.

"Do you want to go first or should I?" Russ asks.

"You first. You know I'm a total coward about the dark."

It has been many years and quite a few pounds since Russ last made this climb, and the first wooden rung groans under him. He pauses, confirms the ladder is actually holding his weight, and then continues upward. He vanishes into the dark. The attic's wooden floorboards creak and whine. There's a thud as he trips on something and sends it flying, but before Erin can ask if he's okay, a dull light flickers and fills the opening above her.

"Come on up," Russ calls. "Watch your step, though. It's really bad."

Erin joins her brother in the attic with the sloped ceiling, the musty smell of departed summers, and hundreds of cobwebs dancing in the shadows as spiders vanish into their hiding places. She barely notices these things, which she was expecting, because of what she *wasn't* expecting.

"What happened?"

A dresser has been pushed over and the contents of the drawers are strewn around the dirty floor. Cardboard boxes are overturned and decades worth of paperwork is scattered. The family's ancient board game boxes have been opened and tossed. Two full-length mirrors lay on their sides like fallen soldiers, their glass shattered. Moth-eaten clothes, including Gram-Gram's yellowed wedding dress, are tattered and torn. Framed family portraits and watercolor paintings bought decades ago at Sears & Roebuck have been freed of their frames and ripped into pieces.

Russ says, "Maybe this was one of Gram-Gram's bad days."

"But what was she *doing?*"

"Looking for something, I guess."

"Where do we even start?"

"Maybe we'll just gather similar things together, you know? Refold the clothing from the dresser, reassemble the games, that sort of thing."

"Okay," Erin says. "I'll fold the clothing since you couldn't get that right to save your life."

"Hey, I tried folding the laundry once. I didn't see the point. The clothes just get unfolded again. No one wears a folded shirt!"

"Whatever, dork."

They don't say much else while they work, but they're not working in silence, either. The floorboards whimper with every movement and the wind assaults the roof, howling in the eaves. Russ and Erin remember these sounds from when the attic served as their secret playroom, but the space seems so much smaller now—and those sounds are somehow louder and bleaker.

When the dresser has been returned to its rightful place with the contents neatly stored away, the twins begin gathering the components of the board games that landed in every nook and cranny the attic has to offer.

Erin is deep under the sloped roof, nearly to the place where the floor and the ceiling meet, when she stops and ponders something she has spotted.

"Russ," Erin says, "come look at this."

"What's up?" Russ asks, crawling in next to her.

"I saw this piece from the Monopoly game," she says, showing him the little silver rocking horse, "but the head of the horse was stuck between these two floorboards. That's when I realized this board wasn't actually nailed down."

She lifts the board and they peer into the dark space. Russ removes his phone from his pocket, activating the flashlight app. Neither really expects to find anything, other than maybe some dust and more cobwebs, so they're both surprised by the wooden cigar box sitting on top of the lath and plaster ceiling of the bedroom below them.

"What do you think it is?" Russ asks.

"A cigar box, you dork."

"I mean, why's it hidden up here?"

"No idea. Should we open it?"

"Well, who else will?"

Erin nods. She carefully removes the box from where it has been stashed away from prying eyes, wipes at the thick layer of dust, and lifts the lid. Russ positions his phone's light so they can see inside. They stare for a very long time.

"What does it mean?" Erin asks, studying the unexpected contents.

"I'm not sure." Russ removes the school ID cards from inside the cigar box. Most of them are plastic, although they're older than the colorful ID cards Russ and Erin carry, but underneath those are even more IDs printed on cardstock, some of which are old enough to only have the student's name, the year, and the school logo.

"Russ. . . the photos," Erin whispers.

Russ understands, but he cannot find the words to reply. The IDs all belonged to women. Dozens and dozens of women over many decades.

And in many subtle but unmistakable ways, these women resemble how their mother and their Gram-Gram look in photos taken during their late teens and early twenties.

In fact, these women are the spitting image of Erin now.

The twins sit at the kitchen table with the IDs spread across the green tablecloth as if they're playing some kind of card game.

The oldest ID is dated 1967 and the faded information is printed on crumpled card stock, no lamination to protect it. The woman's name is Jennifer Mitchell and the University of Pennsylvania issued the card. The newest one is dated 2007 and the student named Cindy Smith bears such a strong resemblance to Erin that the twins wonder if this woman could somehow be related to them. That ID is from Penn State University and it was issued the year before Pop-Pop fell down the stairs and broke his neck.

"Are you going to do it or am I?" Russ asks.

"I don't think I can."

They're staring at their phones, which sit on the table just out of easy reach as if the devices are unwanted, unloved, even hated. Normally, the phones never leave their hands or pockets, but at this moment they represent a true and present danger to Erin and Russ's understanding of their family and the people they love. With one Internet search, maybe two, their suspicions could be confirmed. They've watched enough reruns of *CSI* and *Criminal Minds* to identify a serial killer's trophy collection when they see it. This search cannot end well, but what else can they do?

"Aw shit," Russ mutters, reaching for his phone. He looks at the most recent ID card and then types the woman's name, her school, and the year into the search bar. Seconds later they have confirmation. He slides the phone over to Erin so she can read it for herself.

"Penn State student Cindy Smith missing for two weeks," she says, glancing from the archived news story to the ID card. "*Harrisburg Patriot News*. April 30, 2008."

She takes the phone and types in the information from the second most recent ID card. Within seconds, those results are conclusive, too. She slides the phone back to her brother.

"Slippery Rock student Amanda Miller still missing one year later," Russ reads. "This story is from the *Butler Eagle*, dated April 25, 2005."

Even though they're certain of what they'll learn, they continue passing the phone back and forth, searching for each woman's name and school. It soon becomes clear the missing women have never been found. Some of the stories are from the tenth or twentieth or even thirtieth anniversary of a disappearance. Always in April.

There are countless mentions of loved ones desperately wishing for closure. There are some families who've decided it's better to believe their daughter simply ran away and is living a happy life somewhere. There are even wild explanations to rationalize how a person could vanish without a trace. "Maybe she hit her head," suggested the brother of Julie Dean, a Shippensburg University student who went missing while hiking the Appalachian Trail in April of 1987, "and she forgot her name and she's working in a diner somewhere and she don't even know she's a missing person."

Erin and Russ understand the truth that Julie Dean's brother and many of the others cannot accept. None of these women are in California trying to make it big, or suffering from amnesia in a small town, or traveling through Europe with a rich prince they met on holiday. These women are dead.

"There are years between some of these, and some were in consecutive Aprils," Russ says.

"Is there a pattern?" Those formulaic crime-solving shows are suddenly coming in handy.

"Not that I can see."

The two siblings are so engrossed by their discovery that they don't hear their mother's car roll into the driveway. If she hadn't locked the kitchen door behind herself, obeying a habit established in early childhood when her father warned her repeatedly about the dangers of the outside world, she would have walked right into the kitchen and seen the ID cards on the table. But there's just enough warning for Russ to slide the cards into a pile and shove them roughly into his pocket.

"Oh, hey kids," their mother says as she enters the kitchen, feigning happiness again. "I bought some boxes. Can you get them out of the car for me?"

"Yes!" Erin and Russ answer in unison.

They do their best to act normal for the rest of the day, not giving their mother any indication of the awful knowledge they possess, but she still asks them several times if they're all right.

They say yes, of course, right as rain. What could possibly be wrong?

When the elevator doors slide open, Erin and Russ step into the bright and deceitfully cheery hallway of the fourth floor of the Sunny Days Hospice Home. Their previous visit with Gram-Gram the day before feels like a million years ago. Their shoes seem too heavy, squeaking loudly on the buffed floor. A television blares an episode of *Jeopardy* from one room, but most of the other rooms are silent.

"Are you *really* going to ask her?" Russ whispers.

"We have to *try* to ask her."

"But it's Pop-Pop. He never acted nuts, you know? How could he be a killer?"

"That's what I want to find out." Erin's tone is familiar to anyone in the family. She's made up her mind and nothing can change it.

When the twins arrive at the end of the hallway, Russ has a flash of intuition. Gram-Gram will be dead. Her cooling corpse will be slumped in her bed, highlighted by a beam of sunlight pouring in through the window. He and Erin will be devastated, of course, but they also won't have to ask about their grandfather's horrific hobby — and maybe that'll be a blessing.

His intuition is wrong, though.

When Erin knocks and pushes the door open, Gram-Gram is very much alive. Her eyes are closed and she *is* in a sunbeam as he imagined, but she's sitting in the chair by the window. The sunlight washes across her pale, gray, wrinkled face. She's dressed in a cloth gown and her deflated chest rises and falls.

Yesterday, she couldn't leave the bed and the words she hissed reminded Russ of *The Exorcist*. He has never tried to talk Erin into watching that one, even though he loves to frighten her with horror films. She scares easily. Yet, here she is, being the brave one, ready to ask her unaskable questions.

"Gram-Gram?"

"Oh my," Gram-Gram replies, opening her eyes and turning her head. Her eyes are blue and sharp, not the cloudy and confused orbs the twins saw the day before. "Erin? Russell? Oh, it's so good to see you! You're getting so big!"

"Hi, Gram-Gram," Russ says, forcing himself to speak.

"Please sit." She gestures toward the visitor chairs pushed against the wall under a flat-screen television.

Her chair can swivel and she uses her bony feet to glide herself around to face them. The sunlight makes her glow as if she's more alive than ever, yet even in the radiance of one of her good days the twins recognize how little is left of her.

"How are you? How is school? Not fucking around too much, I hope?"

Her voice is the same as they remember, but the words aren't. The woman they've loved all their lives would never use profanity, not even if she accidentally cut off her thumb while preparing a roast. But their mother has warned them that Gram-Gram's mental filters are gone even on her best of days and she has shocked her own daughter several times by unleashing the crass language she apparently kept locked inside her head for most of her life.

"School is great," Erin replies without missing a beat. "Gram-Gram, how are *you* feeling?"

"Oh, I might be having a good day, truth be told," their grandmother says, her coffee-colored teeth showing in a crooked smile on her too-thin face. She gives them a comically burlesque wink. "Haven't had many of those lately. Oh, I'm just so happy to see you both! Is your mother here?"

"Mom doesn't know we came. Russ and I . . . we have to ask you about something."

"Oh, what's that?"

Erin glances at Russ and he removes the ID cards from his pocket, his trembling fingers nearly dropping them to the floor. He holds them out for their grandmother to see more easily. Her eyes blink and focus. The smile fades and Russ cannot place the new expression that appears briefly on her face and vanishes just as quickly. Guilt, maybe?

"You found those goddamned mementos? Well, I'm glad it was you! Someone needed to and my brain is turning to mush and I couldn't. I searched everywhere. Good for you, kids. Good for you."

"But Gram-Gram, how could anyone do something so awful?" Erin asks.

"It's hard to explain, I'm afraid. Pop-Pop and I had so many fights about that damn ritual and yet I still don't truly understand. Each year April would roll around and if the weather was nice . . . well, things just kind of happened. Once the dirty business was taken care of, life went back to normal. But can you imagine the talk if the neighbors found out? Every year I'd pray for an ugly April. Then the *nastiness* wouldn't happen at all! But some years April would be pretty and sunny and fuck me it's a miracle the police never came knocking on our door. Not even once!"

"But those young women . . . " Erin's voice trails off as the question dies in her throat.

"Yes, dreadful, fucking dreadful. Their families will never have closure and I feel terrible about that. Your Pop-Pop and I argued many times about doing *something* to help, maybe mailing anonymous letters to the families. One of our fights actually got a little too heated and down the steps Pop-Pop went! I wish he hadn't, but he did, and I guess now you know the truth about his death, which is right, I believe. You should know. Maybe don't tell your mother, though!"

Erin and Russ are stunned into silence. They stare at their grandmother, who is smiling and speaking of horrible things they never even imagined possible when they drove home from college just twenty-four hours ago. Nothing feels real, nothing feels right. Not their thoughts and not their world, which they are seeing with cynical new eyes.

"But Gram-Gram," Russ finally says, "*Why* did Pop-Pop kill *those* young women?"

Their grandmother's lips twitch and her eyes fog a bit, glazing over like they did yesterday. Russ fears she's slipping back into the place she goes on her bad days, but then her eyes brighten and that odd expression passes across her face again, the one he saw when she first gazed at the ID cards. It wasn't guilt at all, he realizes. It was *pride*.

"Oh dearie," she whispers with a sly grin, "Not Pop-Pop."

Answering the Call

THE YOUNG MAN must be lonely.

There is something terrible about the look in his eyes, about the way his body slumps over the heavy, black answering machine perched on his lap. He sits on the chair in the middle of the barren room, and he is naked except for his white underwear and his cheap watch. He's drenched in sweat. A single tear hovers on the edge of his pale, trembling lips. He has dark hair and narrow fingers with fingernails chewed to the quick.

The wood floor groans when he shifts his weight. There are no windows, only the door to the hallway and a door to the walk-in closet. A single lamp glows with a yellowed light, but the light does not reach the corners of the room. An extension cord snakes across the floor, powering the lamp and the old, boxy answering machine.

He pushes the button that was once marked ANNOUNCEMENT before years of contact rubbed the word away. The tape crackles, there is a beep, and a woman's voice speaks: "You've reached the Smith Family, we can't come to the phone right now, but if you leave a message, we'll get right back to you."

This is the voice of the dead. The sound has deteriorated a bit with age, but when the young man plays this tape, the dead woman lives on, just for a moment. There is a second beep and the woman is dead once again.

The young man plays the tape one last time, then checks his watch and sighs. He returns the machine to the closet. He wouldn't want to be late for work, and the dead woman isn't going anywhere.

The young man walks with a purpose through the high-class neighborhood. There's no hurry, but he is punctual to a fault when it comes to his work. In his pocket is a special digital recorder and a selection of small tools he has found useful on past jobs.

The houses are old and refined yet clearly updated with the most modern conveniences. Hedges and wrought iron fences border the properties, but the gate to his destination is already open to accept guests. He approaches the enormous front door and hammers the golden knocker with a quick slap.

An older woman answers. She is wearing a black dress, and she's been crying. Of course. They usually cry.

He says: "Hello, ma'am, I'm Mr. Smith. I'm from the funeral home."

"Oh, yes, they said you'd come," she replies, her voice distant, as if she isn't aware what she's saying. The young man understands. A death in the family can be a serious shock to the system, sending a person's world completely out of orbit. She says: "My name is Margaret. Do you need anything from me?"

"No, ma'am. I'm here to help you. Please know that you have my most sincere sympathy for your loss."

She only nods, barely even seeing him.

Twenty minutes later, the woman and her family have left for the funeral.

The young man sits with a phone at the marble island in the center of the spacious kitchen. His presence is meant to deter thieves who might have seen the obituary in the newspaper and decided this would be a good time for a break-in. It's a more common occurrence than most people realize, and often the criminals call first, just to make sure the house is empty.

When the doorbell echoes through the house, the young man makes his way to the three-story foyer with the marble floor, crystal chandelier, and dozens of flower arrangements. The house is very beautiful, but very cold.

He answers the door and accepts more flowers from the delivery driver who greedily eyes the inside of the majestic home. When the delivery van cruises away, the young man stands outside longer than necessary, just to be seen. He scours the neighborhood for anyone monitoring the property. There is no one.

After he closes and bolts the door, he places the flowers on the table and carefully proceeds up the curved staircase.

It's time to do what he really came here to do. His real job.

There is a hallway on the third floor. European paintings line the walls. Definitely old. Possibly originals. They do not concern him.

At the end of the hallway is a locked door.

The young man approaches, removes a tool from his pocket, easily picks the lock, and steps inside.

The floors are polished wood. There is a wide mahogany desk and a dozen bookshelves full of leather-bound books. Thousands of them.

There are no windows.

The room is very, very cold.

The young man crosses the home office and studies the desk, which is neatly organized. There is an old phone with an answering machine on the corner. He won't need the special digital recorder in his pocket, which he's used more often than not lately. So few people have real answering machines these days.

A chill crawls along the young man's spine, poking at him with icy fingers.

This isn't right, he thinks.

He's done this many times, but he's never felt this way before. Perspiration forms on his brow. His nerves scream at him to flee. Yet what can he do? He came here to do a job and there's no leaving until it is done.

When he sits behind the desk, the coldness that started in his spine spreads to his arms and legs, chilling his blood. His head throbs. He feels a sensation like a dagger shoving its way through his skull and into his brain. The pain is simple, precise, and extraordinary.

He wants to run from the office, to run all the way home, but it's too late for that. He will be here until his task is completed or until he's dead, whichever comes first.

The phone on the desk rings.

A scream pierces his mind, making him throw his head back, open his mouth wide and join in. Invisible hands restrain his arms, but he *must* answer the phone. If he doesn't, he will die and the family who lives here will never be safe. No one will ever be safe in this place again.

He struggles with all his might, breaks free and grabs for the phone. Still those unseen hands fight for control. Both of the young man's sleeves simultaneously shred from wrist to shoulder as if the seams have been yanked in a million directions at once. He can see the blue on his pale flesh where fingers are again wrapping around his bony arm, trying to prevent him from answering the call. His watch is ripped away and sent flying across the room.

The young man screams, focusing all of his energy and talent and knowledge, and he breaks free yet again. He gets the phone to his ear and pushes the RECORD button on the answering machine at the same time.

"Hello," he says, and there is a roar like a thundering train in a tunnel as images rush past his eyes, searing into the soft tissues of his brain where the ice pick sensation only grows worse.

He sees:

A woman in 1930s Germany being tied to a bed and raped by her teenage son and his friends; children in a concentration camp suffocating as the poison gas collapses their lungs while a guard watches, surprised by his own arousal; a little girl in Argentina, bloody and dead in a filthy alley; a bride's "accidental" slip and fall in the shower after she nervously laughed at her new, older husband's failure to perform on their wedding night; a young boy, strangled to death on the banks of a river near a famous American city; more dead girls, more dead boys, so many dead children over the years, all over the world; and finally the deceased's chance encounter with a woman named Margaret, a woman who in time learned his terrible secrets and didn't care.

The young man feels the fingers of the dead man push between his lips, grabbing at his tongue, pinching and pulling.

The young man gags and he screams into the phone as those bony hands wrap around his throat again:

"Blessed be the people who dwell within this residence and may they be free of your furious spirit when they sleep within these walls that I bless in the name of Jesus, of Buddha, of Mohammed, of Manitou, of Acolnahuacatl, of Thanatos, and may the people of the world of the living be free of your residual presence as you shall be banished to the tape in this Earthly machine while your mortal frame is interned to the ground forever!"

The hands drop from the young man's burning throat, the icy dagger withdraws from his brain, and the room begins to warm, ever so slightly.

Much later, the young man sits in his chair in his barren room under the yellowed light of the lamp and he holds the new answering machine.

He is very pale and sweaty, beaten and broken, but he's finished his work yet again.

There are burns on his body from the hands and fingers of the deceased, but he doesn't bother to look. The wounds are part of the job.

The woman named Margaret and all others who live in that house will be safe from the fury of the dead.

At least until Margaret dies. The young man has a bad feeling about her.

He presses the PLAY button on the newest addition to his collection.

The room's walls hear a thick German voice say: "You've reached the private line of Mister VonMueller, please leave a message and I'll get back to you as soon as possible."

But the young man doesn't hear those words.

Instead, he hears a strident version of that same voice screaming: "I'LL KILL YOU, *HURENSOHN*, YOU LITTLE MUTHAFUCKER, YOU LITTLE *STÜCK SCHEIßE, VERDAMMTE SCHEIßE*, IF YOU DON'T LEAVE THIS PLACE NOW, AND I MEAN RIGHT NOW..."

The recording goes on like that for almost seven minutes.

The young man had no idea it took him so long to say the required words after he answered the phone, but time is funny when he's doing his job.

The tape plays on, and eventually the words of the deceased slur from German profanities into the language only the dead understand until, near the end, there is the young man's chant, over and over again, and then nothing else until the jarring beep as the recording ends.

He turns off the machine, slides off the chair, and opens the door to the closet.

He steps inside.

The closet extends for as far as he can see. There are hundreds of doors in this endless hallway. Lining the walls of the hall, from floor to ceiling, are answering machines of every make and model ever made, along with boxes and boxes of digital tapes and thumb drives. There are millions, perhaps billions of devices containing the words and spirits of the dead.

The young man walks until he finds an open slot where he adds Mister VonMueller to the collection. Then he returns to his room.

He occasionally sees other people entering and exiting from the other doors, but he is forbidden from talking to them, and that's just one of the reasons why the young man is lonely as hell.

But that's not the *only* reason. He's exhausted and he can't imagine spending the rest of his days ridding the world of evil. There's just so much of it. More and more every minute, every hour, every day. Is that really why he was put on this Earth?

The young man doesn't think so, and he wishes he knew his true purpose. He wishes he weren't so alone all the time.

He thinks maybe there's another call to answer in life.

The dead are dead, after all.

They shouldn't have so much control over his life.

Someday, the young man hopes to be free of this terrible responsibility.

Someday very soon.

But for now there are the dead, just waiting for their chance to return to the world of the living, and he has a job to do.

The Final Lesson

RONALD HAMMERSTEIN COULD FEEL someone watching him as he mowed the lawn in front of his home. The sun was slipping behind the mountains to the west, but just a few more passes and he would be done. Good timing, too, because the bagger on the push mower was nearly full.

The sensation of being watched was unnerving, though. The scrawny little man wiped the sweat from his forehead as he searched the tree-lined street for who might have eyes on him. Normally this was a quiet neighborhood, a nice place to live. The homes were well cared for and he often heard the laughter of children playing in the nearby park, especially in the summer. He wasn't very social, but he liked his neighbors. They were good people.

Maybe that was why he hadn't bolted to start a new life somewhere else, even though the urge had been strong, especially in the months after his wife's death. Some days he still felt like jumping in his car and leaving everything behind, but he couldn't make himself do it. Deep down he knew the loneliness wouldn't be any better somewhere else.

All Ronald had left in this world to care about was his home and his students at work, and both places were haunted by memories both sweet and troubling. He and Jennifer had met as teachers at the Community School—he taught music, she English. At first, they had just casually chatted in the break room during their shared planning period, but those chats grew longer and more in-depth and soon dates followed and a year later they were happily married.

Then, two years ago, Jennifer had been brutally stabbed to death in the side parking lot of the Stop-N-Go mini-mart on the state road that connected their community to the Turnpike. It was late at night, the store was the only one in their sleepy little town still open, and she was there to purchase cough medicine for Ronald when she was attacked. She had been stabbed more than one hundred times. Her purse was slashed open and her wallet was taken.

There were no witnesses and the store's outside security camera had been busted. Because it had been the middle of the night and she was on the side of the building away from the large glass front windows, her body had laid there next to her car for nearly two hours before a townie with insomnia and the munchies found her. Ronald had fallen asleep while waiting for his wife to return and didn't know anything was wrong until the sheriff knocked on his door.

The sheriff had quickly ruled Ronald out as a suspect and focused the investigation on a White Whippet Bus that was at the Stop-N-Go around the same time, but many of the passengers had paid cash and there was no official passenger manifest, so once everyone went their separate ways in Pittsburgh, which happened before anyone even knew Jennifer was dead, it was hard to figure out who had been there.

The entire community mourned with Ronald, of course. An emotional prayer service was held in the school auditorium and a makeshift memorial was created in the gardens. A permanent bronze plaque would eventually be placed there among the flowers. Engraved upon it was one of Jennifer's favorite quotes about why she had become a teacher: *If even one of my lessons changes a student's life for the better, then I will have succeeded.*

Eventually, though, when it became clear the killer probably wouldn't be caught, probably wasn't even a local—*couldn't* be a local because only a monster would have done this sort of thing—interest waned, as if the murder had been a bad dream.

People still consoled Ronald on his loss, even two years later, but they didn't seem to *really* remember how his wife had been ripped from his perfect little world. They spoke as if she had somehow just faded away.

For everyone except Ronald, life had settled down again. Everyone had returned to feeling safe and secure in their quiet little town.

At least until this morning.

The murder of the Derrick couple had the community visibly shaken again. This was a small town in western Pennsylvania, after all, not Pittsburgh or Philly or even Harrisburg. What had been done to the kindly old couple was cold-blooded and horrific, and their deaths had hit Ronald especially hard because he knew them so well.

They were well-respected and beloved teachers at the Community School, and had been for many years, and they were brutalized for an entire night by their attacker. The crime wasn't just murder, it was much, much worse. What had been done to them was inhuman.

Ronald couldn't stop thinking about how their bodies had been found, which was one reason he had decided to do something to keep himself busy this evening, but now he stopped again. That feeling of being watched grew stronger. Invisible icy fingers caressed his spine and he shuddered. Maybe he was just giving in to paranoia, but something didn't seem right. He had barely seen any of his neighbors this evening, as if everyone were staying inside. Maybe, given what happened to the Derricks, they were smart to do so.

He hurried to mow the last strip of grass between the sidewalk and the street, and then he killed the engine and pushed the mower toward his garage where he would empty the bagger into a heavy-duty garbage bag. He wanted to get inside as fast as he could, but the closer he got to the house, the stronger the feeling of being watched became.

Then he realized why. Someone was in the garage, deep in the shadows. Ronald tried to summon his courage, but he wasn't a brave man by nature. He wanted to call out, to make some threat that would scare the person into showing himself. Yet he couldn't think of anything to say, and even if he *did* say something threatening, who would be afraid of a scrawny music teacher?

Ronald opened his mouth, but still no words came. His throat wouldn't allow him to make any sounds. He forced himself to cough and he managed to squeak out a question that wouldn't have scared a mouse:

"Who . . . Who's in there?"

More movement in the shadows, but no answer. The sun was nearly gone and he wished he had started mowing earlier in the day or maybe just stayed inside like everyone else with a lick of common sense apparently had. There was no one to be seen anywhere on the street. Nobody would be coming to his rescue.

"Who's in there?" he asked again, his voice uneven, cracking with each word.

Two teenagers dressed all in black emerged from the shadows. Their rough leather jackets were ragged with holes. Dog collars lined with metal spikes hugged their necks and they wore heavy military boots. One of them was tall, the other short. At first Ronald thought the tall teen had two black eyes, but then he realized the marks were tattoos.

"How's it hanging, Ronnie McDonnie?" the tattooed teen asked.

"Why are you in my garage?"

"We just wanna chat with ya," the shorter teen said.

He grinned, but the expression formed on his face in such a disturbing, awkward manner that Ronald took a step backwards. He knew he had to get away from these two, he understood they meant trouble, but he wasn't sure how he could do that. They were blocking his path through the garage, and if he tried to make his way to the front door, either one of them would be able to run him down if they wanted to do so. He decided he would have to use his words and simple logic to get them to stop trespassing.

"If you boys leave, I won't have to call the cops."

Both teens looked at each other, eyes wide and bugging out comically, and then they laughed. Their cackles were feral, uncontrolled. The sound started guttural and low but grew louder and more shrill. The taller teen bent over and slapped his knee like he had just heard the funniest joke of his life. Then he straightened back up, pretended to wipe a tear from his eye, and looked at the music teacher with cold, merciless eyes that showed no humor at all.

"You just think you're The Man, dontcha Ronnie?"

"Listen, I don't want any trouble..."

"No! *You* listen to *us*. We came here for a reason, and we're going to get what we want."

"I don't have any cash..." Ronald started to say, but before he could finish, the teens reached into their pockets and pulled out knives, which were gleaming and sharp.

"We don't want your cash, dumbass," the short teen whispered. "We want your blood."

As the sun vanished behind the mountains and darkness claimed the world for another night, Ronald came to realize these two had killed the Derricks. The fact was as simple as it was horrifying. They had raped and skinned the couple alive and then left their bodies hanging upside down from the flagpole at the Community School for the entire town to see, blood dripping and pooling in the grass.

Ronald's stomach tightened as hot liquid rushed up his throat. He bent over next to his lawn mower and vomited. He couldn't help himself. Fear filled him, draining the strength from his arms and legs.

The tattooed teen smiled crookedly. "Yeah, you recognize our handiwork, do you? Those old fucks were fun to cut. Oh yeah, we cut them good. We should've played with your wife like that, Ronnie McDonnie."

Ronald wiped the vomit from his lips and stared in horror as comprehension dawned. He thought of his wife lying on the pavement of the Stop-N-Go as a blade penetrated her side again and again, her blood flowing out into the night. She had gasped her last bloody gulps of air while he was home sick on their couch, completely unaware and useless. Sometimes, during long nights spent alone in their bedroom, he could almost hear her gurgling cries for help.

"Ronnie McDonnie, don't you know who we are?"

Even through his confusion, Ronald realized he *did* remember these two. And why shouldn't he? They had been his students...until... until what?

"You failed our asses and so did your bitch," the tattooed teen said. "We dropped out, just to piss everyone off! You all said we'd go nowhere, but oh, the places we've gone."

Ronald knew their names. He had failed so few students that he easily remembered them. They had been in his Basic Music Theory class the year before Jennifer died. They had put no effort into the class, none at all. Yet if they hadn't been so determined to bully the kids they called sluts and fags, Ronald probably would have let them pass anyway. He didn't like seeing students fail. But these two had gone too far and he just couldn't justify letting them slide, not even with a D.

Not that any of it mattered: not their names, not the horrible things they called the other students, none of it. All that mattered was the evil glimmer in their eyes and the knives in their hands.

The tattooed teen raised his blade a little. It sparkled in the light of the rising moon.

"We used the cash we got from your bitch to take the bus to the city. Pittsburgh is great, man, it really is. We've met a lot of people, made a lot of deals, and we're bringing it all back here. We've got some good shit the school kids are gonna love! First, though, we had to get our payback, know what I mean? Gotta settle some scores and make things right."

"Why'd...why'd you kill the Derricks?"

"Well, duh, they failed our asses, just like you did. They're dead, boo hoo, so sad, and now we want to see you die all curled up like a baby and cryin' for your momma just like your bitch."

"Stop it," Ronald whispered. "Stop it."

"We'll stop when we're ready to stop, Mr. Man. Everyone in this goddamned shit town thinks their shit don't stink, but we're gonna teach all you a lesson. Everyone's gonna fuckin' regret treating us like trailer trash shit."

Ronald's heart was pounding so hard he could barely hear anything else. He thought of his wife dying on the warm pavement of the Stop-N-Go. He thought of the skinned couple hanging from the flagpole at the school, their blood pooling under their naked and violated bodies. He wanted to scream.

"Hey Ronnie McDonnie," the shorter teen said. "You still in there, man? You're looking a little pale. You know, I asked your bitch to suck my cock and I think she wanted to, I really do, but she was too busy bleeding out like a sucker."

The tattooed teen laughed and high fived his friend. "Good one! Now let's cut up this little piece of shit and have some fun, what do you say?"

"Stop it," Ronald whispered again. It seemed to be all he *could* say.

"You know what, Ronnie, for old time's sake, we'll make it a fair fight," the tattooed teen said as he tossed his knife at the music teacher's feet. "There ya go. It's the bigger blade."

Ronald stared at the knife laying at the edge of his driveway, next to his puddle of vomit and his lawn mower, which he had completely forgotten about, as if mowing the lawn were something he had done in another lifetime. He thought again about his wife and the Derricks and what a nice town this used to be. He thought about how these two little monsters had destroyed his life by taking Jennifer away from him, how they were now planning to destroy his community with murder and drugs and God knew what else from the big city.

Ronald's outright horror transformed into a new emotion he hadn't truly experienced before in his entire life. Rage rose inside of him like a towering gasoline-fueled inferno. He had never been in a fight in his entire life — he had never even raised his fist in anger — but he wanted to kill these boys. He wanted to make them pay for what they had done.

The blinding fury consumed him from out of nowhere. These two weren't going to get away with their crimes. Not if he had his way.

Rage exploded through Ronald.

And then he snapped.

When the sheriff spotted Ronald Hammerstein sitting on the lawn in front of his home, the career lawman knew there was some element of truth to the frantic calls his office had received.

Not because of how or where Ronald was sitting, exactly, but because of how far away his neighbors were standing. Normally when something bad went down, you had to fight with the public to maintain the sanctity of the scene. These people were keeping their distance without any encouragement.

The sheriff put his hand on his holster and slowly approached Ronald, who sat motionless in the light of the full moon. There were dark streaks on the music teacher's clothes and face. The air was ripe with a sour mixture of blood and vomit.

"Mr. Hammerstein?"

The teacher gradually raised his head like a man coming out of a dream. Once the fighting and the screaming had ended, he had collapsed from exhaustion on the lawn next to his driveway. He had sat there, silently, and hadn't moved since, not even when the screaming around him started again. At times the screaming seemed to be everywhere, but he blocked out the noise and he thought about how much he loved his wife and how much he missed her and how he would give anything for her to be alive again.

"Ronald, what happened here?"

"They attacked me with knives." His words were unhurried and his eyes twinkled like diamonds in the moonlight. "They wanted to fight, and I had to, I had to. After what they did, someone had to show them they couldn't be human monsters, not here, not in our town. I guess I had one final lesson for my former students after all."

"Ronald, *what* did you do?"

"They wanted to fight, but they gave me an advantage."

The sheriff glanced at the overturned lawnmower and the two bulky trash bags on the edge of the driveway. He nudged one bag with his shoe. It was full. The mower must have weighed fifty pounds, but the blades were coated in blood, which was dripping and forming sticky puddles on the pavement.

"Ronald, what was your advantage?"

The music teacher grinned, showing his teeth. "I had the bigger blade."

Loving Roger

EVERYONE MAKES MISTAKES, a truth Patty knew all too well, which was why she believed in the power of forgiving and forgetting. Her mamma always said forgiveness was love and love was forgiveness. In the end, Patty knew Mamma was right. No matter what mistakes Roger had made, Patty could never stop loving her husband.

The city noise pounded against Patty's temples as she slowed the rental car to a stop at one of the many busy intersections between her and the suburbs. The summer day would have been beautiful if she had been anywhere else in the world. A tractor-trailer roared past, horn blaring, engine snarling, black puffs of smoke spitting out of the chrome pipes behind the cab as the driver ran the red light.

Patty couldn't wait to escape the city. She had felt trapped in the rundown motel where she had been collecting her thoughts, and she would never go back there again. That place was loud and dirty and everyone was rude. The walls were made of cinderblock and the neighbors were so dangerous that all of the windows had metal bars on them.

"Everything will be better," Patty said, focusing on her goals. "I've learned from our mistakes."

She reached for the bottle of cheap champagne on the passenger seat, just to make sure it hadn't shifted. She worried about having the alcohol in the car. She wasn't even sure if that was legal and the new

Patty who was driving home again almost didn't care. She and Roger had never imbibed, and she had begun to believe that was a mistake on her part. They needed to loosen up a little.

After confirming the champagne was okay, Patty removed a compact from her brand new purse. The price sticker and bar code were still affixed to the bottom of the peach-colored plastic shell. Her dress was also brand new, as were the lacy red bra and panties and the high-heeled shoes. She had never worn anything like this before. She wondered what her mamma would say and then she pushed the thought away.

Patty flipped the compact open and checked her makeup, lipstick, and hair in the tiny mirror. She felt so much older these days. Lines had formed under her eyes. Their fight had aged her badly, but she thought the makeup hid most of the damage.

Yes, there had been some problems lately, but those problems weren't *all* Roger's fault. Patty was seeing the world differently now. While in the rundown motel, she had found herself with a lot of free time to *really* contemplate what she wanted out of life, and what she had decided she wanted was to fix their mistakes and move forward. She hoped Roger felt the same way. They had to work together if they wanted to get back on the right track.

"Tonight, we'll make up for lost time," Patty said.

The light changed and someone behind her honked.

Patty raised her middle finger to the other driver—another thing she had never done before—and then she headed home, not looking back.

An hour later, Patty slowed to a stop in front of the two-story house deep in the heart of the suburbs. The street was tree-lined and the sidewalks were decorated with children's chalk drawings. Lush lawns dotted with trimmed shrubs and beautiful gardens surrounded the well-maintained homes. Everything was more colorful today than Patty ever remembered it being. More beautiful. More alive.

She realized she really *was* seeing life differently. She checked her watch and smiled. Roger wouldn't leave work for at least an hour. The champagne bottle would be chilled by then, and she would be ready to start their relationship anew.

She stepped onto the lawn. The grass was green and soft. A new-found love for her home and her yard and her neighborhood washed over Patty. Her heart fluttered and her skin quivered with unexpected warmth. She never wanted to leave again.

Patty approached the front door and shifted the bottle of champagne under her arm. As she reached for the doorknob, she stopped dead in her tracks.

She had forgotten her house key.

Panic rose inside of Patty and her breathing became clipped. Her hands trembled. She was so close to making things right again and then something like this had to happen. How could she have been so stupid? Her plan was ruined!

"No," Patty whispered. *"No,* I can do this."

She sucked in two deep breaths and then made her way around to the back of the house, pushing through the flowering bushes that enclosed the brick patio. She crossed the patio and stopped at the sliding glass door. She said a little prayer, reached for the handle, and pushed. The door slid open with a squeal.

Patty smiled brightly and stepped into the kitchen, the bottle of champagne gripped tightly in her hand. The yellow patterned linoleum floor was spotless and the ceiling fan spun in lazy circles. Cool air washed over her sweaty skin.

Something was different, though. On the counter was a wooden knife block holding seven specialty knives. Patty had always wanted a set like that, had pointed them out to Roger a million times at Monkey Ward, but he always claimed they were too expensive. Then she noticed an even more dramatic change: the new Kenmore refrigerator. She hardly believed her eyes. She had wanted a new refrigerator since they first moved into the house so many years ago and Roger always said they couldn't afford one.

Excitement rose inside of Patty and her heartbeat quickened. Had Roger come to the same realization she had during their separation?

Was he making an effort to win her back, too? What else might he have planned? Her mind spun at the possibilities.

Yet, something wasn't right and her heart understood that before her brain. A frown formed on Patty's tired face.

There were comic strips and newspaper clippings and "honey do" lists held to the refrigerator by a variety of magnets. Some of the magnets were shaped like animals, others like clouds, and still others like fruits and vegetables.

None of these magnets or the collected pieces of paper belonged to Patty.

"Who are you?" a woman asked from the dining room. "What are you doing?"

Patty spun around and the champagne bottle slammed into the edge of the kitchen counter. Patty and the other woman both jumped in surprise as the bottle shattered. The liquid inside sprayed into the air as shards of glass skipped across the floor on a wave of foamy liquid.

A moment passed and neither woman moved. Then their eyes rose from the wet mess and locked on each other.

"Who are you?" the woman asked again. She laughed nervously. She was much younger than Patty, with blonde hair and blue eyes and trim legs. The woman reminded Patty of the girls she had known in her college days, back when she first met Roger at a mixer. Patty had seen how Roger looked at those girls.

"*Who* are *you*?" Patty asked. A knot twisted in her stomach.

"My name is Sally." The woman's voice was a little less harsh this time, showing a hint of concern. "Are you okay, hon? What are you doing here?"

"I live here with Roger. What are *you* doing here?"

"I'm sorry. You must be confused," the woman said. "This is my house."

Patty finally realized who this woman was, who this woman had to be. The whore. This was the goddamned whore who had seduced her husband!

The rage Patty had been suppressing for a lifetime boiled over.

Waves of heat flowed through her body and her hands trembled from the surge of adrenaline. A lot of people had taken advantage of Patty over the years, but she had never been so consumed by anger when faced with their betrayals.

Patty's vision flashed red as she reached for the wooden block on the counter and selected the largest knife. When she turned back toward the dining room, she saw the shock on the whore's face.

Patty took a step, kicking the base of the broken champagne bottle across the foamy kitchen floor.

"No, wait a minute," the woman said as she backed away, raising her hands. "What are you doing?"

As Patty moved, she remembered the events of a day much like this one many years ago when she had come home early from work.

She had discovered Roger and that woman from across the street doing terrible things like animals in heat. God, the awful sounds they had made!

Patty's anger and confusion merged with the memory of the endless river of blood splattering everywhere. Patty was home again and she saw every little detail and she had to do *something* to make them stop.

The woman named Sally, now backed into a corner, said: "Please don't hurt me! Please listen!"

But Patty couldn't listen. She had to make Roger and the awful woman stop what they were doing. She had to help Roger understand the mistake he was making.

She loved him so goddamned much. Why couldn't he understand that?

Patty raised the knife and prepared to show her husband exactly how much she loved him, and she would keep showing him until he understood that her love was endless and eternal.

She would love Roger again and again, and she would never, ever stop.

Among Us

I'VE LEARNED A LOT LATELY about the terrible things you can do if you're motivated enough.

Six months ago I was a good, upstanding citizen with a beautiful wife and two amazing children and a great job doing what I loved: standing up for the little guy.

Yes, I was a lawyer, but don't hold that against me. I was the good kind of lawyer, and please don't make any jokes about the good kind being the dead kind. I'm in no mood for jokes these days.

My love for my wife and kids was endless, even though I spent most of my waking hours at work. Like most people, I worked hard because I wanted the best for my family, which was a good deal for the law firm of Jacobs, Michener, and Johnson since my desire and drive made me one of their most loyal and productive employees. Once I set my sights on a goal, I burned the candle at both ends until the job was finished.

So when I arrived at work after the Fourth of July weekend last year and found a message saying I needed to be at an emergency meeting of the Partners, I thought all of my hard work was paying off.

You see, I had recently discovered information that helped us grab a car manufacturer by the ball-bearings: some rather incriminating safety reports they had "misfiled" in one of their subsidiary offices in the middle of nowhere. When the evidence was brought to their attention, they settled out of court and our law firm took our standard 40% of the $1.1 billion settlement.

The message said the meeting was starting in just a few minutes, so I dropped everything and hurried to the ninth floor. I took a deep breath as I exited the elevator and crossed the lobby with marble floors and vaulted ceilings. The opulence was stunning, humbling, and inspiring all at the same time.

An executive assistant was sitting at her desk outside the main conference room, wearing a phone headset and typing away on her computer. Her name was Alice and she handled all of the scheduling for the big bosses. No one saw them or spoke to them without her putting it on the calendar first. She was the gatekeeper to three of the most powerful men in the city, which made *her* pretty darn powerful, too.

Alice glanced up, smiled, and said: "Go right on in, Mr. Smith. The Partners are expecting you."

Just hearing those words made my heart skip a beat.

I pushed the tall wooden door open and entered the conference room paid for with billions of dollars of judgments over the years. It truly was a breathtaking sight.

Chandeliers crisscrossed the ornate ceiling and sparkling rays of sunlight radiated in through the massive windows overlooking the river. The walls were lined with handcrafted bookcases, each twenty feet tall. The shelves held copies of every legal text since the beginning of the written law.

In the middle of the room was a polished table surrounded by plush chairs on the wide oriental carpet. Seven men were already sitting there, but the Partners were nowhere to be seen. These men were senior lawyers I recognized from around the building, although I hadn't worked closely with any of them.

A moment after I sat down, one of the bookcases opened into the room, revealing it was actually a hidden door to the Partners' private offices.

Peter Jacobs, Robert Michener, and Thomas Johnson emerged from the doorway and everyone at the table stood. The Partners were in their early fifties with matching suits, distinguished salt and pepper hair, and handcrafted Swiss wristwatches. Their *shoes* cost what I made in a year.

Someone started to clap and then the rest of us joined in, which was as surreal as it sounds. The clapping echoed around the immense chamber. I guess it was just a nervous reaction. Like I said before, these were three of the most powerful men in the city and they could get into any meeting with anyone, but only the chosen few got to meet with them. They had mansions in the most elite neighborhoods, fabulous trophy wives, and stunningly successful children. They were the living, breathing American dream. Hell, Robert Michener owned his own (albeit small) Caribbean island.

I hadn't spoken with the Partners once during my entire time at the firm and I had certainly never been called to a meeting like this.

Maybe no one had. Something was up. Something *big*.

Robert Michener waved his hand to get us to stop and sit back down, smiling his bright white smile as he did so. The Partners took their places at the end of the table in their ornate, oversized chairs. The rest of us returned to our seats.

Peter Jacobs said: "Gentlemen, we have to be certain this meeting stays strictly confidential. Please put your cell phones, PDAs, and keys on the table."

The eight of us did as we were told without any objection.

Jacobs continued: "I'm sorry to rush you up here on such short notice, but we have important issues to discuss. We're taking all of you on as new Partners."

I was speechless. You're taught to have a face of stone in the courtroom — it should appear as if everything's going just as you expected, no matter what happens, even if your client just accidentally confessed — but this wasn't merely a surprise piece of testimony or a slip of the tongue on the witness stand.

This was *huge*. There were eight of us . . . *eight* new Partners!

My first thought was simple disbelief. Yes, I had worked my butt off for years, but becoming a Partner? Now? Where was the hidden camera, right?

My second thought was so hopeful and full of joy it pains me to even write this: I couldn't wait to call Melinda to tell her the news.

This offer was what we had been dreaming about for so long. It would make up for the long hours I had spent in this building and out on the road working cases. It would justify all of the important moments I had already missed: Alan's first steps, Christy's birth, and almost every other significant landmark in my children's lives to date.

Jacobs continued: "There's been a major change at the firm and we need your help. We've joined with a much larger group."

This was almost a bigger shock than the news that there would be eight new Partners. Jacobs, Michener, and Johnson had merged with another law firm? How could that have happened without anyone knowing? Office rumors bounce around like ricocheting bullets and sometimes they're even somewhat accurate, but nothing like a merger had *ever* been mentioned at the water cooler or via a gossipy e-mail.

Michener said: "It's a much larger cause. One we believe in wholeheartedly. You men are here to represent your departments, to help make the change easier for everyone. But first, you need to join us. You must join us and become Partners!"

He bellowed this last sentence almost theatrically, and something in his voice didn't sound quite right. A sense of unease suddenly nagged at me deep in my gut.

"Join us," Johnson said, standing and removing his jacket. He began unbuttoning his shirt, slowly from the top. I sat there stunned. Now this was *really* too surreal. Was I dreaming? Was there a punchline to come? Men like the Partners aren't exactly known for their sense of humor, and the whispering voice of doubt in the back of my mind grew louder.

When Johnson reached the last button, the entire room lit up with blue lightning. When the flash faded, sunspots floated in my field of vision.

I stood and backed away. The Partners were staring at me, their eyes widening and their mouths dropping open. They were shocked and I quickly realized why. The seven other lawyers who had come for this meeting were sitting motionless, their unblinking eyes locked on Johnson. They looked like zombies... or maybe corpses.

"He's one of *them*," Jacobs stated coldly. "Take care of the rest, Johnson, and I'll deal with this troublemaker."

Johnson finished removing his shirt. He stood there, proudly displaying his pale white skin and graying hair and slightly rolling stomach.

Then something happened.

His abdomen twitched, the muscles twisting through his flesh, forming some kind of horrible face on his round belly. Two ruby-colored eyes popped open below his nipples and a jagged horizontal line ripped across the bottom of his abdomen, revealing a rotting mouth filled with green slime.

The mouth yawned, as if just waking up.

I screamed and backed away, knocking my chair over. I yelled at my colleagues, trying to compel them to move, but it was too late. Their chests were expanding through their shirts, bubbling and mutating like vats of chemicals in some old science fiction movie.

Jacobs reached for me and I did the only thing I could: I kicked him in the groin, sending him to the floor like a sack of bricks. His face turned bright red and a slight cry escaped from between his lips.

I never was much of a fighter, so I make no apologies for my methods.

I ran for the door, turning the doorknob and throwing myself against the door, expecting it to be locked.

It wasn't.

The door flew open and banged against the lobby wall. I stumbled and tripped, sliding across the polished marble floor. The world seemed off its axis as I hobbled toward the stairs while Alice the executive assistant watched in amazement. Her wide eyes suggested either she had no idea what was happening in the conference room or she also hadn't expected someone to escape.

I hurried down the stairs, only slowing when I finally realized no one was chasing me. Why would they bother? Security would most likely be waiting for me in the lobby, after all. That was the quick and easy way to end the situation before it could escalate.

Instead of continuing any further, I exited at the third floor and navigated my way through the rows of cubicles where dozens of clerks worked on cases. Real offices with doors encircled the cube world. One of them was mine, but I never stopped.

My destination was the back stairs to the basement, which was home to the boilers and other mechanicals necessary for a building that size. There were also vast rooms of filing cabinets containing tens of thousands of folders from old cases.

If I needed somewhere to hide, that was a good place, but deep down I knew I had to leave the building fast. Hiding just meant the Partners would find me sooner or later, and I didn't want to learn what they did to "troublemakers."

I reached for my cell phone, not quite sure what to tell 911 and then my wife ("hey, my bosses are monsters and they're recruiting!"), but my pocket was empty. My phone and keys were still sitting on the table in the conference room.

"Fuck," I muttered, hurrying down the stairs.

I ignored the door to the lobby and kept moving, listening for any sound that might indicate my pursuers were closing in.

At the bottom of the stairwell I pushed open the heavy metal fire door and made my way through the maze of storage areas and mechanical rooms until I found the dock door in the rear of the building's basement.

I took a deep breath, reached down, and tugged on the metal handle. The door rumbled along its metal tracks. The intense sunlight pouring in was nearly blinding after being in the dimly lit basement.

Part of me expected security guards or maybe even the Partners themselves to be waiting on the other side, but there was no one in the loading area.

Without keys, my car was useless, so I stuck to the side streets and searched for a payphone to call Melinda and warn her to not answer the door until I got home, but there wasn't a phone booth to be found anywhere. Apparently the city had been getting rid of them for some time since the spread of cell phones really took off. I was too busy working to notice, I guess.

I flagged down a cab and gave the driver my home address. When I asked to use his cell phone, he gestured that he didn't understand me, but that might have been a lie. I must have looked like a crazy man, even in my expensive suit, because the driver kept glancing at me in the mirror while he drove.

My mind spun during the trip from the city to the suburbs. There were so many questions. What the hell had happened to the Partners? When did it happen? What exactly were they? What did they want?

The events of those five minutes in the conference room were too impossible and absurd to truly comprehend, yet I never doubted my sanity for an instant. I was too scared to be insane and my hands were shaking badly by the time the cab stopped in the driveway of my two-story colonial in the picturesque neighborhood my family called home. No real mansions here, but a lot of McMansions for sure.

I paid the driver, jumped out, and ran to the front door, which was unlocked and slightly open. A lump formed in my throat. There was no good reason for the door to be open. None at all. We *never* left that door open.

I stepped inside the foyer. I heard voices upstairs and then Melinda appeared in the doorway of the guest bedroom.

She saw me and asked: "What's wrong? Is it the kids?"

Before I could answer, a cell phone rang in the room behind my wife. She glanced over her shoulder. A voice answered the cell quietly, but I heard him well enough.

I said: "Who's up there?"

A look of confusion crossed Melinda's face as two hands appeared out of nowhere to jerk her back into the bedroom. The door slammed shut.

I dashed up the steps two at a time and kicked at the door, which popped open without any resistance. The privacy locks on modern doors are pretty much useless, just FYI.

On the far side of the room, one of the new Partners held Melinda. His shirt was open and the red eyes below his chest were pulsating. The muscles that formed the monster's mouth were moving and leaking green slime.

"Get him," the monster growled to its host.

The Partner left Melinda where she stood and approached me.

Instead of falling back on the classic kick to the groin, I threw the best punch I could. My fist landed directly on his chin, but he didn't flinch. My knuckles, though, felt like someone had smacked them with a hammer.

The Partner smiled and returned the favor, slugging me in the gut. The pain radiated throughout my entire body. I fell backwards into the dresser and gasped for air.

The Partner motioned at me in a way that said "come here and try it again," so I did. What other choice did I have?

With my stomach and hand still roaring in pain, I inched toward the Partner, sucking in deep breaths.

When I was within striking distance, I punched him in the chest as hard as I could, my fist landing true on the monster's face.

This time the Partner stumbled backwards, the agony obvious in his bulging eyes. The monster in his chest looked even less happy. I grabbed Melinda and backed us out of the room.

"He's ... he's ... " she started to babble.

"Yes, he's one of *them*," I stated, pulling her with me to our master bedroom. I slammed the door shut and opened the closet. My father's service revolver was hidden in a shoebox on the top shelf.

"We have to get Alan and Christy and get out of town," I said, quickly loading the gun. Melinda didn't answer.

I turned. The bedroom door was open and the new Partner stood next to my wife.

"I don't understand why you're like this, but let us try to change you," Melinda said. "We can at least try. The change makes everything better."

My heart sunk and I felt like someone was punching me in the stomach all over again. My wife was one of *them*, but I couldn't believe it. Didn't want to believe it. Didn't even have the capacity in my heart or head to consider the idea.

"Get him, you fool," the monster growled from the Partner's belly.

He moved in my direction. I had never fired the gun in my life, but this wasn't a human being coming toward me. This was a monster that couldn't be reasoned with.

My shaking hand raised the gun and pulled the trigger. The gunshot was louder than I expected and I screamed as the right side of the Partner's head ripped open ... but he didn't die. He actually laughed.

The Partner kept coming for me, half of his brains leaking onto his shoulder. He staggered from side to side like he was drunk. I pulled the trigger twice more. The first bullet hit his open mouth, blowing out two of his teeth and sending blood flying everywhere, stopping his laughter, but still not killing him.

The second bullet, though, found the sweet spot, hitting one of the *monster's* glowing eyes, which exploded in a splash of bloody slime. The monster screamed in pain as the Partner dropped to a knee. Green brain matter poured out of the wound.

I stepped forward and put the gun's barrel directly against the monster's other eye, which widened in terror. The Partner reached for me as I pulled the trigger. The gunshot was loud and abrupt, and the Partner fell backwards against the wall and slumped to the floor.

His chest was a catastrophe of blood and pus and tangled muscles, and his flesh pulsated the same color as the eyes had a moment before. Then there was a flash of blue lightning and the monster's face healed over. The eyes and the mouth vanished, all in a matter of seconds, as if they had never been there in the first place.

Now the man was just a dead lawyer in my master bedroom. That certainly couldn't end well.

I looked at my wife. She had unbuttoned her blouse and she wasn't wearing a bra. The muscles below her breasts began to twitch as she slipped the blouse off.

The monster was emerging from within her beautiful flesh and there was a coldness behind her eyes, a darkness lurking within the woman I knew better than anyone else in the world. It was the monster. A monster inside the woman I loved.

She charged.

A few minutes later the front door of the house swung open.

I was sobbing in my hands when Alan appeared in the doorway to the master bedroom. My five-year-old boy was carrying baby Christy in his arms. His expression was cold and collected. Her face displayed a chilly smile I had never seen before.

They had both been changed.

Now that I knew what to look for, that coldness behind their eyes, I could see the monster inside of them even if they looked normal otherwise. My heart broke again.

"Come join us, Daddy," my son said. "Pretty please? I'll be the best little boy ever if you do. Let us try to change you again. The change feels wonderful."

Sitting there next to my wife's dead body, my wife who no longer showed any sign of the monster that had dwelled within her, I couldn't think of anything I wanted more than to be with my family one more time, to be a real family, to just be together with no worries in the world.

But that wasn't possible.

I had to make a choice: stay and be killed by the monsters when they couldn't change me into one of their own, or go on surviving and try to learn to live with what I had done.

In the end, I made the choice I had to make.

I leapt to my feet and pushed past my son and daughter, throwing myself into the Partner who was waiting for me at the bottom of the stairs, sending him flying across the foyer. My shoulder hurt from the impact. It was like I had run into a brick wall. This was more rough-and-tumble physical activity than I had experienced since my ill-advised attempt to join the football team in seventh grade.

I dashed through the kitchen, grabbed a set of car keys off the hook in the mudroom, and hurried into the garage. As I jumped into my wife's BMW, I heard my son yelling at the Partner in the foyer. He sounded so adult, so *pissed*.

I started the car, shifted into reverse, and floored the gas, crashing back through the garage door. I turned onto the street and floored the gas again as I sped past the black SUV parked at the curb.

I raced for the highway.

I never returned.

A few hours later, I called my house from an old-fashioned phone booth outside a biker bar. Not everyone in the boonies had a cell phone yet, it seemed. Or maybe no one from the phone company could be bothered to drive so far into the middle of nowhere to disassemble it.

I don't know why I called, but I did.

My son answered. He said something in his way-too-adult voice that I haven't forgotten. The words still ring in my mind every morning when I awaken from the nightmares.

He said: "Don't worry, we'll find you, Daddy, and we're not going to change you, we're going to kill you. Wherever you go, one of us will be there . . . soon . . . very soon . . . we're everywhere."

I hung up and cried in the phone booth, holding my head and mourning the loss of my wife and son and daughter. In my mind, they were all dead. That was the only way to keep my sanity, which I thought I was on the verge of losing anyway.

When the tears finally stopped, I made a plan. Planning was what got me through the long years of college and the long days and nights of climbing the ladder at the law firm. Planning for a better future was what allowed me to dedicate so much of myself to my work.

The first thing I had to do would have been easier twenty years ago, but it wasn't impossible.

I had to disappear and drop off the radar. Who knew what access the Partners might have to the government and law enforcement? They *could* find me if they wanted to, I was sure of that, and I was also sure they weren't just going to accept that I was immune to their powers and let me go on my merry way.

That night, I maxed out the available cash advances on my credit cards and emptied my checking account before tossing my wallet in a public trash can.

The next day, in some no-stoplight town that time forgot, I ditched my wife's BMW behind an abandoned house and bought a beaten Ford Bronco from a slimy used car salesman with a gold tooth who didn't seem to care that I had no identification since I was paying cash.

Soon I was traveling the country, stocking up on weapons through private sales. I did everything I could to get better at fighting and hunting and living off the grid.

I'm not only a hard worker, but a fast learner.

These days I can move from place to place without attracting attention, set traps and ambushes like someone born in a war-torn country, and I can hit a moving target at a surprisingly long distance.

I'm not the person I used to be, but I am the person I had to become.

I have to sign off now, but if you haven't been changed, get away from the cities.

Wherever there are people, there is danger.

I have no way of guessing how many of them exist, but they're growing in number every day.

I'm dealing with the ones I can safely dispatch, but it's tough to keep a low profile while you're destroying monsters, so I've had to let many pass by. You can't just shoot a monster twice in the chest in the middle of a diner without compromising yourself. You have to follow him and watch for a good opportunity, which doesn't always present itself.

But if you're reading this, get yourself to safety and be careful. These monsters look like you and me and they won't stop until they have us all.

Maybe it's too late, but maybe not.

Like I said earlier, I've always dedicated myself to my work, even if it meant sacrificing other things I loved.

My work now is simple: to hunt the Partners until they're all dead.

I'll learn everything I can and soon *they* won't know what hit them.

Just remember . . . *they're among us*.

Not Without Regrets

WHEN SARAH WAS A LITTLE GIRL, her grandmother gave her a piece of advice that resonated with her so strongly she never forgot it: make every day count and live without regrets because no one gets out alive.

Those words were spoken in her grandmother's apartment in a retirement community the cheerful old woman called God's Waiting Room, and even two decades later Sarah could recall the conversation with an oddly perfect clarity.

Sarah had taken the advice to heart, but that certainly didn't mean she claimed to have no regrets about her life to date. How could she when her ex-husband was currently living in a padded room in a state hospital? Their lives would never be the same after what he had done to her and their little girl. Emma still loved her father more than anything, probably because she was too young to remember the horror of what happened three years ago. Sarah remembered well enough for both of them, though, and those memories provided her with more than her fair share of regrets.

A fierce thunderstorm was rolling across the valley, but Sarah didn't mind. Nothing much scared her these days, not after what she had been through. The television was turned to the eleven o'clock news, but the sound was muted and she wasn't actually watching. Instead she was debating whether to check on Emma again. Most of Sarah's nights were sleepless and she couldn't help but look in on her daughter again and again, even though the compulsion was bordering on unhealthy.

She sat on the couch in the living room, one hand caressing the ornate wooden cane resting on her lap. Sharp pains still ripped through her whenever she put all of her weight on her right leg, so the cane was a godsend. And although her leg was disfigured, her upper body was stronger than ever. When she was honest with herself, she was surprised by how powerful her arms had become. She didn't discuss with anyone why she spent so much time in the gym. No one else would understand she was preparing for the day when David would be free to come after them again.

Lightning split the night and thunder rumbled, shaking the house. The power flickered, but not enough to turn off the television, and when Sarah glanced at the newscast, she saw something that nearly took her breath away.

The words BREAKING NEWS: RIOT AT MENTAL HEALTH FACILITY were superimposed over a file photo of the state hospital located on the outskirts of town, the place where David had spent the last three years ranting and raving at the doctors.

Sarah grabbed the remote and fumbled with the buttons until the television blared: "...sources within the hospital report at least three people are dead and dozens have been injured. State Police on the scene are not releasing the names of the victims. Several patients have reportedly escaped the facility and could be somewhere on the grounds or in the woods nearby. The State Police are setting up roadblocks..."

Sarah turned the television off. There was no need to hear more. She clutched her cane and staggered to her feet. She wanted to believe this was just another nightmare, but then her knee smacked the corner of the coffee table and the sharp stab of pain told her she was awake.

She hurried to the front door, her mind spinning with panic, her cane thumping the floor like a hammer. She didn't bother with the light switch as she entered the foyer. She could see what she needed well enough in the glow of the nightlight at the top of the stairs. Both the deadbolt and the regular lock were secured. There was no reason for them not to be, but still, she was relieved to see the locks undisturbed. She peered out one of the narrow windows next to the door. The lawn was drowning in pools of water and the world was a dark curtain beyond her home.

You've gotta stay calm, she thought, glancing up the stairs at Emma's bedroom door. She desperately wanted to check on her little girl, but first she had to take care of one more thing if she were to have any peace of mind.

Sarah hobbled to the kitchen, her bad leg screaming at her as she went. She hadn't stretched properly, she hadn't moved in a thoughtful manner, she hadn't obeyed any of the rules for protecting her leg from injury—and it was letting her know there would be hell to pay.

When Sarah reached the kitchen, she checked the back door. Both of those locks were secured, too. Again she felt a sense of relief. She backed into the middle of the kitchen, leaned on her cane, and took several deep breaths.

Gotta stay calm, she thought. *Gotta think clearly. Be cool, be calm, and think.*

The words soothed her, brought her down to a more relaxed state, but then a quick movement in the darkness of the backyard caught her eye. She approached the window above the sink, leaning closer to the glass for a better view. At first she couldn't see anything beyond the torrential downpour, not even the woods. Rain and darkness had swallowed the entire world.

Then lightning split the sky and the backyard lit up, making her jump in surprise.

In the brief moment of blinding clarity, Sarah saw Emma's tire swing spinning wildly and tree branches bending in the savage wind. The rain beat against the window with a marching band's cadence.

But there was no one there.

She caught her breath and laughed. She had been certain David would be standing in the middle of the yard, closing in on the house like a horror movie villain.

She wondered if she looked as silly as she suddenly felt. The state hospital was miles away and the weather was awful. Even if David had somehow managed to escape, which was impossible considering he was on the most secure floor of the entire building, there were roadblocks and cops on patrol and endless ways for him to be stopped long before he reached the house.

Sarah laughed again, putting her hand over her face and rubbing her eyes. She needed to get some sleep. That was the real problem. How long had it been since she got a decent night's rest? Three years? And how many times did she peek into Emma's bedroom each and every night? Dozens? Hundreds?

Then Sarah heard a window shatter in the basement and in that instant she knew all of her worst fears were coming true after all.

Shit, shit, shit, he's here, she thought, the panic consuming her. *I have to protect Emma!*

Lightning flashed and thunder exploded almost instantaneously. They were in the heart of the storm. The power died. No flickering lights. No drama. No warning.

In the dark, Sarah opened one of the high kitchen cabinets and swatted around until she found a small cardboard box she had stashed there many years ago when romantic dinners had still been part of her life. She carefully lowered the box, but it slipped out of her hands and landed on the floor with a loud thud.

She dropped to her knees, sending a howl of pain from her bad leg throughout her body. She groped blindly until she found the thin candle in a metal base and a few loose matches. She struggled to her feet, leaned against the counter, and struck a match. The tip flared to life, releasing the harsh odor of sulfur dioxide. She lit the candle. The yellow glow of the burning wick filled the room with dancing light.

Sarah retrieved her sharpest carving knife from the drawer next to the stove before making her way to the basement door. She paused there, considering her options. Her heart was racing, she could barely think, and she had to do *something,* but what?

She had envisioned so many different scenarios for David's return, but this wasn't one of them, and now that the moment was here, all of the thousands of hours lifting weights and working out didn't feel like nearly enough preparation. Why hadn't she bought a gun? Why hadn't she and Emma changed their names and moved to some other country?

Sarah shook her head. All of that hindsight was academic and it wasn't helping her think clearly. What mattered now was, what was she going to do?

Before she could decide, the basement door swung open toward her, the hinges squealing.

David stood on the top step, nude. He was concentration camp skinny and dripping wet from the rain. His pale, gaunt flesh glistened as lightning illuminated the room and thunder rocked the house again. Streaks of mud covered his legs. Cuts and bruises from his escape marked his flesh.

"Oh shit," Sarah muttered, her eyes widening in horror.

David grinned, grabbed his wife by the shirt, and pulled her forward. Gravity took over from there, sending her tumbling down the steps.

Pinpricks of light erupted inside her eyelids with each blow to her head on the way down, and then she felt nothing.

When Sarah awoke, she wanted to believe David's return had been just another bad dream, but the excruciating pain was all too real. Every bone, every muscle, every nerve in her body shrieked.

She forced her groggy eyes open. The basement was almost completely dark, the only light being from the candle she had dropped at the top of the steps and the occasional flash of lightning outside the high, narrow windows. The storm had moved further east, so time had definitely passed.

Sarah turned her head and winced as a sharp pain tore through her neck, but she resisted the urge to scream. She was curled in the fetal position on the concrete floor at the bottom of the steps. Blood trickled from a wound in her forehead.

She realized she was naked. David must have stripped her while she was unconscious, but how long had she been here? And where was he now? If something happened to her daughter, she didn't think she could go on living with the guilt.

"You awake, Sarah?"

David emerged from a darkened corner where he had been watching her. He was still naked. He circled her with his hands hidden behind his back.

"Please, David, don't do this."

"Sarah, Sarah, Sarah," he said, dragging out her name long and slow. "Do you have any regrets about what you've done?"

"David, you don't want to do..."

"No, Sarah, no! I *do* want to do this! I need answers, goddammit."

"What kind of answers?"

"For one, do you regret putting me in that place?"

"David," Sarah replied cautiously, "You tried to kill me and Em. I couldn't let you hurt our daughter. You were out of control. You needed help. You *need* help."

"Fuck you, Sarah. You're the one who needs help."

David brought his hands out into the open and Sarah's carving knife gleamed in the candlelight. He knelt and lowered the blade to her throat. The knife's tip pushed into her flesh, just a little, but he didn't go for the kill. Not yet.

"Sarah, I don't think I can forgive you, do you understand that? At least not until you explain why you betrayed me."

"You know what, David?" Sarah said, a righteous rage suddenly welling within her. "*Fuck you.* How's that for an explanation? Fuck you for what you did."

David backhanded her across the face, sending a wave of stars through her field of vision. Her head rolled loosely on her neck, which roared in pain.

"Fuck *you*, Sarah, how do you like *that*," David said, slamming her head sideways into the concrete floor.

Her lungs ached and she coughed, a ribbon of blood spitting out between her lips. With her head turned and blood pouring out of her mouth, she spotted something that seized her attention. She had to force herself to look back up at David, so he wouldn't know what she had seen.

"Don't hurt yourself," David whispered. "That's my job. I'm here to make you pay for what you did."

Sarah knew she had to buy herself some time to make her move. She sucked in a painful breath and asked: "Why are you *really* doing this?"

David's eyes widened and his face twisted with rage.

"Sarah, you dumb bitch, you blamed me after you killed Em and those goddamned police *believed* you! You ruined our lives, you ruined *everything*, and now you're going to pay for it!"

Sarah hadn't realized how bad her husband's delusions had become, but she didn't have time to think about that. While he ranted, her right hand blindly reached for her cane, which had snapped in half during the fall, landing just a few feet away. Her fingertips found the rounded grip and she grabbed on tight.

Lightning flashed, illuminating David's nude and blood-spattered body poised over her like a native preparing a ritual sacrifice. His eyes were bright and wild. His mouth was expelling insane thoughts that made no sense. His ribs showed through his pale flesh. He began to bring the knife down in an arc toward her chest.

Time slowed as Sarah pulled her arm back as far as she could, using the same motion she practiced when thumping the heavy bag at the gym. When her elbow smacked the concrete floor, she drove the broken cane forward with all her might.

David's ranting ended in a deep sucking sound as the jagged end of the cane slammed into his abdomen. As his hands reflexively came together in front of his body, the knife flew off to the right and skidded across the floor. A sickening yelp escaped his throat as his flesh ripped open. Sarah screamed and twisted as hard as she could.

David stared into Sarah's blazing eyes as if he couldn't figure out what had suddenly happened. Then he tipped backwards, the cane sticking out of his belly like an arrow, his hands still clutching it. His head hit the floor with a loud crack.

And then there was silence, except for the rain and the thunder.

Sarah stared in horror at her husband. She couldn't look away. She had to make sure he was really dead.

She also couldn't stop hearing David say that she had *killed* their daughter. That was ludicrous. He had truly gone insane.

Yet she carefully circled around the statement again and again, as if it were a dangerous animal.

She watched David's cooling corpse and she couldn't quite bring herself to ask the questions forming in her aching head...like why hadn't Emma been woken by the storm, and when was the last time she had actually seen her daughter, and what would she find when she went upstairs to check the cute little pink bedroom next to her own.

Sometime later, Sarah got her answers.

What They Left Behind

S COTT SODERMAN STOOD in the open dock door as rain pounded the warehouse's parking lot and the forest beyond. To his right were the rented trailers waiting at the other doors to be emptied. Below him was a storm drain clogged with leaves, debris, and trash that had collected during the years the Timlico complex sat abandoned. Dirty water pooled like a lake.

By the entrance to the parking lot, nearly lost in the overgrown grasses, was an enormous and faded sign: *Office/Warehouse/Flex Space For Sale/Lease*. The realtor had nailed a hopeful and bright *LEASED!* banner across the front just yesterday. Scott suspected she was probably the talk of the local real estate community for finally landing a tenant for this place.

The Timlico Logistics Corporation had built the warehouse and the attached offices as their east coast operations center in the 1970s. It was state of the art at the time, but the property had been deteriorating for years, sitting unoccupied since the sudden closure of the company a decade before. The remnants of the offices next door were rotting within the vine-covered walls and roof. The warehouse was still solid, though. Steel, concrete, and sheet metal endured the ravages of time better than drywall and carpet, although nothing man-made could last forever. Eventually, Mother Nature would have reclaimed all of this land.

"What a way to spend a Saturday," Scott muttered.

A voice behind him replied: "Yeah, the storm's getting worse."

Scott spun around as George stepped onto the loading dock.

"Jesus Christ man, don't sneak up on me!" Scott dramatically clutched at his chest like he was an old man instead of just shy of turning twenty. "If you kill me, I'm pretty sure my sister will have to dump you and my dad will probably fire your ass and send you back to New Jersey."

George laughed. "Sorry 'bout that. Thought you heard me coming."

"Christ, now I need a smoke. You got a light?" Scott pulled a pack of cigarettes from his pocket. His lighter was in the car and he felt no desire to brave the elements to retrieve it.

"Nada. Those things will kill you before you're fifty."

"If I live that long." Scott returned the pack of cigarettes to his pocket for later. "They calm my nerves."

"If you say so."

"I do. Anyway, there's not much I can actually do here, so I may as well get busy getting cancer."

"Why'd you agree to help then?"

"I would have been dragged along one way or another, but I figured my old man might go easier on me if I volunteered first."

George laughed. "Maybe, maybe not. He's been in rough shape since we lost his biggest client. I just wish we'd had two more weeks to prep for this move. We're trying to get too much done this weekend, which means I'll have to spend the next month fixing our mistakes *and* doing my regular job."

"I guess there wasn't much choice. Dad's getting evicted from the old building on Monday, right?"

"Correctamundo."

"So you guys leased this place on the cheap, but as part of the deal you have to demolish that office building next door?"

"Yep, we agreed to tear it down within the next six months since it'll never be up to code again and our rent was reduced to compensate us for that work. Why?"

"Don't tell anyone, but I want to go find something in there before you get started. A souvenir or whatever, something they left behind. It'll be cool."

"If you say so, Scott. You're a weird guy sometimes."

Mary sped by on the forklift, sounding the horn as she passed, although they heard her coming a mile away. She was busy unloading pallets and crates from the trailers lined up at the dock doors. Scott and George shared a single responsibility that could have been handled by one reasonably competent person: checking the incoming inventory numbers against a master list to ensure each delivery was recorded properly. It was *almost* as if Scott's father didn't trust either one of them not to fuck up the most basic task.

Every hour or so a truck driver brought another fully loaded trailer from the old warehouse where Scott's father and the rest of the employees were busy closing down operations. While Mary unloaded that trailer, the driver returned one of the empty trailers to the other side of town and the process repeated itself. There was a lot to move and it would have been a hectic day even without the bad weather.

Mary stopped the forklift near where Scott and George stood watching the rain. The yellow machine's weary engine growled. The stink of oil and grease emanated from under the hood.

Mary shouted: "Dad called! He says the power keeps cutting out at the old warehouse and we need to check the generator here to figure out if it actually works!"

"Okay, I'll go!" Scott said.

Mary tossed her brother a flashlight. "Take that and watch yourself! You don't want to fall through the floor! George, why don't you go with him and make sure he gets back in one piece?"

Without waiting for an answer—the question had been rhetorical anyway—Mary gunned the forklift's engine and rolled into a trailer to grab the next pallet, leaving a cloud of black smoke hanging in her wake. There was no time for chitchat.

George and Scott made their way across the warehouse to the double doors that served as a gateway to the offices. Tacked onto the wall next to the doors was a map of the complex. At first glance the lines on the dusty, oversized paper resembled a giant maze, but the color-code system helped bring some order to the chaos.

"According to the realtor, the generator should be in the basement under the offices," George said. "None of us went down there, though. Hell, we didn't even go into the offices. She said it was too dangerous."

"Looks like the stairs to the basement are on the other side of the building," Scott replied, pointing at a square labeled MECHANICAL ROOM #7/BASEMENT ACCESS. "It's a straight shot, though."

"Okay, let's go. I don't want to spend too long in there."

"Scared of the dark?"

"Don't ask."

"Too late."

They opened the double doors and stared into the pitch-black void while Scott swatted around the wall, finding damp drywall and a series of switches. He flipped them. Some of the lights flickered to life, but not many.

"Holy crap," Scott whispered.

The hallway was eerily cloaked in shadows, but he could see the mess well enough: piles of discarded paperwork, water-stained ceiling tiles that were crumbling and falling onto the carpet, and colorful graffiti on the walls. The trapped stench of mold, mildew, and standing water seeped into the warehouse.

"Watch your step," George said.

Scott used the flashlight to guide them through the wide gaps of gloom where the overhead lights were broken or burned out, but he stopped at the first office with an open door.

A high-backed chair was overturned behind the metal desk, a framed aerial photograph of the property was smashed on the floor, and two filing cabinets were stripped of their drawers. Paperwork, discarded beer cans, used condoms, and crumpled fast-food bags littered the office. Water dripped from a blackened ceiling tile in the corner.

They started walking again. Dozens of offices, conference rooms, and several hallways branched off to their left and right. If there had been any twists and turns along the way to their destination, they surely would have gotten lost for hours. Everything looked the same after a while.

"Why'd they leave all this stuff?" George asked, pointing at another filing cabinet tipped on its side. Yellowed, wet piles of paperwork covered the floor. "I mean, why didn't Timlico take it with them?"

"Shit, you don't know, do you?"

"Know what?"

"I assumed you knew, but I guess not since you didn't live here back then."

"Well, what happened?"

"There was a freak fire about ten years ago. Some people were killed and the company closed because of the lawsuits."

"Lawsuits? How many people died?"

"Nearly forty."

"Jesus, how?"

Scott pointed the flashlight at a MagCard slot next to a closed office door. "See these panels?"

"Yeah?"

"The doors worked on an electronic passcard system, but when the fire started in the basement, the computer system froze. Apparently, Timlico had used some fly-by-night company out of China for the system and it always had problems. A bunch of people got trapped in their offices while the smoke was sucked through the ventilation ducts. They didn't burn, they suffocated. And then some of the maintenance workers in the basement fucking drowned. They were locked down there and the sprinkler system malfunctioned, filling the room with water."

"Holy shit! How'd the fire start?"

"Some kind of freak accident. It was never explained, I don't think, but I was just a kid, so I don't really remember."

"Damn! This might have been a bad idea."

They had reached the end of the hallway where the door marked MECHANICAL ROOM #7/BASEMENT ACCESS–RESTRICTED ACCESS awaited them. Looking back, Scott agreed with George. The building was seriously creepy and everything left behind was a reminder that people used to come to this place every morning, never realizing that a day would arrive when they wouldn't go home alive.

They felt safe in this building, but that feeling had been a lie. Death was waiting, biding his time, and the Timlico employees were oblivious until it was too late.

"Do you want to go back? I can handle it myself," Scott said, even though he really didn't want to continue alone.

"No, let's just get it done."

Scott nodded and opened the door to reveal a narrow set of concrete stairs leading down to another door. He and George exchanged a look, but they said nothing as they descended, both of them gripping the railing tighter than they would ever admit. The metal was cold and rough.

Scott opened the door at the bottom of the stairs, the hinges squealing from disuse. He reached inside and found a light switch. Several yellowed fluorescent bulbs throughout the basement grudgingly sparked to life, but many did not.

The space was much larger than Scott had expected. Hundreds of steel posts supported the offices above. Endless pipes and metal ducts crisscrossed the ceiling, and the few flickering lights produced a million shifting shadows, creating an unsettling effect, like there were tiny movements everywhere in your peripheral vision.

Just inside the doorway were benches and lockers for the maintenance crew. A broken television with twisted rabbit ears lay on the floor next to a fungus-covered milk crate.

Beyond the lockers were hundreds of desks, filing cabinets, and conference tables, and after that was a graveyard of forgotten office equipment including ancient computers, printers, copiers, and fax machines. The building managers for Timlico had apparently been pack rats. Everything was saved, just in case.

On the far side of the basement were metal stairs leading to a landing and a door marked GENERATOR ROOM. That was where they needed to go, but Scott couldn't make himself take the first step.

There was water on the floor, and that troubled him for reasons he couldn't articulate. A chill crawled across his flesh. Shivering, he wanted to turn back, but how would he explain that to Mary? He didn't check on the generator because he got scared of the dark? There was some spooky water on the floor? He'd never hear the end of it, not if he lived to be a hundred.

"What do you think?" George asked, studying the basement from over Scott's shoulder.

"I think we'd better do what we came to do."

Scott stepped through the doorway and onto the concrete floor, his work boots sending little ripples of water in every direction. The water wasn't deep, but still, he didn't like it being there. Maybe because people had drowned in this room once.

They started walking, glancing into the lockers that had belonged to the maintenance crew. Most of the doors were hanging open. A few still contained moldy clothing on hangers and there were family photos taped inside a couple of others. One locker still had a lunchbox sitting on the top shelf, undisturbed since the morning of the fire.

Scott and George continued onward. After a couple of minutes, the water had reached the top of their boots and slithered down inside, soaking their socks. The sensation was revolting.

"What the hell?" Scott asked. "Is this water getting deeper?"

"Seems like it. Maybe the floor is sloped?"

"Christ, I hope not too much."

Soon they were slipping on rotting papers and other things they couldn't see below the water's black, slimy surface. They touched the timeworn and scarred office furniture as they passed, as if to confirm it was real. Next they were into the land of forgotten computers. There were more than enough Packard Bells, Acers, Dells, and eMachines to stock a few hundred Radio Shacks just in time for Christmas 1998. The monitors were bulky yet the screens were tiny compared to what Scott and George were accustomed to working on.

They weren't too far from the stairs to the generator room when the working overhead lights died without warning.

"Shit," Scott muttered. He lifted the flashlight, shining it on George.

"Let's go back," George said. "I hate the dark."

"Why didn't you say that when I asked?"

"I didn't know it would be *this* dark!"

"The generator room isn't much further," Scott said, pointing the light at the stairs. "Let's get the generator started and then we'll haul ass out of here. We'll be quick."

George didn't look convinced, but he started moving again. Scott did his best to keep the narrow circle of light focused on their goal, but something was wrong. The air was growing colder and heavier. The water had also gotten deeper. It was to their knees and he couldn't recall when that had happened. Then he realized the water was still rising, reaching his waist within seconds.

There was a splash behind them. Scott whirled around, waving the flashlight high and low, left and right, but he saw nothing.

From the darkness came an anguished moan. Then there was another. And then another. Soft at first, then getting louder. None of the sounds seemed real.

Scott opened his mouth to say something, but his lungs filled with smoke. He coughed and gasped. Suddenly there was very little clean air to be had. Thick ribbons of smoke wafted along the top of the water and encircled him like a python.

"Let's go!" George said, diving toward the stairs. Scott followed, coughing and struggling to keep the flashlight out of the water, the circle of light swinging wildly.

The two men hustled up the stairs to the door marked GENER-ATOR ROOM. Scott pointed the flashlight back to where the waves from their panicked swim were still spreading across the water.

There was no smoke and no one in sight. The basement was silent again, except for the sound of water dripping from their soaked clothes onto the metal landing.

"What the hell was that?" George asked, his words turning to fog in the chilly air.

"I have no fucking clue," Scott replied. "I want to say our imaginations got away from us. Can you believe that? I want to believe it."

"That wasn't my imagination. Something's very wrong. We need to keep moving. Try the door."

Scott did. The door opened without issue. He searched the generator room with his flashlight before entering, just to be safe. For some reason he had expected to find a small generator like the one at his father's hunting cabin, but instead there was a control panel that NASA might have used to launch rockets in the '60s and a wide metal door labeled: RESTRICTED AREA! ACCESS TO BACK-UP GENERATORS 1 THRU 5! AUTHORIZED MECHANICS ONLY.

Scott approached the workstation. There were gauges, buttons, switches, knobs, and a few tiny, blank screens. None of the controls made much sense to him, but there *was* a green button labeled ON. Scott pushed it.

Nothing happened. No sputtering. No revving of power. None of the gauge needles even twitched.

"Damn. Should have figured as much, I guess."

"Broken?" George asked, flipping a few switches as if that might help.

"Something like that. Maybe no fuel. Or maybe I just don't know how to run this thing, ya know?"

"Okay, we tried. Let's get the hell out of here, okay?"

Scott returned to the door, but he stopped dead in his tracks as fear tightened around his throat like a noose. The stairs were being submerged by quickly rising water. Yet that wasn't what made a shriek escape his throat before he even knew it was coming.

They weren't alone.

Smoke filled the basement, and in the smoke were shadowy forms moving toward the stairs, their arms flailing above their heads. Forgotten cries and screams bounced off the ceiling, the ducts, the foaming water.

This isn't right, he thought, his mind going numb while trying to process what his eyes were showing him. *This isn't right!*

That was when Scott discovered he couldn't move, couldn't even remember how to walk. It was as if his body was an unfamiliar foreign land in which he was trapped behind enemy lines. He urged himself to *move, move, move,* and yet nothing happened.

The smoke figures were closing in. The first of them stumbled at the bottom of the stairs. Scott's eyes were wide as his brain kept sending fervent signals to flee that his body simply ignored.

"Holy mother of God," George whispered, grabbing onto Scott's shoulder to steady himself.

The paralysis broke. He turned, pushed George back into the generator room, and slammed the door shut. The flashlight slipped from his hand and the bulb shattered when it skidded across the floor. Instant blackness washed over the two men as boots clanked on the stairs outside the door.

"What the hell is going on?" Scott said, his voice cracking. "I mean, seriously, what the fuck!"

"I think . . . I think they're ghosts."

"Ghosts aren't real!"

"Maybe you should tell them that."

Scott stared into the pure black nothingness of the room as the shouts continued outside. Angry hands pounded on the door, scratched at the doorknob. Hoarse screaming followed. Water slipped under the door like a thief and lapped at their boots. Every beat of Scott's heart was a jackhammer pounding his ribs.

This isn't right, he thought, *this isn't right, this isn't right, this isn't right.*

His mind spun and he couldn't stop the words repeating in his head. *This isn't right.*

His head began to ache from the pressure, as if his skull might crack open.

This isn't right!

Esto está todo mal.

This isn't right!

Esto está todo mal.

This isn't right!

The words were all-consuming, but then he realized they weren't just *his* thoughts. He was hearing different voices. Men, women, young, old. Some in English, some in Spanish. Strangers in the dark gathered together by the unknown hand of death.

Then came a moment of surreal clarity.

This isn't right.

His first thought when he saw the people in the smoke had been the same thought the workers had when they realized they weren't going

136

home again. They perished repeating those words and now all they could do was forever attempt to escape the inescapable. But they weren't *real*, and that was what mattered.

"I don't think they can hurt us!" Scott said.

George didn't speak right away. Then he whispered: "We're not alone."

Deliberate, wet footsteps approached them. There was a distinct *click, click, click* that reminded Scott of all the times he had mindlessly played with his lighter, flicking at the sparkwheel, causing the flames to jump.

Click, click, click...

The footsteps were getting closer. More clicks. A spark briefly split the darkness.

Click, click, click...

"We have to get out of this room," Scott said, fear overwhelming him. There was another spark, even closer. He stammered, cleared his throat, and forced the words: "Those things out there, I don't think they can hurt us. But whatever's in here..."

"Let's go then, let's go fast," George whispered, directly into Scott's ear, nearly causing him to shriek with fright.

They pulled the door open, stepped onto the landing where the smoky shapes of dead people raged, and dove blindly over the steps. They hit the water hard and began to swim, coughing and choking and splashing. Their arms and legs collided with objects in the water, but they pushed through the darkness threatening to swallow them whole.

After a while, they had no idea which way they were headed, but they kept moving. The smoke was smothering, the water was freezing, and there was heat above them, as if the ceiling were on fire but shedding no light.

They pushed on, side by side, gasping for air and swimming, their hands and arms sometimes colliding.

Then suddenly George was gone.

Scott stopped. His feet settled on the floor. The water was up to his chest, but that didn't tell him where he was. He remained very still and listened. The screams were muffled and distant, and the smoke wasn't as bad here.

"George?" Scott whispered. "Where the hell are you?"

There was movement to his right. Something broke the surface, splashing wildly. Then silence. Then more splashing and a wordless scream ending in a wet squeal as George vanished underneath again.

Scott moved in that direction and a flailing hand grabbed his arm under the water. He yelped in surprise but clutched the hand with both of his, pulling as hard as he could. He felt the resistance of the water as if a substantial weight were being lifted and then he heard another splash followed by coughing and gasping as George surfaced.

"Something pulled me under," George cried, spitting, choking. "Something so *cold!*"

He didn't wait for Scott to reply and he didn't take a moment to catch his breath. He started swimming again, even more frantically than before, and Scott followed, not wanting to meet the cold thing that had grabbed George under the dark water.

Soon their hands struck the floor. They stumbled to their feet and ran, the water sloshing around their knees as they smacked into furniture and equipment. They still had no idea where they were, but now the water was only ankle deep.

They kept running blind, and Scott pulled slightly ahead of George just in time to slam into the maintenance crew's lockers. He howled, the metal edges pushing hard into his flesh. George crashed into the locker next to him with a dense thud and a hiss of pain.

Scott staggered backwards, holding his face with both hands as if to squeeze the agony away, and he muttered curses that would have made a sailor blush. He didn't know how long he stood like that in the dark but finally the worst of the pain dulled enough for him to think straight.

"Come on, I know where we are!" Scott said.

He used the lockers as a guide to locate the door where they had entered the basement. They rushed up the stairs, their soaked clothes weighing heavily on them, and Scott shoved the door to the hallway open without slowing down. He stumbled and hit the opposite wall hard, collapsing as the last of his energy was sapped from his legs. George tripped as he passed through the doorway and landed on the mildewed floor next to Scott, gasping in short breaths.

The door slowly closed behind them.

Scott and George lay there, stunned and exhausted, as the storm raged against the ceiling above them and their heartbeats echoed in their ears. Time passed. Part of Scott expected the door to fly open to reveal some monster charging after them, but nothing happened. They were alone in the hallway again.

"Jesus H. Christ," Scott whispered. "Let's get the hell out of this place and never come back."

They pushed themselves to their feet and didn't stop moving again until they passed through the double doors at the end of the hallway, where they stopped only long enough for Scott to slam the doors shut. Then they crossed the warehouse and made their way to the loading docks. Mary was on the other end of the building and Scott had no idea what he would tell her when she returned, other than maybe how goddamned happy he was to be alive.

He stepped out onto the dock plate and turned his head up toward the storm. Lightning flashed, thunder rumbled, and rain pelted his face, but everything about the moment was revitalizing. The clean rain was a godsend after being in that disgusting basement water. Deep down he felt like he had been born again. He realized he was crying.

"George, I believe we're two very, very lucky guys," Scott said as he wiped the rain from his face.

When George didn't reply, Scott turned to ask if he was okay, but the words never left his lips.

George stood in the shadows near the loading dock, his head tilted down and his chin resting on his chest.

This isn't right.

His thumb flicked at the sparkwheel of a silver lighter—*click, click, click*—until a flame jumped to life in the darkness.

When George's cold eyes rose to meet Scott's gaze, Scott wanted to scream but he couldn't. Besides, he knew screaming wouldn't help him now. Screaming wouldn't help at all.

This isn't right.

Scott had learned an important lesson from the shadowy ghosts in the smoke, the echoes of the workers whose deaths were seared into the memory of the building. Screaming wouldn't open locked doors, it wouldn't extinguish flames, it wouldn't stop rising water, and it certainly wouldn't prevent whatever terrible horror was about to transpire.

As death approached from the darkness, Scott also realized something else.

George had found what they left behind.

PART THREE

DREAMLIKE STATES

"Every single day of life truly was a miracle…"

The Temperament of an Artist

THE PRISON SUPERINTENDENT sits in his high-backed leather chair and pretends to read a document in the folder containing my personal records.

He's not reading anything, though, he's just making me wait because he can.

That's okay.

He'll play his games and I'll play mine.

"When can I have my art supplies back?" I ask.

He pretends not to hear me just like he's pretending to read that report from his guards about the illegal contents of my cell.

Of course, of course, I get it, I really do.

He wants to control the room. He's gotta be The Man.

That's fine. Let him be The Man.

I've never met a prison superintendent before but I've met plenty of people who thought they could bully me, push me around, and tell me what I was supposed to do with my life.

Some of those assholes are dead now.

Smoke curls into the air from the cigar resting in the ornate crystal ashtray on the superintendent's desk.

What a nasty habit. It could kill him someday, it really could. An educated man should know better.

Behind his chair is a window overlooking the prison recreation yard.

The usual chorus of bullshitting and hustling is audible even through the glass.

I don't need to see the yard below to picture the other inmates walking the dirt track, playing basketball, lifting weights, and generally proving how much of a waste of flesh they are.

Humanity is right to leave these beasts behind.

They aren't artists, like me.

The burly guard in a blue uniform behind me snorts some snot back into his throat.

What a fearsome brute.

He's one of the four men who came to the prison's farm to haul me back behind the barbed wire and fences after my cell was searched.

Four big, strong guards to retrieve scrawny little me.

A bit of overkill, but then again, when people see the scars on my skin, especially the ones on my face, they're often scared of what hides inside of me.

They don't understand I'm but a humble artist and all I want is to be loved and understood in my own time.

This waiting is getting boring, but sometimes boredom is the price of admission for the best moments in life.

"*When* can I have my art supplies back?" I ask again to move things along.

The superintendent glances up as if he's just finally processed my question.

"Sonny, given what we found in your cell, it'll be a very long time before you even get a bunk to sleep on. I'm thinking we might need to strip that cell of yours down to the bare walls."

He's referring to the items hidden deep inside my mattress, which were discovered during an unplanned inspection.

Someone tipped the guards off.

I'm not supposed to have my art supplies inside the prison, but I can't help myself.

I'm an artist and telling me not to create art is like telling a bird not to fly.

Ludicrous, right? Every creature on this Earth is meant to serve a purpose.

Even odious fellows like the superintendent.

Besides, the threat of removing my bed from my cell doesn't concern me.

The law says I have to have *something* to sleep on or I get to call the ACLU.

We both know that.

And that's why he has my art supplies sitting there, on the corner of his desk, teasing me.

Those are things he *can* take away.

He knows that I know that, but he wants to make sure I understand he's the Big Boss. The Man.

Yeah, yeah, I get it, I get it.

I'll play my part in this stupid charade.

"But I need to make my artwork," I say, pretending to plead like he pretended to read my file.

I have a good idea of how this conversation will go. I've heard it inside my own head many times.

But before the superintendent can reply, there is shouting in the hallway.

A dispute between two inmates working on the janitorial crew has boiled over.

They bellow and curse as they struggle.

"End that shit," the superintendent orders the guard.

The brute in the blue uniform quickly opens the door, steps into the hall, and yells: "What in the holy fuck are you two assholes doing?"

The commotion only grows louder after that insightful line of questioning.

"Those animals have no finesse," I say, sighing. "Untamed beasts!"

"As for you," the superintendent says, ignoring my comments as his attention returns to the matter at hand. "We're going to have to do something about you, aren't we?"

"But my art," I beg again.

He isn't listening.

He doesn't understand what it means to be an artist.

He doesn't have any idea how someone can love something that springs forth from within to become bigger and grander than himself.

I stare at him and remember how I came to be in this prison.

Five years ago, I was a free man.

Back then, I created my art whenever I wanted.

The sun was almost gone from the sky and I had worked my way through the neighborhood for much of the afternoon searching for the subject of my next work.

Several of the homes were nearly what I needed, but none of them were perfect.

Eventually, though, I found the house I had been dreaming about all week.

The two-story colonial sat on a wooded cul-de-sac with a faded *For Sale* sign by the curb.

The lawn was wild and full of weeds.

No one had lived there for years.

There were overgrown bushes along the side and a ground-level window that looked into the basement.

I dropped to my knees and cleaned the dirt and dust off the window with my gloved hand.

Always wear gloves to protect your hands, a voice in my dreams had told me. *Your hands cannot create great works if they've been damaged.*

In the dim orange light of the setting sun I saw the bundled newspapers piled on the basement floor.

A dog howled in the distance, setting off the other dogs of the neighborhood in response.

I checked for curious neighbors or other witnesses as I selected a rock from the weed-filled garden.

There was no one.

This couldn't be better if I had planned it myself.

Of course, the dreams told me to seek this house.

The dreams always knew what was best for my art.

I smashed the rock against the dirty window, careful to shield my eyes.

Fragments of glass fell to the basement floor.

I glanced toward the street again, scanning for anyone who heard the noise and came to investigate.

No one appeared.

Perfect. So perfect.

I carefully lowered myself through the broken window.

It was a tight fit and some of the shards of glass embedded in the wooden frame scratched me, but I had been cut before. Cuts didn't bother me.

I dropped to the concrete floor and knocked over an antique record player on a milk crate I hadn't seen from outside.

My legs and back hurt from the fall, but I had work to do and no time to whine.

Besides, everyone knew great artists suffered for their art. It was just one of the laws of the universe.

I opened a bundle of newspapers, removed the business section from each one, and spread the pages into the correct design.

The process was complicated and precise.

The dreams had showed me what to do, and I couldn't let my fans down.

You see, the world loved my art.

Every time I opened a new exhibit, there would be a story on the front page of the newspaper the next day.

I worked very carefully.

I couldn't make any mistakes.

That would disappoint my fans.

Once the design was ready, I opened a red container of gasoline that had been waiting for me in a dark corner of the basement.

Why that gas can was there, I didn't know, but the dream had told me it would be and the dreams were always right.

I spread the foul-smelling liquid over my design.

I removed a pack of matches from my pocket and broke one free.

I spared just a moment to study the match's natural beauty.

So thin, so tiny, but containing enormous raw power like a star waiting to be born.

Time passed, I don't know how much. That happened to me sometimes when I was really deep in the process of creating.

Finally, I struck the red top of the match against the long black strip on the pack.

A flame burst to life.

I lobbed the match where it had always been meant to go, ever since the moment a machine in some Mexican factory had assembled the matchbook.

The flames raced along the trail of gasoline-soaked newspapers until a glowing pentagram erupted to life in the center of the basement.

The dark space filled with flickering orange light that reminded me of the setting sun.

So powerful, so beautiful.

I stood in awe of my work.

This was by far my greatest, most glorious achievement yet.

But something wasn't right, and I realized my mistake too late.

The flames jumped onto the red gas can, which was too close to the fire.

And to me.

I turned to escape, but the explosion ripped through the basement and flung me against the wall as if I weighed nothing.

I was on fire, my skin burning off my body.

Part of my face slid away from my panicking hands.

My legs were being charred like a steak forgotten on a grill and my blood boiled.

I screamed but no words escaped my mouth.

Then everything faded to black.

I've been told a man walking his dog witnessed the explosion and called the fire department.

The firefighters pulled me from the inferno and took me to the hospital where I spent six months in the burn unit.

It's because of that passerby I'm still alive.

I owe that person my life, as do all my fans.

But as I stand here behind the superintendent's desk, I think of how sad my fans will be today when they hear the news.

They're going to miss my newest and greatest exhibit.

I gaze at the superintendent's body sprawled next to the desk and I barely even hear the guard pounding on the office door.

He isn't a fan.

He doesn't understand.

I study the wet design on the superintendent's heaving chest, which I made with gasoline siphoned from a tractor on the prison farm a few days ago. I had filled a plastic sandwich container with the fuel and then concealed it in my mattress.

What I see before me at this very moment is the same image I've been receiving in the dreams that have haunted me since I arrived in this place five years ago.

Haunted me, I say, because it seemed like such an impossible piece of artwork to bring to life in the real world.

I feared it could never be done.

But the dreams have always been right, have always been very fair to me, have always shown me the way.

How could I get the superintendent alone in his office with the right supplies?

Well, tricking another inmate to snitch me out to the guards for my contraband was the first step.

Inmates are stupid, but we all know who the rats are, and I went to the biggest, dumbest rat in the yard yesterday to casually brag about my lair of hidden treasures.

The guards searched my mattress this morning and found the gasoline, just as I had hoped.

The next step was to bribe the inmates on janitorial duty here in the main administration building to start a fight to distract the guard.

The bribing was easy, as I said my fellow inmates are stupid, but they had to time their commotion correctly or the effort would have been pointless.

Still, though, even with getting my supplies into this office and tricking the guard to leave at the right time, I wasn't truly sure if I would be able to create my masterpiece in the end.

But then the superintendent's attention had been drawn to the altercation in the hallway, which had grown into quite a brawl, and I took the opportunity afforded me.

I brained him with the heavy crystal ashtray from his desk and I locked his office door, so we could have some time alone.

Blood trickles from where his skull cracked.

His breathing has become raspy and he stares off into space with eyes that are trying to focus in different directions.

Now everyone in the hallway is silent, even the guard waiting for someone to bring the key.

They want to find out what happens next, I guess.

Well, I don't want to disappoint my fans.

I strike one of the superintendent's absurdly gigantic cigar matches against the desk.

The tip flares into brilliant, pulsating life.

I stare for a few seconds, unable to pull my eyes away from its beauty.

I have so much artwork inside of me, so much to share with the world.

Now it's time to paint.

The Gorman Gig

"JIMMY, YOU'VE GOTTA TIE the ropes tighter than that."

"I don't know if this is such a good idea."

"Listen, we came here for the money, and we're gonna get the money, you understand me?"

Jimmy put his head down and got back to work. He knew better than to argue with Mike. He tried his best to secure the woman to the chair, but he had never been good at tying knots and the woman was still squirming and twisting her hands. She probably had a pretty good idea what was happening, even if she didn't know the specifics yet.

Moments earlier Mike had caught her off-guard and pushed her down from behind, stuffing a dirty rag into her mouth and forcing a paper grocery bag over her head. She had struggled until she felt the butcher knife against her throat—then she whimpered and did as she was told.

Jimmy yanked on the end of the rope and checked the knot again and found it was as tight as it was going to get.

"What do we do now, Mike?"

"Don't use my real name."

"Sorry, Mike. I mean Jake."

"Jesus, Jimmy, you're a real idiot. Is your brother watching the street? He's your responsibility, remember?"

"Randy's fine, he's fine. Do you want me to check on him?"

"No, I need you here. This might get messy. Just remember, if your retarded brother screws the pooch, you take the fall."

Mike studied their surroundings. He hadn't expected to see the upstairs of the house. That wasn't part of the plan. The bedroom looked like it belonged on one of the decorating shows his ma was always watching on the premium cable channels. The woman tied to the chair was dressed appropriately for the posh neighborhood, that much was for certain. The bags she had been carrying when she arrived home were scattered on the floor. Mike checked for anything good, but only found expensive shoes and a new leather handbag.

He watched the woman struggling in the chair, trying to wiggle her way out of the knots, and he felt something stir inside him. He used the knife to cut a few buttons off the woman's fine silk blouse. She flinched. Tears dotted the paper bag covering her head. Mike reached out and squeezed her breast. She squealed.

"Lady, shut up, okay?" Mike said, startled back into action. "I don't want to have to shut you up. *You* don't want me to shut you up."

This wasn't how the gig was supposed to go. Mike and Jimmy were just going to grab the cash and get out of there fast—they hadn't even originally planned to bring Randy along—but the woman had come home earlier than expected.

At least her husband wasn't with her, but considering she had deviated from her routine, who knew when he might arrive. They probably didn't have a lot of time. The husband owned a restaurant and some people said it was a front for something else. For what, Mike wasn't sure, but he knew the guy was loaded and he knew some of the cash was in the house.

"Mike, let's just go. Let's forget the money."

"Jimmy, if you use my real name again, I'll cut you and leave you to bleed, you understand me?"

Jimmy shuddered and nodded. This wasn't his style at all. This wasn't what they had planned. This wasn't how the other gigs had gone.

"Listen to me," Mike said, putting the knife to the woman's throat again. "We just want the money from the basement and we'll let you live, okay? Just tell us where your husband stashed the money and everything will be cool."

The woman mumbled something, but Mike couldn't hear her. He reached under the paper bag and ripped the dirty rag out of her mouth.

"Say it again, real slow, and don't try to scream," he said. "I can kill you before the scream even leaves your throat."

"I don't know what you mean," she whispered, out of breath.

Mike punched the woman in the stomach and she cried a breathless cry. Jimmy jumped backwards, as if he had been hit. Mike glanced over and saw his partner trembling and chewing on his fingernails. It wasn't a good sign. He needed Jimmy on his toes. He certainly couldn't depend on dumber-than-dog-shit Randy.

Mike said: "Tell me where the money is *now*."

"We don't have much in the house," she whispered, sobbing. "I might have a twenty in my purse."

"You lie to me again, I'm gonna hurt you *real* bad."

From the doorway came the familiar stutter: "Mi-Mi-Mikey?"

Mike turned and saw Randy standing there, holding the duffel bag they had brought to carry the money. Mike shook his head and glared at Jimmy, and he didn't have to tell his partner that he was pissed.

Jimmy said, "Randy, you need to watch the front door like we told you. Go back downstairs."

"Bu-bu-but Jimmy? I don-don-don't understand?"

Mike gave Jimmy another look, and this one said, *If you don't handle your retarded brother, I will.*

"Randy, just go downstairs and watch the road, okay? I'll explain everything later. You gotta trust me."

Jimmy could see the confusion in Randy's eyes, but finally his little brother turned and started back downstairs, his head dipped forward, his eyes locked on his feet.

"If he comes up here again," Mike said, but Jimmy put his hands up in the air, as if to answer, *I know, I know, you don't have to say anything, don't worry about it.* Mike returned his attention to the woman. "Okay, lady, you've had some time to think about my question, yes?"

"We don't have a lot of money."

"Wrong answer." Mike moved to the other side of the chair and put the blade of the knife between her ring finger and her middle finger. She whimpered and pleaded with him to let her go, and he shoved the rag back into her mouth to stop her from screaming. He didn't want any neighbors getting suspicious and coming over to see if everything was okay. Things were definitely not okay.

Mike pressed on the knife, gently splitting the flesh between the woman's fingers. She screamed but the sound was muffled. Blood sprayed onto the white carpet.

"Mike, no," Jimmy said as he turned away, but he never finished the statement. He fainted and hit the floor like a sack of potatoes.

"Christ, what a bunch of losers I'm working with," Mike muttered. He stared at the blood dripping between the fingers of the woman's tightly-held fist. The puddle was soaking into the carpet. "Lady, I don't want to hurt you more than I have to, you understand? Just tell us what we want to know."

"Mi-Mi-Mikey?"

Mike's head snapped up at the sound of the stutter and he was already starting to tell Randy to go back down the fucking stairs when he realized his unwanted partner-in-crime wasn't alone. A man wearing a suit stood in the doorway beside Randy. A big man. Taller and heavier than Mike remembered.

"What are you doing, you son of a bitch?" the man asked. The woman reacted strongly to the sound of her husband's voice, struggling against the chair and calling his name in a muffled cry. Mike swiftly placed the sharp blade of the bloody knife against her throat. She became still again.

"Hey man," Mike said. "Put your hands in the air. We just want the money in your basement and we'll let her live." He glanced over at Jimmy, who was lying next to the bed, disoriented from his fall. "Jimmy, get off the fuckin' floor."

"Oh crap," Jimmy whispered, blinking his eyes and trying to stand. He saw Randy. He saw the husband. "Oh shit!"

"Listen, I don't know what you mean," the husband said, holding his hands up. "What money?"

"I overheard you talking about it at your restaurant, so don't lie to me again," Mike said. "You lie and your wife gets a new hole to breathe through. I heard you say you put twenty grand into your basement and I want it."

"No, you misunderstood. I meant renovations. I finished the basement into a rec room and that's what it cost me. Twenty grand. There's no cash in the house."

"Mike, let's just get out of here," Jimmy said. "Mister, you'll let us go if we don't hurt your wife, right?"

Mike turned to tell Jimmy to shut the fuck up, but the moment his attention shifted, the woman's husband leapt across the room and knocked him down, moving faster than Mike ever imagined possible.

The knife flew from his hand and the big man recovered it before Mike even understood it was gone. The man braced his knee on Mike's chest, easily holding him on the floor.

"Sit over there, in the corner," the man said, pointing the bloody knife at Jimmy and Randy. They complied without hesitation. This wasn't right. This wasn't how the gig was supposed to go and they had no idea what to do without Mike telling them. Randy started to cry. The front of his pants turned dark when he wet himself.

The man pulled the paper bag off his wife's head and removed the rag from her mouth. With one precise movement of the knife, he cut the ropes and freed her hands. She jumped to her feet, backing away from her attackers.

"You okay, hon?" the man asked.

"I'll live." She clutched her hands together tightly, massaging her bloody fingers. "Thank God you came home when you did."

The man pushing down on Mike's chest was heavy and strong, and Mike had to battle just to keep breathing. He saw the terror growing on the faces of his friends and he realized he was probably going to see the inside of a police car for the first time in his life.

"You know the cops ain't gonna do shit to us!" Mike said, coughing out the words as the heaviness inside his lungs grew worse. He was terrified, but he didn't want to show his fear. "They ain't gonna throw the book at a bunch of middle school students!"

One Way Flight

WHEN HE AWOKE, the man in seat 36-B had three very clear and terrifying thoughts go through his mind all at the same time.

The first thought: he had no idea who he was or how he got on the plane.

The second thought: the other passengers were either dead or asleep, and considering it was a bright sunny day outside, he had a pretty good idea they wouldn't be waking up anytime soon.

The third thought: 82726782B might be faulty.

That didn't make a lot of sense, but considering he had no idea who he was or how he got onto a plane full of dead people, that seemed to be the least of his problems.

Panic gripped the passenger and his stomach turned at the mere thought of what he needed to do to confirm his situation, but he did it fast before he lost his nerve. He touched the face of the overweight man next to the window—not breathing, flesh cold—and then he touched the baby lying on the seat between him and the aisle; tiny eyes open and staring at him like black marbles, but also dead. No sign of visible trauma or blood on either of them.

The passenger turned away from the baby's accusing stare and he searched the compartment again for any sign of life. There was no movement. He heard nothing other than the hum of the engines and the hiss of air coming through the vents. The plane was full of dead people. He still couldn't quite wrap his brain around the idea. He didn't have a clue who he was and *all the other passengers were dead*.

Passenger 36-B shook his head, trying his best to organize his thoughts. How did this happen? Was he the only person left alive? What would he do if that were the case? Did he know the overweight man? What about the baby? He didn't remember having a kid ... but then again, he didn't remember very much at the moment. He didn't feel any sort of recognition when he looked at the tiny child, only fear and pity.

Passenger 36-B unbuckled his seatbelt, stood, and inched out into the aisle, moving carefully so his hand wouldn't come close to the dead baby again.

Everyone is dead.

His heart jumped at the thought, as if some true understanding of his predicament were finally setting in. He was in a world of trouble.

"How could this have happened?" he asked. He didn't expect an answer, but it felt good to speak aloud, even if he didn't recognize his own voice. Hearing the words made him feel alive among all the dead. It reminded him that he *was* still alive, and if he wanted to stay that way, he needed to find some answers fast. So he asked himself again: *How could this have happened?*

The most obvious conclusion was terrorism. Nerve gas pumped in through the air system? It might explain all the dead passengers and maybe why he, apparently the lone survivor, was suffering from amnesia. Not that he knew anything about nerve agents. Or anything about anything for that matter. Right now he was simply happy to be alive and aware of his surroundings—bizarre and terrifying as they were.

Passenger 36-B checked his pockets for a wallet or some form of identification. At least then he would know his name, and maybe that knowledge would jog his memory of how he got on the plane and where he was headed and maybe what had happened. He searched all of his pockets, but they were empty. Not even a stick of gum.

Where was I traveling without any identification? How'd I get on the plane? he wondered as he double-checked to make sure he hadn't missed something. There was nothing to be found.

A thought entered his mind, although he had no idea what it meant: *This is a one way flight.*

"One way flight?" he repeated. Again his voice sounded alien to him. "What the hell does that mean?"

Even though he had no credit card, Passenger 36-B reached for the nearest air-phone. He figured it couldn't hurt to try. There was no dial tone. Was that normal? He wasn't sure, so he dialed a variety of numbers, including good old Zero for the Operator, but the phone didn't connect him to anyone. He dropped it with a sense of regret, feeling that his best chance for answers had slipped away.

But should he have been so surprised? If someone had been able to slip something into the air system to kill everyone onboard, surely they could have disabled the phones, right?

The plane shook a little as it hit a pocket of turbulence. A second later Passenger 36-B heard a thud at the rear of the plane.

"Hello?" he called out, moving in the direction of the sound.

There was a restroom after the last seat. The little panel in the door was green and said VACANT, but Passenger 36-B opened the door anyway. Maybe someone was hiding inside and hadn't locked the door.

There *was* someone inside, a tall man leaning against the sink, his arms folded, his head turned and pushed against the wall. Like the others, he was dead and there was no blood and no sign of any visible wounds.

Passenger 36-B closed the door and surveyed the section again. He leaned over to a window and peered outside.

It was a beautiful day, barely a cloud in the sky. Field after field passed by below, but there was nothing to identify where they were flying over . . . not that landmarks would necessarily tell him anything given the state of his memory.

The plane began a slow bank to the right, and Passenger 36-B put his hand against the overhead compartment to brace himself. That was when the most important question of all popped into his head: *Who is flying the plane?*

He hurried to the front of the section, pushed aside the curtain, and stepped into the plush luxury of First Class. There were more dead passengers here, sitting on bigger seats with better legroom for their useless legs.

As the plane nosed downward sharply, he reached out to grab a seat to brace himself, but at that moment the plane hit another pocket of turbulence and tossed him to the side. He nearly cried out in surprise, but he just barely stopped the sound in his throat. He wasn't sure why, though. He could yell as loud as he wanted to, for as long as he wanted to, and he wouldn't wake anyone up.

Maybe there's someone onboard who shouldn't hear you coming.

The thought popped into his mind, speaking in a voice he had never heard before (as far as he could remember), and although he had no idea where the words came from, he had to agree with the logic. For now, staying as quiet as possible might be a really good idea.

The plane continued to descend.

Passenger 36-B climbed to his feet and turned his attention to the cockpit door, which was closed. He approached it slowly, listening for any sounds that could indicate who was inside. After all, maybe *that* was where the terrorists had gone. They could be flying the plane!

If there were three or four terrorists in there, he'd be outnumbered. Then again, he would have the advantage of taking them by surprise, however limited such an advantage might be. Was he willing to sacrifice himself if terrorists really were in control of the cockpit?

He didn't think he had much of a choice. If they had murdered all of the passengers and crew, they wouldn't hesitate to kill him if they discovered he was alive. And if they had been willing to murder all these innocent people in cold blood, who knew what else they had planned with the plane?

The plane was pulling up from the dive, just a little bit, but Passenger 36-B's stomach turned from the forces exerted on him and the numbing terror of the situation. There was an alarm coming from the cockpit, but he heard no voices in response.

As he put his hands on the door he realized it was probably locked. Wasn't the cockpit door supposed to be secured during the flight? That sounded right to him. He must have heard the fact somewhere along the way, maybe in his travels.

He tried the latch anyway.

As the door opened, this thought popped into his head again: *82726782B might be faulty.*

He looked through the doorway, found the pilots slumped over in their seats . . . and he saw why the proximity alarms were sounding.

A runway was rushing toward them at a tremendous rate of speed.

The world shredded around Passenger 36-B in a flash of flames and crunching metal.

As the team completed their final search through the wreckage of the commercial airliner and documented the last details for their research, two facts became very clear.

The first fact caused a great deal of joy: the remotely-controlled crash of the jumbo jet had gone exactly as planned and valuable lessons would be learned.

The second fact wasn't as simple and it might cost someone their job: not only were the electronics in Passenger Simulator 82726782B faulty, as one engineer had suggested, but someone had misplaced the crash test dummy during the prep phase.

The chewed-up remains of the new deluxe Passenger Simulator were nowhere near his assigned seat at the rear of the plane; in fact, he had been found in the burned-out wreckage of the *cockpit* of all places.

Who the hell would have put him there?

Monster Night

LIKE EVERY HALLOWEEN Jonathon could remember in his short life to date, his mother spent the weeks leading up to the big day making his costume by hand.

When Jonathon asked her why everyone wore costumes to go trick-or-treating, she said the costumes helped little kids blend in with the real ghouls and goblins walking around on October 31st.

"If the kids look like the ghouls and goblins," she explained, "the ghouls and goblins won't know the kids are really just kids!"

This made sense to Jonathon, but his friends had costumes their parents bought from the Party City store in the strip mall at the edge of town. Would the monsters be able to tell he was human?

"No," his mother patiently replied. "A costume made by loving hands has extra-special protective powers."

His mother often smiled sadly when she spoke to him. Once, when he asked her how she could look happy and sad at the same time, she said it was because he reminded her so much of his father. Jonathon couldn't remember his father, who was killed by a drunk driver on Halloween night when Jonathon was still in diapers, but he understood his mother was lonely. He wished she could be happy.

Sometimes she was even sadder, like in the weeks after the bad person broke into their house and stole their television and the change in the swear jar. Jonathon and his mother discovered the smashed kitchen window when they arrived home from a walk to Dairy Queen.

His mother made him wait outside while she investigated. She cried a lot in the days that followed.

She *had* been a little happier the previous summer after she made a new friend named Dave, but that friendship didn't last long and Dave didn't come around anymore.

Jonathon thought maybe his mother and Dave had a *fight*. He hoped it wasn't about him.

He knew his mother hadn't liked how Dave would show up at the house so late at night sometimes. He would smell funny and talk too loud and Jonathon's mother would say, "Don't wake Jonathon," not realizing he was already awake from the noise.

The last time Dave had come to the house in the middle of the night, his mother had yelled, "Leave us alone and don't come back!" and slammed the front door. That had scared Jonathon pretty badly, but he didn't dare tell his mother.

He understood the topic of her friend Dave wasn't something he should bring up. She had hated some of the things Dave told him, especially the time Dave had warned Jonathon about the Pumpkin Eater.

As Dave explained it, the Pumpkin Eater wasn't someone who ate pumpkins, as the name might suggest, but was instead a giant living pumpkin who ate *little boys*.

In their sleep.

In their beds in their darkened bedrooms.

If the little boys were too nosy or asked too many questions, that was.

The Pumpkin Eater was awakened every October by people stealing his friends to carve them into jack-o-lanterns. This angered him and he pulled himself free from the ground and roamed the town each night seeking revenge. Little boys who asked too many questions gave off a smell that the Pumpkin Eater could detect from miles away like a good hunting dog. He would catch and eat the nosy little boys until he was full, and then, once Halloween was over, he would return to the farm where he would rest until the next year.

Jonathon's mother had tried to convince him the Pumpkin Eater wasn't real, but no matter how much he wanted to believe her, he couldn't stop thinking about what Dave had told him as summer turned to fall and the leaves on the trees began to change colors and drift to the ground.

Thoughts of the monster pumpkin filled Jonathon's mind while the cold October wind howled outside. He should have been asleep hours ago, but Halloween was tomorrow and the Pumpkin Eater was out there somewhere *right now*.

Lurking. Waiting. Hunting.

Jonathon's bedroom was on the second floor, next to his mother's, and that should have made him feel safe, but what if the Pumpkin Eater found a way inside?

The full moon rose behind the skeleton branches of the tree in the backyard, projecting bony shadow fingers through the window of Jonathon's bedroom.

These fingers crawled across his walls.

They waved, they shook, they trembled.

"Go away, Pumpkin Eater," Jonathon whispered, his blanket pulled to his chin, his tiny fingers clenched tightly. "Leave us alone and don't come back."

Tomorrow was October 31st. After that the Pumpkin Eater would return to the fields to rest for another year.

Just one more night and Jonathon would be safe.

The children at school the next day couldn't contain their excitement. Most of the teachers couldn't, either. Halloween brought out the little kid in everyone.

The best part of the day was the school's Halloween parade.

It was a *big* deal.

The parade was also the first time Jonathon got to see his costume, which his mother worked on in her room after his bedtime. She said the costume had to be a surprise or it would lose its protective powers.

Jonathon would lie in bed and listen to the hum of the sewing machine, which sat on a table at the foot of his mother's bed. He understood she lost a lot of sleep trying to get his costume just right and he loved her all the more for it.

When the time of the parade arrived, Jonathon and his classmates happily made their way to the cafeteria where their parents waited with their costumes. There was talking, shouting, cheering. No one was able to move in a straight line as they had been taught. Not today.

Jonathon passed through the double-doors of the cafeteria and began searching for his mother.

At first he couldn't find her in the chaos. There were parents and kids and teachers everywhere. The room was hot and loud.

His heart sunk a little—had she forgotten?—but then he spotted her standing in the far corner, holding a big black trash bag.

Jonathon rushed to her, waving and grinning. He hugged her.

"Love you, kiddo," she said, smiling as she pulled his costume from the bag.

He felt his face twist into a grimace.

His mother held a pumpkin costume as big as the biggest pumpkin they had ever seen in the farmer's field outside of town. The costume was made of soft velvet and there were black stripes, a brown stem, and a traditional jack-o-lantern face stitched on the front. Narrow eyeholes would allow him to see where he was walking.

The costume reminded Jonathon of the Pumpkin Eater so much that he was *terrified* by the idea of wearing it.

He looked from the costume to his mother's face and he saw her disappointment. He forced a smile, and his mother forced a smile back, but he could tell she was heartbroken. That made him feel heartbroken, too.

"I love it," he said softly, but she didn't reply.

He locked the fake smile on his face as his mother draped the costume over his head. He felt like he was being smothered, but he kept his mouth shut tight and didn't complain. The costume was heavy and he had trouble walking, but he told his mother again how much he loved it.

As Jonathon marched through the school hallway with all his happy classmates, a deep sadness grew inside him, one unlike any he had experienced before, not even when their television was stolen or on the many nights he listened to his mother crying through the bedroom wall.

That evening, as the growing shadows stretched across the neighborhood and a cool breeze blew between the trees, the trick-or-treating hour drew closer and the butterflies of anticipation were eagerly dancing in Jonathon's stomach.

His mother helped him dress and this time he was certain he had done a better job of convincing her that the costume was his favorite ever. Once he was ready, they walked to a neighbor's house where he met up with a group of other kids. They were dressed as vampires and werewolves and zombies and Superman and Batman and Harry Potter.

Some of them had fancy decorated sacks for their loot, but Jonathon carried a generic plastic pumpkin with a black plastic handle. He hoped it was big enough for all of the candy he would be hauling home. His plan was to have enough to get him through Thanksgiving, which was when he and his mother would spend the better part of a day making a huge batch of Christmas cookies.

Jonathon and the other kids rushed from door to door, knocking and waiting and then yelling, "Trick-or-treat!" as the door opened and someone appeared, ready to distribute pieces of factory-wrapped candy to all of the little ghouls and goblins of the neighborhood.

Most people gave you one piece, some people gave you two, but the very best house on the block was Doctor Brown's house. Mrs. Brown sat dressed as a green-faced witch in the rocking chair on the front porch and she let you take your pick from a fancy crystal punch bowl filled with *full size candy bars.*

When given the choice, Jonathon always grabbed a Butterfinger. They were his favorite.

As he and the other kids hurried from house to house, Jonathon couldn't help but wonder who among them were the real ghouls and goblins. This was the one night of the year when there were more strangers than friends on their street. He didn't recognize most of the monsters carrying sacks of candy. This worried him, but he knew his costume would protect him, just like his mother had promised.

Like always, she was correct.

Jonathon and his mother arrived home safe and sound at eight o'clock. Porch lights were turning off across the neighborhood and the streets were almost empty again. Forgotten pieces of costumes dotted the lawns and sidewalks.

Jonathon's mother helped him out of his costume and she carefully placed it in his closet where it would wait to be prepared for proper storage in the attic. She inspected his candy and allowed him to select one piece for a pre-bedtime snack. He snagged a Butterfinger, of course.

Twenty minutes later, Jonathon was in bed, happy and content to dream about the candy his mother had stashed on the high shelf in the kitchen to dole out over the next few weeks.

He hoped no one would break into the house and steal his candy, but he also knew that wasn't the worst thing that could happen.

It was still Halloween night, after all, and there were real monsters out there, prowling in the dark.

A few hours later, Jonathon couldn't tell if he was awake or asleep. He certainly felt awake, but dreams could be tricky.

He was about to pinch himself when something thumped on the side of the house.

He turned his head.

Pumpkin vines tapped on the window glass, highlighted by the full moon glowing brightly in the starry night sky above the tree in the backyard.

A massive brown stem rose into view as the Pumpkin Eater climbed upward.

The pumpkin skin was dark orange and wrinkled.

The eyes were slits that glowed from an angry fire burning within. The Pumpkin Eater was grinning, too, a most awful grin.

"I've come for you, Jonathon," the monster growled. "I've come to split you open and eat your pulp and your seeds!"

"No," Jonathon whispered as he pulled his blankets above his head. "Please leave me alone. I told you not to come here again."

The window glass shattered and then the Pumpkin Eater was inside his room, slithering across the floor. The vines snatched Jonathon's covers and pulled them back as the Pumpkin Eater towered over him. One of the vines was waving a jack-o-lantern carving tool. Then the Pumpkin Eater lowered the plastic tool to Jonathon's belly, pushing into his pale flesh...

And that was when Jonathon flopped out of bed, tangled in his covers, landing hard on the cold floor. He blinked his eyes open, confused about what was real and what wasn't. His heart raced.

He rolled and looked toward the window, which was not broken like he feared it would be. The full moon *was* out there, though, watching over him, illuminating his room with a brilliant white light.

"Just a dream," he whispered. "It was just a dream."

As his breathing returned to normal, Jonathon started to crawl back into his bed when he heard a gruff voice say something on the other side of the wall. He stopped and remained as still as he could.

"Leave Jonathon alone," his mother answered.

After a moment, Jonathon understood: The Pumpkin Eater hadn't come for him. It had come for his *mother*!

Jonathon had to help her and *fast*. But what could he do? He was just a little boy. He had no idea how to defeat the Pumpkin Eater, but he had to do *something*. His mother needed his help! What kind of son wouldn't be able to help his own mother when a monster was in the house?

The answer came to Jonathon in a panicky rush of jumbled thoughts. He hurried to his closet, grabbed the orange velvet pumpkin off the hanger, and pulled it over his head, stumbling under the sudden weight. He could barely see through the eye slits, but that hadn't stopped him from traveling to every house in the neighborhood for candy and it certainly wouldn't stop him now. His mother needed his help!

Jonathon gently opened his bedroom door, tiptoed down the hallway as quietly as he could, and listened outside his mother's bedroom door.

"Please leave us alone," his mother said.

Jonathon's heart thudded in his tiny chest, but he had no time to waste on fear. He turned the doorknob and pushed the door open a few inches.

The first thing he spotted through the narrow eyeholes was that the window had been broken, just like in his dream.

But there was no Pumpkin Eater.

Instead a man stood by the bed, towering over his mother, who wore just her nightgown.

The man held a gleaming hunting knife.

In some ways, this man looked like his mother's friend Dave, but the greasy hair sticking out from under his backwards Budweiser hat was longer, his clothes were dirty and torn, and his face was hidden behind a scruffy beard. He waved the knife, punctuating the air as he said something about getting what he was owed. The man sounded a lot like Dave, too.

Jonathon's mother was crying.

The man was as scary as any monster Jonathon had ever seen on TV or in picture books, but he had to do something. He was the one with the protective costume, not his mother. He pushed the door open the rest of the way and rushed into the room without the faintest idea what he would do next. He trusted the costume would protect him like it had during trick-or-treating.

The man turned and said, "What the hell?"

"Jonathon, no!" his mother cried, her eyes widening in terror.

As Jonathon got closer, he realized the man smelled a lot like Dave had on the nights when he came to the house way too late. The odor was harsh and pungent as it seeped into the room with every breath the man exhaled.

The man stepped forward and shoved Jonathon, sending the little boy in the pumpkin costume tumbling back across the room.

Jonathon yelped, reaching for anything that might stop his momentum. He smacked into the door, slamming it shut. Pain arched through his small body.

The man returned his attention to the bed just in time to see the sewing machine smash into his face. The impact was hollow and thunderous at the same time. He roared in pain.

Jonathon's mother dropped the sewing machine and pushed the man backwards through the broken window. He screamed again, but this scream ended suddenly with a loud thud.

Jonathon's mother hurried to her son, dropping to her knees beside him. She rolled him over so he was sitting up.

"Are you okay?" she asked as she helped him out of the costume.

"I'm a little dizzy."

Jonathon rubbed his head and regarded the room with blinking eyes. His mother kissed him on the forehead. She was crying harder now. She wrapped her trembling arms around him and held him tight.

"That was very brave of you," she said.

"I thought the Pumpkin Eater had come for us. Was that a different monster?"

"Something like that."

"It's the worst part of Halloween. I can't wait for the monsters to go away."

"Me, too," his mother said softly, kissing the top of his head again. "Me, too."

Tomorrow Could Be Even Better

A S KATHY WALKED HOME from her job waiting tables at the Old
West Buffet, she considered how quickly life could change when
you were least expecting it.

A decade ago, her father had dropped dead of a stroke while golfing
on a beautiful spring day. Three years ago, Kathy's husband had left
her without any warning at all. She had walked to work without a
worry in the world only to come home and discover him gone. No note,
no goodbye, nothing. And today... well, she still wasn't sure exactly
what had happened today, but *something* certainly had happened. Not
something she was expecting, that much was for sure.

The armpits of Kathy's black shirt were soaked in sweat and she
stopped frequently to wipe her brow and then wipe her hands on her
smock, which hugged her swelling waistline. There were no clouds in
the sky and the scorching summer sun was as hot as the fryers in the
restaurant's kitchen.

(today is the day you leave the past behind)

Days like this had always made her wish she could find the
willpower to skip the free meal at the end of her shift. Given how
she viewed the customers—future graduates of Bovine University, she
called them, referencing some television show she couldn't quite
remember—resisting the temptation to indulge should have been
easy.

Yet after every shift Kathy found herself sitting alone in a corner booth with plates of macaroni and cheese, chicken wings, chicken strips, narrow slices of pizza, mashed potatoes with gravy, cake, two plastic cups of pudding, and anything else she desired from the all-you-can-eat buffet. Three glasses of Pepsi washed the slop down.

Kathy ate until she hurt, knowing she would hurt worse later, and not really caring. That was later. The act of eating filled a void greater than her stomach. Deep inside, the food soothed her pain.

(today is the day you take control)

Only today was different. Kathy had done what she had always thought she could do with the proper motivation. She hadn't stuffed her face at the end of her shift. She hadn't even filled her water bottle with diet soda for the walk home. In fact, she had skipped her meal, and the soda, for the first time she could remember.

Kathy contemplated all of this as she approached the looming brick apartment building she called home. There had once been a colorful canopy draped over the main entrance, but all that remained was the rusted metal skeleton. She climbed the cracked concrete steps, opened the oversized door, and stepped into the ancient lobby, which was even hotter than the street outside. At least she had escaped the blinding eye of the sun.

(today is the day you learn about real change)

Kathy crossed the lobby, pausing to check her mailbox. Nothing but bills and sales flyers for luxuries she couldn't afford. She closed it without removing the contents. She wasn't going to *fret*. She was taking *control*.

Kathy started toward the elevator, then saw that a note had been taped to the closed doors. *BROKE USE STAIRS.*

Kathy felt anger rising, but she took a deep breath and said: "No, this isn't a big deal. Not today."

With sweat dripping from her hair, Kathy pushed open the door to the stairwell. Stagnant air smacked her in the face. Each breath shuddered from deep within her chest as she trudged up the seven flights of stairs. She rested often, but she didn't swear and she didn't complain.

Not today.

Today, she knew, was going to change her life forever.

Today was going to be different.

Once inside her apartment, Kathy noticed how empty the place felt without someone waiting to greet her. John hadn't even taken anything with him when he left without a word of explanation. When she finally understood he really wasn't coming back, she had tossed out his clothes so she could have the bedroom's only closet for herself.

(today is not a day just like yesterday)

Still, the apartment seemed to be missing something important. Something more significant than her husband, the man who had loathed so many of the things Kathy had once loved: going to the movies, walking in the park at sunset, meeting friends for coffee and gossip, or doing anything that required him to miss his favorite primetime shows.

"No, forget all that old crap," Kathy whispered, shaking her head. She removed her dirty smock and tossed it on the floor. A few dozen coins spilled out of the pocket and scattered across the carpet.

She sat at the table in the tiny kitchen as her plump cat came strutting out of the bedroom. Mr. Whiskers stretched and yawned and rubbed against Kathy's legs, but she barely noticed. She loved her kitty, but she had more important things on her mind at the moment.

Change.

Someone had once said change was the only constant in life, yet what had changed around here since John left? Nothing positive, that was for sure.

(today is the first day of the new you)

Kathy reached into her pocket and removed a folded sheet of paper, which was oddly sized and thicker than normal stationery. She tried again to remember the customer who had dropped it on one of her tables, but his face wasn't there in her memory.

"Today is not a day just like yesterday," Kathy said.

The note had been left in lieu of a tip and she was beginning to believe the words were infinitely more valuable than any pile of quarters and nickels she had ever received in her many years at the restaurant. She felt a tranquility she had never experienced before. The words in the note echoed through her mind, flowing in her veins like powerful antibodies attacking an aggressive but now vulnerable disease.

Today really *was* going to be different.

"Damn right it is!" Kathy said, jumping to her feet, knocking her chair back against the wall with a sharp crack. Mr. Whiskers sprinted for the bedroom, his claws slipping and skidding on the linoleum floor.

Kathy rummaged through her cabinets and found the box of trash bags. She opened the refrigerator.

"Today I take the first step," Kathy said, reaching for a two-liter bottle of diet soda.

When Kathy finished, there was no food to be found. Not a box of cereal, not a candy bar, not the snack-sized pudding cups she loved, no chips, no ice cream, not even the gallon of milk she had just purchased the previous day. It was all stuffed in trash bags in the foul-smelling trash chute outside her apartment. The food was dinner for the rats, not for Kathy.

"I couldn't start my diet without purging my home," Kathy said to Mr. Whiskers, who was sleeping on his fuzzy bed under the table. At the sound of his owner's voice, the cat purred and his paws twitched. "I need to flush my system of all the impurities to begin my new life."

(today you take the first step)

Kathy was considering her next task when the phone rang. She frowned. She knew who was calling—the same person who always called at this time of day. She wanted to ignore the phone, but that would be worse than answering it.

"Today is the start of tomorrow and tomorrow will be a better day, so I have to take this call," she said, paraphrasing several lines from the note. Kathy couldn't help herself. The strange poetry was running in the background of her thoughts, a hidden current charging her mind.

"Hello, Mother," Kathy said, putting the phone to her ear.

"Hello, dear! How was work?"

"It was fine. Same old, same old."

"You could always find a nice job here, you know."

"I know."

"You could even live with me. I can have your old room ready whenever you are."

"I know, Mother."

"There are plenty of good, single men around here, too."

"I *know*, Mother."

"Did you at least manage to control yourself?"

Kathy shuddered. Why did her mother have to ask that question in that tone of voice? It made Kathy sound like some kind of crazed sex offender!

She closed her eyes and pictured her mother sitting in the air-conditioned comfort of her living room on the other side of the state, one hand on the remote control for the muted television and the other hand holding a lit cigarette. The house probably hadn't changed one bit since the last time Kathy had been there a decade ago for her father's funeral. Why *would* it change? Her mother was perfectly happy in her routine with her snobby circle of friends and their gossip and drama and their love of boxed wine and cheap smokes.

(today is the day you leave the past behind)

"Mother, why do you always say that?" Kathy asked for the first time. "You know how that question makes me feel, don't you?"

Silence.

"Mother? Why do you *enjoy* making me feel bad for being overweight?"

"I don't *make* you feel bad," her mother replied. "You feel bad *because* you're so fat, not because of anything I do or say."

"Well, that's going to change."

Kathy hung up without saying goodbye.

The phone rang again almost immediately. When the ringing didn't stop, Kathy grabbed the cord and ripped it out of the wall.

———

177

As Kathy stood in the tiny shower that evening, the water cascading over her, she closed her eyes and her memory conjured an array of sounds: the clicking of silverware, the excited voice of an exercise infomercial host, Mr. Whiskers whining when she was late to fill his bowl, and John complaining that she was blocking the TV.

The memories made Kathy's blood boil. She wanted to tear her hair out, she wanted to scream!

Instead she recited the note's message like a prayer, over and over, and soon she felt cleansed, inside and out.

By the end of her shower, she was grinning and humming a song.

Kathy fell into bed, exhausted. Piled on her dresser were dozens of diet and exercise books. This certainly wasn't the first time she had contemplated correcting her bad habits, but she had never made much progress. It was just so easy to fall off the wagon.

Did she really believe she could be as firm and trim as the blissful models with dazzling white teeth who graced the covers of the books?

Yes, she did.

She truly did.

She hadn't before, not really, but today was different.

(today you shed the vices you sow)

Kathy drifted into the land of dreams as the car horns blasting back and forth on the street below faded into nothingness.

The nothingness grew darker and then it became the loud murmurs of people engaged in conversation while eating.

The next morning, Kathy decided not to go to work.

There was no way she could be around all that food, all those future graduates of Bovine University, and keep her sanity. Yet it had been nearly sixteen hours since she had eaten her lunch the day before and now an intense pain throbbed in her belly.

Wouldn't a burger be delicious, Kathy baby? her stomach whispered, calling her by John's pet name. *One piled in bacon and slathered with ketchup and mustard? Or how about a candy bar? One dipped in delectable Hershey's chocolate?*

"Today I take the first step," Kathy muttered as she made her way to the front door.

Mr. Whiskers meowed at her, his morning feeding nearly fifteen minutes late, but she didn't want to stop for anything. She had momentum, dammit, she was finally making progress toward a better life and she couldn't let anything stop her.

"When I return, kitty love," she said, slamming the door behind herself and not looking back.

Kathy found herself smiling while she walked to the end of the block. She would have whistled if she could have, but she had never learned how. She decided to add that to her new *Kathy's Life Goals* list, which would contain anything she wanted to do before she died. There was also another list forming in her head of the things she was never going to do again.

"So many vices," she muttered as she walked, nearly out of breath. "So many vices holding me back."

The stranger's note had told her it was time to shed the vices she sowed, but she hadn't understood what exactly that meant until now.

At first she had thought those vices were simply the junk food in her kitchen and how she engorged with her free meal after work, but those weren't the only things that had been preventing her from improving her life, were they?

How much time did she spend watching television? Surfing the Internet? Playing stupid apps that cost money just to make it to the next level when there never was a real ending to the game, no sense of accomplishment?

When was the last time she had gone for a walk like this?

When was the last time she struck up a conversation with a stranger?

Kathy had locked herself in a cage of her own making without realizing it. It had taken some stranger leaving her the weirdest tip of her serving career to open her eyes to the desperate nature of her situation.

No, the stranger had done more than that.

He had left her more than a tip. More than a note. More than the peculiar poetry she heard humming in the back of her mind.

The stranger had left Kathy a set of keys to unlock the invisible cage she had built for herself.

(today is the day you take control)

Kathy walked around the block twice before she needed to take a break and sit on the concrete steps outside her apartment building, but she loved every moment of it. She soaked up the rays of the blazing sun and she couldn't wait to go around the block again.

Later that day, when Kathy should have been preparing herself lunch, she instead was opening the window to the fire escape. The air out there stank, but the humid breeze felt wonderful.

She made her way to the middle of the living room and pushed the coffee table out of her way. The TV remote fell to the floor, the back cover popped open, and the batteries rolled under the couch, but she didn't care. Watching so much television had been part of the problem in the first place.

(today is the day you learn about real change)

Kathy still remembered some of what they had taught in her grade school gym class, back in the days when you actually still *had* gym class, and that would be enough to get her started. She took some deep breaths.

"And one," Kathy said, bending over, touching her toes. "And two. And three."

On her fourth toe touch, just as her fingers brushed her shoes, pain raced along Kathy's spine as if she had been zapped with a cattle prod. She shrieked and tumbled forward, landing next to the television. The pain grew worse and she vomited.

Darkness washed over her.

Kathy awoke to Mr. Whiskers licking her face. The sounds of the city streamed through the open window. Sunlight sneaked across the room, the fiery hues of sundown. Most of the day had passed while she was unconscious.

"What do you want, kitty love?" Kathy asked, rolling away from the dried vomit next to her head. Mr. Whiskers scampered into the kitchen in answer to her question. Kathy struggled to stand, but her back ached too badly.

She crawled instead.

By the time she reached the kitchen, her body was shuddering. She sat against the refrigerator.

Mr. Whiskers stood demurely by his food bowl, which he had licked clean. He pawed at the emptiness, as if to clue in his oblivious owner.

"Oh," Kathy whispered. She jerked open a cabinet. Mr. Whiskers scrambled away, but he quickly returned when he saw the bag of Cat Chow. Kathy ripped open the bag, tipped it, and poured the brown nuggets onto the floor. Mr. Whiskers pounced on the food in delight.

Kathy watched her happy kitty eat and then her world faded to darkness again.

Kathy blinked her eyes open. Daylight again. Morning, maybe, but it was hard to tell through the blinds in the tiny kitchen window. How long since she last ate? She wasn't sure, but her belly burned, her flesh itched.

Mr. Whiskers had devoured the cat food on the floor, his water bowl was dry, and he was sitting next to the nearly empty bag of Cat Chow, tapping at it impatiently with his paw.

With the last of her strength, Kathy emptied the Cat Chow onto her lap. Mr. Whiskers pawed at the food, but Kathy smacked him away, bared her teeth, and growled.

She picked up a brown nugget and placed it in her mouth. She chewed. The cat food crunched with unexpected flavor.

Her hands were heavy and her eyes wouldn't stay open, but she ate as much as she could before the darkness returned.

Mr. Whiskers was crying and he wouldn't stop.

Someone was pounding on the door.

More darkness.

The next time Kathy awoke, Mr. Whiskers was sitting on her lap, sleeping, purring. The gutted remains of a mouse lay nearby.

"Good boy," Kathy whispered, reaching for the bloody lump, putting it into her mouth.

The first bite tasted like the chicken fingers on the all-you-can-eat buffet.

No, that wasn't quite right.

The mouse tasted better than anything she'd ever had in her life. The mouse tasted divine.

Eventually, the darkness came again.

For a long time there was nothing but sweat and hunger and the pitch black of a sunless existence in the void of space.

Then:

Light appeared in the distance. As the world came into focus around Kathy, she found herself standing outside the Old West Buffet. The sun was blinding but she felt no heat. There were no cars, no people, no noise at all, as if the city were abandoned.

"Hello?" Kathy called. "Is anyone there?"

Her chubby cat meowed in reply from where he sat at the restaurant's front door. A wide grin spread across Kathy's face and she started toward Mr. Whiskers. Only then, when every step didn't feel like she was moving a mountain, did Kathy realize how thin she was. She hadn't felt this light on her feet since middle school.

When Kathy reached Mr. Whiskers, she knelt and stroked his fur. He purred and nodded at the door, which Kathy opened, allowing him to waddle ahead of her. The waiting area was empty and Mr. Whiskers strolled past the hostess station as if he owned the place, but Kathy stopped dead in her tracks, not quite able to comprehend what she was seeing.

She was already sitting at *every* booth. Not the thin, beautiful dream-Kathy, but instead a Kathy who had never turned her life around. Two hundred pounds overweight, eyes glassy and mouth full of grimy teeth.

On each table was a television displaying a different specialty of the Old West Buffet: cakes and pies and fried chicken and French fries and salads and thin cuts of bargain-basement steaks.

Every Kathy moved in sync, reaching in through the television screens. Their hands came back full of food that they shoved into their wide mouths, which stretched and expanded in unnatural ways.

"Mr. Whiskers, I don't understand," Kathy whispered in horror.

The cat was suddenly huge. Ten feet tall. He sat on the salad bar, his back legs crossed like a businessman waiting on a bench for a bus.

In his paw he held a remote control. He pushed a button and the televisions changed channels, flipping from the food to exercise infomercials to a home video of Kathy's prom night.

She had forgotten how *young* she had once been. The teenage Kathy on the television screen morphed into a live shot of Kathy standing there in the doorway of the Old West Buffet.

Every Kathy at every booth reached into every television and dug in, grabbing at her flesh and eating as fast as they could.

Mr. Whiskers towered over Kathy, raising the remote control above his furry head like an offering to the gods.

"I love you, Kathy," the cat said, "But I've been holding you back and you know it! Today is the day you release the last of the vices you sow! If you don't let me go, you'll die!"

The walls of the Old West Buffet pulsated, bulging in and out. The floor creaked and rolled.

The numerous Kathys fell out of their booths and flopped around on the floor like fish on a boat.

Mr. Whiskers grinned with huge teeth as the walls of the restaurant crumbled and the windows exploded inwards.

As the building collapsed, light burst from every direction and blinded Kathy.

A bright light flashed directly into Kathy's eyes.

"Ma'am, can you hear me?" a paramedic asked as he checked her pupils. He was just a fuzzy dark spot floating in front of Kathy's bloodshot eyes. The kitchen was all shadows and dimmed colors. Darkness encroached, trying to force her to yield to sleep again.

Before the darkness could win again, the mysterious customer appeared in the doorway from the living room. Kathy could see him very clearly even though the rest of the room remained a blur. He wore a cheerfully bright red overcoat, his hair was golden and flowing like that old romance novel cover model Fabio, and his flesh glowed with a beautiful inner light.

Then Kathy blinked and she saw the truth: the man's features were ugly and distorted as if viewed in the shards of a broken funhouse mirror, his overcoat was the color of dried blood, his hair consisted of hundreds of hissing snakes, and his flesh wasn't glowing, it was burning from the heat of the dark embers inside the dead body he wore like a cloak.

Kathy blinked and saw the beautiful man again, and she cowered and asked: "Where did you come from?"

"A place I hope you'll never see for yourself, Kathy baby. The past few days have been hard on your body and your mind, but you have shed the last of your vices and you will sow them no longer."

"I don't understand."

"You've freed yourself. You can move on. You can now experience *real* change."

Kathy recognized where she had heard the voice before, although neither version of the man in the doorway looked anything like he had during their courtship and marriage.

"*John?*" she asked. "Where have you been?"

"I love you so much, Kathy baby, and I hope I've made amends for how I treated you," the man said.

Then he was gone.

Two paramedics shifted Kathy onto a stretcher and rolled her through the apartment. The living room window was still open and Kathy thought maybe she saw the distinctive movement of a cat descending the steps of the fire escape.

"Mr. Whiskers, I'll never forget you!" she called, knowing she couldn't return to the apartment. Even though she would miss her kitty dearly, he would never again be her excuse for heading straight home after work, for avoiding people, for declining a free gym membership.

Today, Kathy could become whole again.

Today, she could leave the past behind.

Today, she could take control of her destiny.

Today, she could begin her new life.

Today, she honestly and truly believed, was a very good day, and tomorrow would be even better.

Nine Months Later, a.k.a Kathy's After Time.

Sometimes when Kathy saw a photo of her Old Self, taken back in what she thought of as her Before Time, she wondered who that person could possibly be. She had trouble remembering the years prior to her life in the suburbs and those old photos confused her. That's why she had tossed most of them in the trash months ago, with a single exception. There was one she just couldn't part with.

The organic grocery market where Kathy worked was exactly four miles from her apartment and she loved her daily walking commute. She pushed herself hard, trying to beat her best time without actually running. Running would be cheating. She sweated a lot and the sweating felt great.

Some of the neighborhood kids called her Skeletor, but Kathy didn't understand what they meant. She couldn't see her bony face and arms and legs, or her gaunt, tight skin. All she saw in the mirror was the beautiful woman who had emerged from the dark pit of despair at the end of an all-you-can-eat buffet.

The Kathy who had lived in the Before Time was dead, as far as the Kathy who lived in the After Time was concerned, and she felt that was no great loss to the world.

Kathy slipped into her apartment without even fully opening the door. There was a bed, a kitchenette, a bathroom, and enough room on the floor for her yoga mat. That was all she needed to be happy. She didn't even own a television or a phone.

When Kathy spotted the folded piece of paper waiting for her on the dining room table, her heart sank.

She unfolded the note, which was written on paper that was oddly-sized and too thick. She read:

I'm very sorry, Kathy baby, but the original prescription I wrote you was much too strong. I'm still getting the hang of this, but I'm learning more every day. I hope you'll live a long and healthy life.

There was a flowing postscript, almost as an afterthought:

Today is the day you truly leave the past behind for good.

Something clicked deep inside Kathy. She could no longer remember any of the soothing, comforting words she had been repeating over and over again for the last nine months, the words written in the original note.

A tear trickled from the corner of her eye, curving in and out of her sunken cheekbone. She reached for the lone photo on the refrigerator, the only one she hadn't been able to part with: her and Mr. Whiskers sitting on the couch in her old apartment.

Kathy tucked the photo into her pocket, went outside, and started walking again. She needed to find somewhere to eat. She hadn't been inside a restaurant in nine months and she had a craving for something she could really dig her teeth into, maybe a juicy steak with a side of roasted vegetables. But she would eat *just* enough to feel full, no more, no less. She understood that without giving the matter a second thought.

After dinner, Kathy decided she would go to the animal shelter near her work to adopt a cat. She couldn't replace Mr. Whiskers in her heart, but she could give another little furry friend a happy home.

Today, Kathy knew, was the day she would truly leave the past behind for good, and tomorrow could be even better.

One More Day

MICHAEL WASN'T SURE how long he had been chained naked to the floor of the Big Man's Punishment Room, but he did know the Big Man would be coming back. Then the bleeding and the screaming and the torture would start again.

The smooth concrete floor and the metal drain near Michael's bare feet were stained with blood. He was a young man, but his back shrieked at him from the strain of sitting in the same position for days on end. Directly across from him was a wide mirror that relentlessly showed his reflection. He couldn't help but stare into it, watching himself deteriorate.

There were no windows in the Punishment Room, of course, just that damned mirror, so Michael had lost track of time. The hours between the Big Man's visits were horrible and his sleep was full of its own terrors, but the nightmares weren't nearly as bad as what happened when he was awake. In fact, the nightmares were almost comforting in their own bizarre way. At least in his dreams, he was in control. He didn't have to do the terrible things the Big Man demanded or face the consequences for non-compliance.

Assuming Michael managed to escape this hellhole with his sanity and his life—and those odds were looking worse and worse with each passing visit of the Big Man—he wasn't sure if he'd be able to go on living with the knowledge of what he had done to survive. Then again, that was a dilemma he wouldn't mind being forced to deal with, given the finality of the alternative.

Each time the Big Man entered the Punishment Room, he gave Michael the same two options, and Michael hated the vacant eyes staring back at him in the mirror as he made his choice. He never stopped staring at himself, judging himself for what he had done, contemplating how he had ended up here in the first place.

Michael knew he might eventually escape from this endless hell—there was always a slim chance—but there was no escaping his own judgment of himself. Some days he gazed at his reflection until he felt like he was watching someone else. He barely recognized the man in the reflection, sitting upright against a bloodstained cinderblock wall. His hands were chained to heavy anchors in the floor, but he had enough range of movement to do what the Big Man demanded—if he didn't want to choose his other option.

Day after day after day passed. The nightmares grew worse and the Big Man's terrible choices became more maddening.

Michael's body and mind were exhausted. His eyes burned from the awfulness of the things he had seen and done. Soon there was movement in the mirror when he was all alone. Shadows shifting and jumping in the corners. His own eyes, big and bloodshot, peered back at him, searching for some escape from the terror. The eyes in the mirror moved while his own eyes remained still.

And as always, after another string of endless hours spent staring at himself, watching those strange eyes he didn't recognize, Michael heard the footsteps echoing down the stairs. The door hidden in the corner of the room opened.

Michael's heart raced and he closed his eyes for the first time in hours. He didn't want to know what the next punishment would be, and he definitely didn't want to see who the Big Man might have brought with him today.

Yet keeping his eyes closed didn't matter when he heard the small voice whisper: "Mikey?"

Michael's eyes flew open and he stared in horror. His little sister stood next to the Big Man, who was dressed all in black with the mask protecting his face. Alicia wore her best Sunday dress and she had obviously been crying.

"No, no, no," Michael said, his voice a low growl like some kind of trapped animal.

The Big Man towered above Alicia and he led her by the hand. His gloved hand was huge, engulfing her tiny fingers, but his grip wasn't tight and Alicia didn't struggle the way Michael had when he first awoke in this terrible place. Her eyes were big, yet she showed no fear.

In her left hand, Alicia held a pair of pliers.

"Oh, Alicia, no," Michael whispered. He tried to believe she was a hallucination—maybe he had finally lost his mind for good, maybe this was just another nightmare—but he had known the truth the instant he heard her voice.

The Big Man released Alicia's hand and she crossed the room and sat down on the floor in front of her big brother.

"I'm sorry," she said, her eyes locked on his face.

Michael began to cry. So did she.

The Big Man watched the events unfold with his usual detached silence. This was *his* room—he controlled what happened and when, yet he said nothing.

"I am, too," Michael replied, staring at the grimy metal drain in the concrete floor. He couldn't even look his little sister in the eyes as he considered his options.

He could take his own life and end the pain for good, which would also allow his little sister to go free without suffering through the terror of what was to come, or he could accept what the Big Man silently demanded.

These were the same two options Michael was presented each time, just with a different person waiting in front of him, holding a different tool or weapon. As Michael grew more tired, as the eyes watching him in the mirror across the room became dimmer and more foreign, the two options seemed more and more similar.

Alicia tried to hand him the pliers. She was closer to him than anyone in the world, but deep down Michael knew he wanted to live for another day.

Another hellish, terrible day.

Another day of hoping to escape.

Another day of praying to live to regret what he had done.

Just one more day.

Michael watched in the mirror as the stranger he didn't recognize took the pliers and began to work.

Later, after the Big Man had disposed of yet another body, the pool of Alicia's blood continued to drip down the metal drain in the middle of the floor while Michael stared at the alien eyes in the mirror.

He didn't blink, but his mouth moved silently and slowly.

After a few minutes of this unspoken conversation with his reflection, Michael grinned and pulled his left hand close to his face, the chains growing taut between him and the heavy anchor in the floor.

He chewed on his wrist.

The blood came soon after.

"Oh my God! I can't watch this anymore!"

Like always, the gray-haired lady had been given the best seat in the house: a stiff, plastic chair directly on the other side of the two-way mirror facing the prisoner.

The viewing room was climate-controlled and extraordinarily sterile, and the witnesses for the State murmured at the latest development. Michael Cooper, prisoner 4105885901, really *was* chewing at his wrist.

"That's acceptable, Mrs. Lawson," the Government Official said from his leather chair in the control booth. "Mr. Cooper's punishment ends as soon as you tell us he's been rehabilitated and your family is satisfied that society has been repaid for his crimes. Is this what you're saying?"

The little old woman rubbed her face with her brittle fingers and contemplated what had happened since the trial ended, what had been done on the other side of the mirror.

"I just never imagined it would be so ... gruesome. The way he keeps staring at me ... "

"You can set him free whenever you'd like. That is how the system works, after all."

The old woman sat behind the mirror, watching the boy who had killed her granddaughter. She watched him and her heart dropped into her stomach and she heard her granddaughter's sweet laughter at a Thanksgiving dinner lost to the past.

The old woman flinched as she watched the boy chewing at his bloody arm, and she asked herself again how much more she could really stand to see, to hear, before she'd go mad. How much more punishment did this boy deserve until everything had been made right?

Then she thought about the day she had heard the piercing scream outside her home and she had rushed to find her granddaughter's bloody and broken body in the middle of the street. The little girl never had a chance against Michael Cooper's souped-up sports car that he had been driving way too fast.

The old woman considered her options and finally said: "I think I can stand the sight for another day. Just one more day."

And then she watched the prisoner consume his own flesh while the witnesses for the State whispered their words of reassurance.

The Christmas Spirit

"*H*AVE YOU SEEN THE *M*ILLERS LATELY?"

As a child and then a teenager, Adam Tanner never really understood the Christmas spirit, but surviving a close call with death in his early twenties gave him a fresh perspective on life.

He had been rebellious in his youth, dabbling in drugs and rock 'n' roll and defying his elders, and entire weeks would pass without him knowing where he had been or what he had done. Ultimately, if it hadn't been for the kindness of a neighbor who took pity on him, Adam would have died alone on a sidewalk one frigid December evening. Maybe, Adam later realized, he had actually wanted to die. Yet the neighbor brought him a blanket, a thermos of soup, and a red button imprinted with **Remember the REASON for the SEASON!** The unexpected and unfamiliar display of kindness turned Adam's entire life around.

The very next morning, he took his first steps to becoming a better person and a productive member of society, and if you asked him, his recovery was nothing short of divine intervention. Every day he walked on the planet felt like a miracle. He kept the red button to remind himself of how one good neighbor could change a life, and he embraced the Christmas spirit with every fiber of his being.

Now Adam was nearly forty and his wild days almost seemed like someone else's memories. His hair had gone prematurely gray from the years of hedonism, but his loving wife Jennifer didn't care a bit. They had two wonderful children, Christopher and Emily, who were both teenagers, yet had stayed pleasant and engaged and devoted to their parents. The family lived in a quiet neighborhood in a quiet part of town in a quiet part of the world. Their neighbors were friendly, their jobs were secure and fulfilling, and they wanted for nothing. Blessed might have been too light of a word to describe Adam's life.

Today, as was their yearly ritual, his family was spending the first day of December decorating their home for a picture-perfect Christmas. Everyone had jobs to do, and they approached their work with the reverence of people who truly loved what they were doing. The morning turned to afternoon, and the property was as festive as any year Adam could remember, but there was still much to be done.

Christopher was in the cobweb-strewn attic above the garage searching for the red container that protected the front door's Christmas wreath for the eleven months of the year that weren't December. He was combing through the shadows and dust, moving boxes of forgotten clothing and pushing aside furniture that should have been offered in the last community yard sale. When all hope seemed to be lost, he spotted the wreath box deep in the gloomy rafters.

"Found it!" he shouted in triumph.

"Took you long enough!" Emily playfully called up the wooden ladder. She was waiting in the garage with her shoes planted firmly on the concrete floor. She had no intention of venturing into the attic unless absolutely necessary.

"Hey, you were the scaredy-cat who didn't want to look for yourself because there *might* be spiders," Christopher replied as his smiling face appeared in the rectangle of darkness cut into the white ceiling.

"When you two are done gabbing," Adam said with a grin from where he was stringing lights around the garage door, "how about you help your mother hang that wreath?"

"Yes, Dad!" the teenagers said in unison.

Christopher descended the attic ladder in a hurry and they scurried off, Emily carrying the huge red container and both of them laughing. Adam returned his attention to the colorful lights.

"Merry Christmas, neighbor!" a voice called from the end of the driveway.

Without even glancing to see who it was, Adam replied automatically with a wave: "Merry Christmas to you, neighbor!"

"Adam?" the voice said a moment later, this time closer. Adam turned and saw George Smith was halfway up the driveway, his white poodle Molly prancing at the end of her leash. The older gentleman, who lived two blocks over, didn't look as healthy as Adam remembered.

"Howdy, George," Adam said, approaching his neighbor and gently pushing away the lively greeting of the enthusiastic dog. "Everything okay? You're a little pale."

"Oh, I have a touch of the flu, that's all." The two men shook hands. George's grip was as strong as you might expect from a retired carpenter who had helped build many of these very homes. He glanced at the decorations already arranged on the property. "You're going all out this year, aren't you?"

"Well, we really want to win the grand prize in the decorating contest. I think this might be our year!"

"That's why you always wait until December 1st to start, isn't it? So no one else has time to copy anything new you dream up?"

"Got me there, neighbor," Adam said, grinning. "It wouldn't be a competition without a little friendly strategy. When the judges make their rounds tonight, we're going to wow them."

"I suspect you're right. You're doing beautiful work, and I don't want to interrupt your day, but I do have a question for you."

"No worries here, George. What's your question?"

"Have you seen the Millers lately?"

Adam's smile faded as he considered the last time he had seen the owners of the Victorian-style home on the wooded lot near the curve in the street.

William and Barbara Miller were an aloof older couple who kept to themselves, so much so that the neighborhood children told scary stories about the pink and yellow house being haunted, but that was just kids being kids. The Millers were simply introverts and probably night owls from what Adam had observed. They walked their dogs after dark, and they would say hello if you happened to be out and said hello to them first.

Most of all, they were virtuous about maintaining their property's appearance. Yet Adam saw the lawn hadn't gotten a final mowing before the first frost, so the grass was long and brittle. There were several damaged pickets in the little white fence encircling the yard, dangling from the top rail like broken teeth.

The Millers didn't embrace the spirit of the season like everyone else in the neighborhood, but they always placed a wreath on their front door after Thanksgiving like clockwork. There was no wreath there today.

"Now that you mention it, I haven't seen them in a while. I hope they're okay."

"You know their son and all their grandkids died in September out in Los Angeles, right?"

"No!" Adam said, feeling sucker-punched. "I've been working long hours, trying to get all of my accounts in order before the end of the year, so I've been out of touch. What happened?"

George was a hard man, but his voice wavered. "Murder-suicide. Thomas Miller checked his family into a seedy motel, then he shot his wife and each of his kids in the head, and then he shot himself."

"Oh no," Adam said, his hand rising to his mouth. "That's... that's just awful! Why would someone do that?"

"Well, he left a rambling note blaming the government. Crazy conspiracy stuff. That's how we know what happened. It made the news."

"Oh... Oh, that's really sad."

A long silence played out between the two men, neither knowing what to say next. They gazed at the Millers' house, which did seem darker and more distressed than Adam remembered. He touched the red button on his jacket, the one a good-hearted neighbor had given him when he had been at his lowest point in life.

"Okay," Adam finally said. "Thanks for getting me in the loop. I'll keep an eye out."

He and George shook hands again, and then his neighbor continued his walk with Molly the poodle pulling ahead. Once George was down the street and out of sight, Adam studied the other homes around his very carefully. If there ever had been such a thing as the war on Christmas, the good guys had certainly won here. Every house, with the exception of the Millers' desolate Victorian, was alive with the spirit of the season.

"Everything okay, Daddy?" Emily asked, returning to the garage to search for a hook for the wreath.

"Yes," Adam said, faking a smile. There was no reason to alarm his daughter or the rest of the family. "Just trying to remember the lyrics to Jingle Bells."

"Oh Daddy, that's an easy one!" Emily replied, and she hummed the melody.

Adam sang along, but his eyes kept finding their way back to the Millers' house. He thought about what good neighbors did for each other, and he touched the red button on his jacket again, but he didn't know what to do. He felt frozen in place. What could he do? What was the right thing to do?

In the end, Adam threw himself back into the task at hand, humming and singing Christmas songs while he worked. He was more and more confident they just might have the most beautiful display in the neighborhood this year. There were more lights than ever before and more Christmas spirit everywhere you looked. Adam had even added an inflatable waving Santa, his sleigh, and reindeer to the roof, although Jennifer had been seriously concerned he might fall and break his neck. The height on top of the house *had* been worse than he expected, but he did what needed to be done and the finished effect was remarkable.

The afternoon sun slid down the sky to the west and Adam glanced toward the Millers' house again as he fixed the last of the candy-cane lights along the sidewalk. Sunset wasn't far off and there still wasn't any sign of the old couple. His heart grew heavy and a voice in the back of his head told him he needed to do something. He touched the red button again. But still, he couldn't decide what to do, so he continued with his decorating.

At five o'clock, just as Emily and Christopher were putting the finishing touches on the new Santa's workshop they had built together over the summer, a police car slowly passed by their house. The teenagers waved and the officer inside waved back. It was Dean Shepherd, the town's sheriff.

"Kids, come over here," Adam said. He and Jennifer had just plugged in the final strand of pulsating and racing lights on the evergreen bushes under the living room's bay window. In the window itself was a neon red sign that loudly and proudly proclaimed *Merry Christmas!* to the world.

The Tanner Family's house represented a glorious monument to Christmas excess. There were tens of thousands of blinking lights and an army of inflatable characters. One Santa waved to you, another beckoned you to sit on his lap, and yet another was busy supervising his hardworking elves in the workshop at the North Pole. Red and green were the primary colors, but there was also an abundance of gold and silver. Plastic icicles dangled and glowed from the gutters. There was a wreath and an electric candle for every window. Green and red spotlights moved busily across the front of the house, left to right, up and down, never stopping. Movement and light were everywhere.

Emily and Christopher dutifully joined their mother and father as requested. Adam put his arm around Jennifer's waist, pulling her in tight. Once the kids were standing with their parents, Adam decided it was time to talk to them about the Millers, but he didn't get a chance. He had waited too long.

"Daddy, look," Emily said, pointing.

The sheriff had parked his patrol car and he stood on the sidewalk facing the Millers' house, inspecting it like a crime scene. He pushed through the white picket gate, his eyes scanning for anything out of the ordinary, his hand on his holster, ready to release the strap securing his firearm. The sun had reached the horizon and the sheriff's shadow was drawn out behind him. The melancholy house loomed over him like some kind of beast.

The front door swung open with a squeal and a dense darkness leaked through the doorway. The Millers stepped out onto their porch. They had American flags draped around their bodies, upside down with the white stars on the blue field at the bottom. The elderly couple made it to the bottom step before the startled sheriff reacted.

"William and Barbara Miller, stop right there," he said, drawing his revolver.

They did as they were told and the sheriff approached them carefully. They said nothing.

Adam glanced up and down the street. All of his neighbors had emerged from their homes to watch, as if summoned by the appearance of the police car. Maybe he had been the last one clued in. Maybe everyone else had seen the signs all along, but he had apparently been too focused on his work to notice what was happening on his own street these past few months.

"William and Barbara Miller," the sheriff declared loudly enough for everyone to hear. "You have been reported by your neighbors for failing to embrace the Christmas spirit. As I witness with my own eyes, you are guilty of violating the Christmas Spirit Religious Freedom Act passed by the United States Congress and signed by our beloved President. Will you reconsider your transgressions against our nation?"

"No!" William shouted while raising his fist into the air. "We will no longer be forced to believe in . . . "

His words were cut short by a bullet from the sheriff's revolver, which removed part of the old man's forehead in an explosion of blood and gray matter. The gunshot echoed in the silence of the neighborhood. Another bullet hit Barbara between the eyes. The elderly couple slumped backwards onto the steps as the thundering gunshots faded into silence. Their mouths slipped open to show yellowed teeth, creating a pair of dreadful grins. Blood pooled under their flag-draped bodies. They held hands in a death grip.

The sheriff holstered his weapon and returned to his car, waving to the onlookers, who jauntily waved back. He drove away, flashing his emergency lights for the little kids, who cheered in response. Once he was gone, everyone remained where they had gathered. There was much discussion and a sense of relief to be shared.

Night finished descending upon the world like a heavy blanket poked with the pinpricks of stars, concealing the dead bodies in darkness. The bodies would wait where they had fallen until the coroner claimed them in a few hours to be cremated. Probably right around the same time the judges from the neighborhood association were announcing this year's winner of the Christmas decorating contest, in fact.

"Daddy, can we please go inside?" Emily whispered.

"I'd like to go in, too," Christopher said.

"Yes," Adam replied. "Yes, I believe it's time to trim the tree."

He ushered his family into the house, stopping to adjust the wreath on the door to get it perfect. He glanced out at the quiet neighborhood one more time. Their wonderful, peaceful, safe neighborhood.

Adam touched the red button on his jacket and he thought about how every single day truly was a miracle. Yes, it was. A big miracle indeed.

You couldn't help but feel the Christmas spirit when you remembered that.

Silent Attic (Amy Walker)

M Y NAME IS AMY WALKER and my mother died three years ago on a sweltering August day during the worst heat wave in decades.

Any time spent in the direct sunlight that week risked a quick burn. Walking outside was like being wrapped in a wool blanket.

I was fifteen.

My little brother was just three.

My father was forty going on forever.

He worked two shifts at the factory to keep the bills paid and we rarely saw him. He worked so hard because he loved us, but also, I believe, because the work allowed him to pretend his wife wasn't dying.

The cancer started in my mother's breast and spread quickly, undetected. She was never the same person after the doctor appointment when she received the bad news.

Sometimes I think she actually died that day.

The rest of the time, the time spent in the upstairs bedroom of our little house, the time spent wasting away, didn't count for anything.

My mother had been so full of life, so energetic before the cancer. She deftly juggled kids and work and mortgage payments and car insurance and everything else, and she did so with a smile and an easy laugh.

After that visit to the doctor, she was a shell of a broken woman.

Within days she looked weak and pale and near death, as if she had been holding back the grim reaper without ever knowing it, but now she had given up the fight.

I spent a lot of time by my mother's side that summer, but I also had to watch Daniel, and he was a handful.

Caring for your three-year-old brother when you're a teenager, when you spent the first twelve years of your life as an only child, is strange, to say the least, but you learn to play the cards you're dealt, as one of my dad's poker buddies from BC (before cancer) used to say.

As my mother got sicker, I took over her responsibilities the best I could.

I'd clean the house and do the laundry and make sure dinner was ready when my father arrived home at nine o'clock each night.

He'd drag himself in through the door, his blue overalls black with grease, his face and hands caked with smears of oil, his legs moving like pillars of granite.

He'd wash his hands for half an hour to get the grit out from under his nails and then we'd eat in silence at the little table in the kitchen. Daniel was already in bed.

I'd wash the dishes while Dad showered and I'd pack his lunch for the next day, just like my mother used to pack my lunch when I was a kid, and then Dad would go upstairs and spend the rest of the night holding my mother while she slept.

I'll never forget how their attic bedroom smelled of a painful illness that summer.

I loved my mother, but I hated that smell.

The bedroom was small and cozy, with a box fan in one of the windows blowing hot, humid air across the room. There were white, lacy curtains in the other window, which was usually left open for ventilation.

The queen-sized bed was against the far wall, with two matching nightstands and an old-fashioned alarm clock with a green glowing face that freaked me out at night. There was also a chair from the kitchen.

I'd sit on that chair and hold my mom's hand and she'd sleep and sometimes she'd want to talk but speaking was difficult for her in those last weeks.

I'd sit there and try not to see how small my mother was, how the cancer had hollowed her out.

Every day she lay under the covers, under the heavy Amish blanket my father had bought her for Christmas the year before.

The house was sweltering, but she was always cold.

On the day she died, my mother could barely speak, but she whispered she was thirsty and needed a drink of water.

I dutifully went downstairs to the kitchen, got a clean glass, and filled it halfway.

I thought about checking on my brother.

He was napping in his room and the visit would give me a little more time away from that awful attic.

From the smell of impending death.

But I couldn't move. My legs wouldn't let me take a step.

I stood in the kitchen, closed my eyes, and found myself sinking into the memory of a trip to Black Rock Lake on a beautiful summer day.

The sky was blue and cloudless, the breeze was light and pleasant. Birds chirped in the trees, fish practically leapt from the sparkling lake water, and the sandy beach by the campground was golden and perfect in every way.

That was the last time my family had gone to the lake before the cancer, and I wished with all of my might that I could travel back in time to that day and grab myself and yell: "Don't let go of this! Stay here, forever! Life will never be better than this day!"

The memory was so real and so strong that I was disappointed when I opened my eyes and found myself standing in the stifling, humid kitchen.

Half an hour had passed.

The movement of my legs as I climbed the steps to the attic bedroom felt wrong, like I was trapped in slow motion.

Something inside me stirred, trembled.

The fan in the window had turned off again, but that wasn't unusual. The motor had been dying for years and often overheated.

My legs shook and when I pushed the door to the bedroom open far enough to see the bed, I stopped.

I looked into the room, which was lit by the sunlight sneaking in around the curtains.

Dirty, blinding light.

My mom's eyes were open, glassy and staring at the ceiling, but she wasn't breathing.

I had known this was coming but I wasn't ready.

I hadn't truly believed the end was near or that the end was even really going to come.

Maybe I was waiting on a miracle. Or maybe I was just a dumb kid.

I made my way to the bed, although I don't remember taking a step, and with a trembling hand I closed my mother's eyes.

Her papery skin was cold to the touch and yet sweat still beaded across her brow.

I sat on the edge of the bed, soaking in the sweltering heat, and I listened to the silence.

I had never heard the house so quiet.

I sat and I sipped from the glass of water, both sad and happy and devastated and relieved.

My mother had been in so much pain.

I sipped the water until the glass slipped out of my hand, shattering on the hardwood floor.

Then I cried.

Downstairs Daniel began to cry, too. The noise had scared him.

I stood, careful not to step on the broken glass, and I made my way down to my brother's bedroom.

I held Daniel and I told him about Mom and I comforted him as he cried.

I called my father and he rushed home.

A very nice man from the funeral home picked up my mother less than an hour later, and the funeral came and went the following afternoon, and we all cried and the days passed in a blur.

And then, before I knew it, I was home alone watching my brother while my father returned to work.

I'd watch Daniel and I'd sit on the couch and I'd fight the urge to go upstairs to check on Mom.

While Daniel napped, I would lie on the couch and close my eyes, sometimes falling asleep thanks to how exhausted I was that year.

Maybe that's why I've had these bad dreams since my mother died, four or five times a week for the last three years.

In the nightmares I'm fifteen again, filling a glass of water half-full in the kitchen. The glass is for my mother, and I have to go and find her dead body.

I know this and I can't stop myself.

One moment I'm in the kitchen, the next I'll be standing at the top of the stairs holding the glass of water.

I push on the door.

My mother is in the bed, lying under dusty covers that haven't been changed in three years, her body frail and thin.

The light coming in through the windows is dirty and the room is so hot the air shimmers like the distant horizon of a desert.

My mother's face has been covered with the blanket.

She has died again and yet again, I wasn't here.

"Mother needs her water," I whisper, my voice cracking like I'm a small child.

"Yes, I do," comes the raspy reply.

My mother growls as she sits up, the sheet wrapping around her like a burial shroud, the blanket sliding off her face.

She asks, "Why did you leave me up here to die? Why didn't you help me?"

The window flies open and a winter wind, the antithesis of the heat that enveloped me all summer, gusts through the space, blowing the sheets off my mother's corpse.

I shriek at the sight.

My mother has been waiting a very long time for me to return.

Her ribs poke through her gaunt belly and her breasts are deflated, saggy.

Her face is tight and dry like a mummy. Her eyes are glassy and fogged.

A single, bloody tear trickles along her crooked nose.

She opens her mouth.

She points one bony finger at me and says: "If only you had brought the water faster, I wouldn't be dead!"

"No, no, that's not true!" I whimper, the terror inside me as real as anything I've ever felt.

Usually that fear is enough to wake me before she gets out of the bed and stumbles across the room, but not always.

Every now and then she'll get her skeleton-like arms around me for a hug.

Often I wake up screaming.

I don't find sleep easily after the nightmares.

Sometimes I'm awake the rest of the night.

Sometimes I'm so thirsty.

I hate that dream.

I think of the silent attic and I miss my mother.

My family is hollow without her.

Danny Dreams (Daniel Walker)

WHEN DANNY WALKER WAS A CHILD, in the weeks after he finally understood his sister Amy was never coming home again, nightmares consumed his nights—even the nights when he couldn't sleep at all.

He would lie in bed with the covers pulled to his chin, his overactive imagination wildly analyzing the shifting shadows created by the light in the hallway outside his room.

His closet door would creak open and glowing eyes would stare at him from behind his shirts and pants.

Broken fingernails would tap on the hardwood floor under his bed, and he was certain he could hear something breathing down there.

When Danny did finally fall asleep, usually from sheer exhaustion, the nightmares were often as bad as the monsters he had imagined in the darkness of his bedroom.

Sometimes they were worse.

In one of the nightmares, he followed his sister to where she was preparing to commit suicide.

The actual location changed from dream to dream.

Sometimes it was the basement of the community school, in one of the hidden places among the pipes and boilers.

Sometimes it was out at Black Rock Lake, standing on the cold sand of the public beach as a snowstorm barreled toward them.

Sometimes it was in the kitchen of the Black Hills Diner where

Frankie the cook should have been working but wasn't for some reason and Amy had awful plans for the red-hot grill.

Danny would yell at Amy to stop, that she couldn't kill herself, that he and Dad needed her so badly, and she would turn and stare at him with a confused look on her face.

"Kill myself? Silly Danny, I came here to kill *you*."

And then she fell upon him, ripping at his face with fingernails as sharp as cat claws.

He would awaken in a cold sweat, usually screaming, and sometimes he wet the bed.

Eventually, the idea of even entering his room at bedtime became more and more ridiculous, but his grieving father was in no shape to help him and Danny knew he had to find his own way through the nightmares.

Sleep became rare and often he could only huddle in his bed, wide-awake and terrified, listening to his father sobbing in his own bedroom.

He would count the minutes and he would wait for the dark to close in around him.

Then one night he had an idea, an idea so strange he couldn't believe it was his own.

He decided he would create an imaginary world to escape into as night descended.

A safe house in his mind.

A walled fortress to keep the demons at bay.

His heart raced as the plan took shape.

He pulled the blanket up to his chin and closed his eyes.

Instead of seeing his dead sister or any of the other monsters of the night, he forced himself to think of anything else he could, anything even remotely happy.

Images formed behind his eyelids, blurry and indecipherable at first, until a series of fractured memories came into focus: his mother and Amy placing a blanket on the grass in the backyard while his father cooked hotdogs on a charcoal grill; Miss Wilson, his kindergarten teacher, handing out modeling clay; Mr. Whiskers, the neighbor's chubby cat, stalking a bird through the lawn; a lion with funny-looking fur at the Pittsburgh Zoo; and finally a trip to Black Rock Lake on a beautiful summer day.

Danny seized this last memory with all his might.

The sky was blue and cloudless, the breeze light and pleasant.

Birds chirped in the trees and fish practically leapt from the clear, crisp water.

The sandy beach by the campground was golden and perfect.

The woods hummed; everything seemed to glow in the sunlight.

Best of all, Amy was there, holding Danny's hand.

Her skin against his was electric. She was alive again.

They stood by the wooden sign at the entrance to the gravel parking lot that served both the beach and the nearby campground.

Beautiful flowers bloomed at the base of the sign, full and yearning toward the blazing summer sun.

In the real world this sign said: WELCOME TO BLACK ROCK LAKE.

In Danny's new imaginary world the sign said: WELCOME TO THE DARK COUNTRY.

Although the name was sinister, the land was not . . . and for a while Danny *was* able to sleep soundly through the night if he closed his eyes and imagined himself into The Dark Country.

He would swim in the clear water and lie on the sandy beach under the hot sun and play with as many friends as his imagination could invent, always with Amy by his side.

Those nights were wonderful and carefree and his imaginary world was as real as any place he had ever visited.

He was happier there than he had been in a long time.

But one day, Danny made a critical mistake, one he couldn't be blamed for, not at his tender age.

He told his father about The Dark Country and how Amy lived on there.

His father, who had been drinking heavily in the months after his daughter's suicide, was in no mood for his son's make-believe bullshit, as he put it.

"Your sister is *DEAD!*" he slurred. "She fucking killed herself and left us here alone to rot. She up and quit on us just like her mother and don't you *ever* forget that!"

Danny had run crying to his room, slamming the door shut as if to block the words, but the damage was done.

That night when he closed his eyes and took himself to The Dark Country, Amy didn't appear.

Hours passed.

His invented friends—the boys, the girls, the astonishing creations straight out of the liveliest part of his imagination—simply stared at him, confused and speechless and no help at all.

Distraught to the point of tears, Danny called for Amy until his voice cracked from the strain—and just once he thought he heard her whisper back from beyond the trees of the forest.

He ran to the edge of the woods but he couldn't travel any further; a forbidding presence stopped him dead in his tracks.

The woods were much darker than they had been before, as if it were night under the trees, the complete opposite of the happy and safe world around the lake.

He feared what might be lurking in there.

Danny called to Amy again and again, but she didn't reply.

He begged her to return, he promised to fix whatever he had done wrong, whatever he had done to drive her away...but she never appeared.

When he awoke in the morning he was terrified and soaked in sweat and he wasn't the least bit rested.

Danny realized he missed his sister even more the second time around and he traveled to The Dark Country every night, desperate to locate her again, but the imaginary world was changing.

His friends looked exhausted and rundown like old machinery left out in the rain.

Over time, their features slowly melted; their eyes glazed over and turned red; their skin became leathery; their fingers grew into sharp claws.

The sun crept toward the distant horizon, shifting the world from a mid-afternoon day in August to the dim nothingness of a cold March evening.

The lake water grew dark . . . and murky . . . and cold.

And then, when Danny thought he couldn't take it anymore, something even worse happened: the sun slipped below the mountains, a blood moon rose into the sky, and night descended on The Dark Country.

His imaginary friends finished their transformation into the monsters of the dark, growing into the horrors they were always destined to become.

And yet Danny couldn't stop himself from traveling to The Dark Country; he felt compelled to return, to search for his sister.

He simply wouldn't let her go without a fight this time.

He returned to the haunted land, the place where the monsters bided their time until the moon set and total darkness claimed the land.

Then they would pounce.

The red moonlight shimmered across the black waters of the lake as the monsters slipped in and out of the trees, moving with ease through Danny's mind, circling him, closing in as the moon began to set.

Still, though, he went back to search for Amy one last time, knowing it would be his final chance.

When Danny closed his eyes in his bedroom and opened them in The Dark Country, the world was pitch black, full of the worst sounds: the growls of the beasts, the screams of their victims.

The only light came from the glowing eyes of the monsters swarming toward him.

They had been waiting.

The remaining barriers protecting him had crumbled and the imaginary world had turned poisonous.

Danny couldn't see anything, but he knew their razor-sharp teeth were ready to rip his flesh and their claws were extended to slice him apart.

He screamed and fought to open his eyes, and he felt the teeth and claws and the sickening scales against his flesh just as he threw himself out of bed and onto the cold floor.

He would never be able to return.

He would never see Amy again.

Years would pass and Danny would eventually forget The Dark Country, but the original nightmares returned with a vengeance, as if to punish him for trying to push them away.

Danny's dead sister waited for him each night when the darkness came.

Peaceful sleep never truly returned, not even after he graduated high school and fled the town where his personal demons roamed like gods.

He moved to the city to attend college, but still, every night, in his dreams, he watched as his sister died again, and again, and again.

Then one night, after drinking too much and thinking too little, Danny got a tattoo of a famous quote that summed up how he felt about his life:

The life of the dead is placed in the memory of the living.

Amy was always dead, never living, and she would remain that way for the rest of his life.

Sometimes, he thought, the nightmares were worse than the memories.

Other times, he thought, the memories were worse than the nightmares.

Mostly, he missed the sister he had loved so much who was taken from him before he could ever truly express how much she meant to him.

His life was hollow without her.

All he had left were the broken dreams, both hers and his own, and that wasn't enough to be worth the horrors he lived with.

But that was all Amy would be to him until the day came when he would meet her again one final time in The Dark Country.

PART FOUR

LOST AND LONELY

"The sun will rise, the sun will set, and there isn't anything they can do but wait..."

Ice Cold Dan the Ice Cream Man

A S THE GLASS PANES in the oversized garage door distorted the first fiery hues of another sunrise, Daniel raised his face off the steering wheel of the ice cream truck. His head hurt from the previous night's drinking, which was the only way he could get to sleep anymore, and maybe he should have been surprised to find himself at the wheel of his truck, but he wasn't. Not really. This was hardly the first time he had woken here.

He used to wonder what the guys he had served with in Afghanistan would say if they could see what he did now, but those thoughts rarely crossed his mind anymore. They had been brothers in war, that was true, but Dan was a loner and everyone in his unit had known it. They hadn't given him the nickname Ice Cold Dan *just* because of the time he stood there cool, calm, and collected firing an M249 into the windshield of a suicide bomber's out-of-control truck, although he *was* all of those things in that moment.

In fact, a photo of Dan during the attack, taken by an embedded journalist working for *The New York Times,* was often mistaken for a promotional still from one of the Rambo movies. He was actually sort of famous after the photo went viral, but the notoriety did nothing for Dan. What he mostly thought about was how no one seemed to care the suicide bomber had been a twelve-year-old kid forced to drive against his will. In his nightmares, Dan still saw the boy's terrified face and huge eyes in the moment before the windshield exploded in the hail of bullets. The truck had rolled safely to a stop, Dan was a hero, and the kid was dead. Life in Afghanistan went on as usual. It all came to the same in the end, didn't it?

Dan cracked his back, slid out of the driver's seat, and started his day. After stretching to test the extent of his aches and pains, he filled a metal bucket with soapy water. He could have skipped washing the truck if he wanted to. His head felt like an exploding bowling ball and he didn't have a boss looking over his shoulder, but he still wouldn't deviate from his routine. He simply wasn't wired that way.

His father had always said there were no shortcuts to anywhere worth going, and Dan believed that was true. "You do the hard work, even if no one else will, because the hard work needs done," was another of his father's truisms Dan had taken to heart. Maybe a little too well, if he gave his life's journey much thought, which he tried not to do if he could help it.

Once the exterior of the truck was clean, he inspected the engine and the tires for any signs of impending problems. After he crossed those items off his mental checklist, he opened the back doors and stepped inside. There was a portable refrigerator with bottled water and cans of soda, a soft-serve machine, two freezer cases with glass tops, and a serving counter. Above the counter was the sliding glass window through which business was conducted.

Dan reviewed the contents of the freezers, which he had reloaded the night before. He felt it was best to be ready to go at a moment's notice, whether you were bunking down in the battlefield, taking in some R&R in the Green Zone, or even operating your own little ice cream truck.

You could never *make* more time, but you *could* use the time you had wisely. That was another of his father's famous sayings and Dan certainly had plenty of free time in the evening these days to prepare for the next day—no wife, no kids. Not anymore. His prep work also helped delay the drinking, which he both needed and despised. After what he had seen and done, he knew no one would blame him. Still, he blamed himself more than enough for everyone.

Once he was confident the truck was ready to go, Dan returned to the driver's seat. His work was about to begin.

Dan never took the same route twice, a strategy born of his time in Afghanistan, and he found himself traveling to towns further and further away. There was also one neighborhood he always skipped, no matter what, even though he passed the entrance daily and he knew there were enough families there to keep him busy for hours. It was the neighborhood with the little Cape Cod he had called home with Shelly and their two kids, Anna and Adam, after he left the service. His family had been dead for six months and he hadn't returned to the house once. He couldn't bring himself to do it.

Today, Dan drove to a town forty miles east and he felt robotic as he went about his day, but that was okay; the sensation was calming. No thinking required. Drive for a while, flip the switch to activate the speaker on top of the truck, park somewhere, and get to work. The only song programmed into the sound system was a Muzak version of "Camptown Races" and Dan hadn't learned how to change it, but that wasn't a problem. Kids of all ages recognized the soulless bleating of the sound system for what it was: a siren's call from the ice cream gods.

Dan parked and waited for the kids. That was his day. That was his routine. That was his life.

Eleven hours later, Dan's legs and hands ached and he was ready to return home, even though there was some daylight left. He *could* go home if he wanted. He certainly didn't need to clock any extra hours.

Still, as he navigated his way back across his hometown, he *knew* there was time for one more stop and a nagging voice in the back of his head told him the job wasn't done yet. He debated whether to visit the community park and pool, in case someone might still be there, or maybe swing by one of the big box store parking lots.

He continued to drive, almost as if he were on autopilot, barely seeing the road, and he didn't realize where he had decided to go until he turned onto the street where he had lived the happiest years of his life. Dread rose inside Dan when he recognized the neighborhood, but then something like relief washed over him, too. This could be a turning point, perhaps. A chance for him to move on with his life. Maybe.

Dan activated the music as he parked in front of the little Cape Cod, but he didn't look at the house. Not yet. He stepped into the back of the truck, past the soft-serve machine, and he opened one of the ice cream freezers. In the very bottom was his M249, just like the one he had used in Afghanistan on the day he became semi-famous as a heroic soldier. He lifted it with great care.

Dan inserted his earplugs, slid open the serving window, and glanced at the sidewalk next to the tree-lined street. The kids were coming, just like always, with adults in the mix. There were more than he expected, maybe because he had never brought his truck here.

Once the group was close enough, Dan leaned out the serving window and opened fire. He barely felt the recoil anymore, but he made himself watch as the rotting children were ripped to pieces, arms and legs flying in different directions, heads exploding in a terrible mist of decaying brains and congealed blood. He also mowed down the decomposing adults with ease, his hands making minute adjustments to keep control of his weapon.

Within seconds, the living dead were living no more and there was only silence and the acrid bite of his spent ammunition. The street would remain quiet until the next wave of zombies appeared, which usually wasn't too long. They'd hear the music and start toward him, their atrophied muscles carrying them forward with the awkward gait of the dead.

Dan calmly reloaded the weapon, his tired hands moving smoothly through the steps like a well-oiled machine. Would Shelly and Anna and Adam be among the next group of corpses? Perhaps. Perhaps not. It all came to the same in the end, didn't it? Someone had to do the hard work, even if no one else would or could, and Dan certainly had a lot of work to do these days. Tomorrow he would visit another town and start all over again.

I'm Ice Cold Dan, he thought as he prepared to do what needed to be done.

Losing Everything Defines You

(Recording begins.)

I F YOU'RE LISTENING TO THIS, I must be dead.

I have to wonder: Who are you and how did you discover this tape?

Are you my agent's assistant searching for one last usable scrap of manuscript to sell?

That fifteen percent is tempting enough that he'd fly you down here to dig up whatever you could, isn't it? And depending on how the media covers my death, my work might be more popular than ever by the time you hear this recording.

Or are you a police detective trying to explain what happened to me? Maybe you don't think I had a heart attack, like the coroner will probably report. Or maybe my death will be far more gruesome than I can imagine and you're hunting for the sicko who killed me.

Or are you simply someone who wants an answer to the question so many people have been asking these past few months:

Did I kill my wife and son?

I've never been arrested, never been charged, but I've certainly been questioned.

The accusations have been made both publicly and privately, even as everyone has admitted I had no reason to hurt my family.

It's been three months since Wendy and Andrew vanished after an afternoon spent with friends at Black Rock Lake.

The police have no real suspects. My wife and son disappeared without a trace.

Well, unless you consider leaving our car where they left it to be a trace. That and the blood.

Did I kill my wife and son?

Every morning, those words ring in my ears.

Every night, those words echo in my mind.

The answer?

I don't know.

I wish I could explain what happened.

Maybe then sleep would come a little easier at night.

Maybe I wouldn't hear the noises in the hallway outside my bedroom.

The slow, deliberate footsteps hitting every creaky floorboard like some Halloween-horror soundtrack.

Each night I cower in bed, the covers pulled up to my neck, the darkness wrapped around me like the grip of a dead lover.

I stare at the ceiling and I listen to the rumblings in the hallway.

There's no one else residing within this house, not anymore.

But I know what I'm hearing each and every night: my wife and son are coming home to me.

These sounds are driving me mad . . . yet I've learned waiting can be easier than knowing the truth.

These days I'm waiting to face my worst fear, which is better than actually confronting myself about what might have happened.

The whispering voices continue to ask:

Did you kill your wife and son?

It's a hard question to answer.

After all, they might not be dead.

No bodies were ever found.

(A click on the recording indicates the tape has been stopped and then started again.)

I miss Wendy and Andrew. I miss them terribly. At night, I wonder how I can continue on without my family.

People ask: *If everything was okay, why didn't you go to the lake with them that day?*

They ask this question when I say Wendy and I couldn't have been happier, when I say life was like a fairy tale.

We had a beautiful child, my books were selling well enough to pay our bills, and Wendy was preparing to quit her job at Happy Homes Realty to manage my business affairs full-time.

People ask this question even though our friends, the ones Wendy and Andrew spent the day with, repeatedly insist she didn't mention anything that would indicate we were having problems.

That day, when our friends asked where I was, Wendy told them the same thing I tell people now.

I was deep into writing a new book and I didn't want to lose the story, so I stayed home to work.

People believe that.

It certainly sounds like a good reason for a writer to skip a day at the lake with his beloved family.

Most days I *am* so drawn into my work that I can't escape the gravitational pull of the words. The world I'm creating becomes my reality.

But in this case, that answer isn't completely true.

Life wasn't as perfect as Wendy and I wanted people to believe. We lied to everyone, but not to ourselves.

Our personal divide started slowly, years ago, with me writing later and later into the night, pulling myself out of the real world until I wasn't even aware of my surroundings.

My son was growing up fast and I was missing all the important moments in his life but I couldn't help myself.

My work consumed me.

My imagination took me places my body never could.

The need to transcribe those stories on paper was bordering on the compulsive nature of an addict.

In the months before Wendy and Andrew vanished, I barely spent any time with either of them.

I was too busy here in my office, hunched over my computer or talking into this tape recorder.

But please don't misunderstand me.

Even though a passionate fire no longer burned in my heart for my wife, it wasn't like I wanted to be with anyone else.

Wendy and I never discussed ending our marriage.

We talked to no one about the situation and we did the best we could with what we had.

I loved my wife and my son, even if I was becoming a stranger in my own house, and I would have done anything for them.

Yet if I told anyone these things, the accusations would get worse. You understand that, right?

The police have already questioned me as many times as you would expect given the circumstances.

The husband is always the number one suspect, but this is a small town where everyone knows everyone.

I am well-liked and I had no motive.

My wife was well-liked, too.

No one could have imagined things ending badly between us, but no one has an imagination quite like mine.

I've imagined a lot of things in my lifetime, and I understand the intensity of the spotlight I'm standing under.

After I called the police the day my family vanished, the men in blue searched the area and I was questioned about where I had been, what I was doing, and when I last heard from my wife.

The FBI arrived early the next day and soon after the media descended like vultures, attracted by the Amber Alert.

Within hours I was standing on the steps of the Sheriff's Office before the cameras, begging for help, pleading for the person who had my wife and son to let them go, since they had to have been kidnapped, right?

I repeated the special phone number the FBI had arranged so the kidnapper could contact us.

No one ever called.

(Another click on the recording indicating the tape has been stopped and started again.)

Can you hear the storm?

I don't know if this tape recorder is powerful enough for you to hear those sounds, but it's raining outside and the rainfall is steadily tapping at the window.

The sound gets inside my head.

I wonder if I'm losing my mind.

Maybe I already did.

But here's what I've told anyone who will listen:

That morning, Wendy and I had breakfast and then she and Andrew departed for a day at the lake with our friends.

I headed upstairs to my office on the second floor of our home.

From ten in the morning until I awoke from an unplanned nap in the hour before sunset, I was lost in another world writing my new novel.

But when my wife and son didn't return from their afternoon at the lake, I went looking for them.

We live in a secluded house in the woods and our front door is nearly a mile from Rural Route #324, the main road to town.

My search didn't take long.

Wendy's white BMW was sitting at the end of our gravel driveway, parked like she had stopped to check the mailbox on her way home.

The driver's side door was open.

The right turn signal was blinking.

That yellow light, flashing on and off, again and again, was hypnotic through the gloom of nightfall and spring fog.

The dome light inside the car glowed like the moon.

My wife and son were nowhere to be seen, but there was blood on Andrew's baseball glove in the back seat.

Just a little. A couple of nickel-sized spots.

One of Andrew's flip-flops lay torn and tattered on the gravel nearby. Just one.

But there was no other sign of my family.

I yelled their names.

No one answered.

Panic consumed me.

I had forgotten my cell phone and the nearest neighbor was miles away.

I rushed back to the house and called 911 from the kitchen, wasting no time.

Less than ten minutes later, the sheriff arrived and the questioning began.

(Thunder is audible in the background. The recording stops and starts again.)

Hold on.

There was another creaking floorboard in the hall.

Can you hear it?

I don't want you thinking I'm crazy. I'm not.

Everywhere I look, the world is closing in on me.

Maybe death would be better than my life, than living this haunted existence.

Do you really want to know why I'm recording this?

The *real* reason I feel compelled to spill my guts?

I'll tell you why.

The footsteps in the hallway are closer than they've ever been and I don't think the lock on the door will be of any use.

Maybe if I tell you everything I know, I can cleanse my soul.

So is it possible I killed my wife and son?

Yes, of course.

You just have to use your imagination a little bit and anything becomes possible.

(Another click. When the sound returns, the storm is considerably louder.)

Here's the truth about that day three months ago:

I really *was* caught up in writing a new novel, but there was another reason I stayed home and it's a good thing no one knows.

Wendy and I had a fight that morning. The cause of the disagreement isn't important. It really isn't.

But we *were* fighting and I'm sure you can understand why I haven't told anyone.

Instead of going to the lake, I stayed home and I wrote.

What I was writing will make me sound even guiltier, but I must be honest, at least now, at least on this tape for you, whoever you are, if there's even a chance this declaration will protect me from what I fear will happen soon.

My new novel was called *Losing Everything* and it was the story of a man who decides to kill his wife and son. He doesn't love his family and he needs the insurance payout. He plans and he plots, trying to determine the best way to get rid of them, and it finally occurs to him that people wreck their cars all the time. What could be less suspicious? So he disables the brakes on his wife's Camry.

But that's not a *confession*. Can you see the differences here? The differences are *huge*.

I loved my wife and son. Even if my love for Wendy wasn't the same kind of love it had been once upon a time, I still cared about her.

And my son? Andrew meant the world to me.

The insurance? I didn't need the money and I haven't gotten any, either.

Wendy and Andrew are missing persons.

They weren't killed in a freak auto accident like the mother and son in *Losing Everything*. They disappeared at the end of our driveway.

But no one can ever know about *Losing Everything*, which is why I deleted all of my files from my computer and the cloud, and I burned the only paper copy of the manuscript in the fireplace.

No one would understand that the things I write about aren't based on my real feelings or real events.

If someone discovered *Losing Everything*, there would be even more questions and accusations, and I would prefer to do without both.

That's the last thing I need.

I'm having enough trouble staying sane as it is.

After being asked certain questions a million times, you find yourself questioning your own answers.

Some people asked why the police aren't tearing up the woods around my house searching for the bodies.

But the police *did* search the woods.

They searched for three days using cadaver dogs without finding anything.

No bodies, no fresh graves, no footprints, no nothing.

I might have been neglectful of my family's needs, I might have spent every waking hour alone in my office, but I *never* would have done anything to hurt my wife and son.

At least ... at least I don't think I could have.

(Another click.)

Can you hear that?

The storm is getting worse. The wind is whipping around the house, the rain is smacking at the wooden siding, and the slow creaking in the hallway continues.

Two heavy footsteps.

Two lighter footsteps.

Can you hear that?

They're getting close, I think.

It's so cold in here.

Thunder just crashed outside the window, shaking the entire house like a bomb exploded.

Did you hear it?

I'll lose the lights soon, I just know it.

(Another click.)

There's one more truth I've kept hidden, denying it even to myself most days, but this might be my last chance to clear my conscience.

I've told you the day had turned to dusk, on the verge of night, when I awoke in my office, right?

But what I didn't tell you was this: I awoke to a whispering in my ear.

You understand why I've told no one about this, right?

Why I've even denied it to myself at times?

People would say: *If he hears voices in his head, who knows what he might have done to his wife and son!*

That's what they'd say and you damn well know it.

But the voice was very real.

The voice whispered: *If you hurry, you can save them.*

I jumped to my feet and ran from the room as if maybe the words had come from God himself, not even fully awake and not knowing why I was running but understanding there wasn't a second to waste.

I took the stairs two at a time, tripping at the landing and slamming into the wall, knocking the framed print of "Cutting the Stone" by Hieronymus Bosch to the floor, where the glass broke.

A red handprint greeted me when I pulled away from the wall.

There was blood on my hands.

I was surprised by the cry rumbling from my throat as I stumbled through the foyer and into the living room, wiping my hands on my shirt as I moved.

The sounds my voice box was making were foreign to me. A wild animal caught in a trap might squeal like that.

My hiking boots by the living room couch were caked in mud. The mud was fresh.

The voice in my head screamed: *You have to go now!*

I didn't think, I just ran to the garage and jumped in my Jeep, starting the engine with a trembling hand.

Time was moving all wrong like I was stuck in slow motion.

I floored the gas and shot out of the garage into a strange night fog that had descended upon the woods.

The gravel driveway crunched under the Jeep's tires and the engine roared and I drove much too fast with my limited visibility.

The woods blurred past like something I might have dreamed the couple of times I experimented with drugs in college.

I spotted the car's yellow turn signal blinking through the fog in the distance.

The glow of the headlights.

The open driver's side door.

The tattered flip-flop.

The spots of blood on the baseball glove.

I screamed my wife and son's names into the night; I screamed until my lungs burned.

My heart sank.

I thought of the mud and the blood back at the house and I realized what I had to do.

My imagination is very vivid, but you don't need to be a natural-born storyteller to understand how the police would connect the dots upon their arrival.

Leaving that mess would result in a trip to death row at Black Rock State Prison for sure.

I sped back to the house, leaving my wife's car exactly as I had found it.

Cleaning up the blood, the mud, the broken art print, and disposing of my shirt took less than thirty minutes, and then I called the police.

I called as soon as I could and . . .

Oh, God.

Are you still listening to me?

The power has died and the room is pitch-black except for the lightning, which sends splinters of light across the room.

That light splashes my shadow onto the wall like an accusation.

I hear someone outside the door.

My heart is pounding.

Can you hear my heart?

I can!

I can!

Throbbing inside my head like a bass drum!

The doorknob is slowly twisting.

The damn lock didn't do anything!

I can't look, but I know what'll happen next . . .

The door will swing open and Andrew's small voice will whisper something through his throat filled with mud and water and bugs, something about the ghastly realm that is his life after death.

Another creak!

Here they come!

Oh God!
The voice!
The door!
Oh God!

(The recording does not stop, but there is thirty-three seconds of storm sounds and nothing else. Then:)

"Daddy, why are you hiding in the dark? Mommy and me really miss you."

(end recording)

As She Lay There Dying

THE CAMPUS WAS DAMP from another morning of April showers and the co-ed freshman convulsing on the road was missing part of her head, but she was still alive. Just barely. Her legs were twisted in opposite directions and there was blood everywhere. One of her tattered running shoes had landed on the other side of the street, knocked clear of the scene of the accident. A broken iPhone lay just beyond her hand.

The dying girl wore mesh shorts and a pink shirt featuring the Haverton Field Hockey logo. She was sprawled next to the curb at the entrance to the school's grounds, directly in front of the big stone wall with the sign proclaiming *Welcome to Haverton College*. The car that had hit her was nowhere to be seen.

"Oh shit," Sam whispered, turning to the bushes and vomiting. The English professor wasn't alone in his horror.

Students on their way to one o'clock classes gathered around the dying girl. Some held their hands to their faces while others texted their friends and a few livestreamed the scene to their social media accounts.

The dying girl moaned. Her disfigured head rolled loosely about and blood spit from her broken mouth, staining her teeth red. She turned her face blindly toward Sam and whispered in clipped breaths: "Sammy...we can't...run...anymore."

Sam blinked, startled by the sound of his name. He stared into the girl's glassy eyes. He didn't recognize her, but no one called him

Sammy, especially not students. The only person who ever called him that had been dead for six months.

Sam heard the artificial click and whir as a camera phone snapped a photo.

"Get out of here, you ass," Sam said, turning and shoving the young man with the phone in his outstretched hand and a backpack slung over his shoulder. The student stumbled backwards and then just stood there, off-balance and stunned. Sam yelled and shoved him again, up against the stone wall with the school's name.

Next came more shouting and pushing as the campus police arrived. The girl was dead by then, and the questioning began.

According to one of the department secretaries gossiping in the third-floor hallway of McGrove Hall, the dead girl's name was Lauren Redman, a first year Math Ed major who had come to the school on a field hockey scholarship.

Sam listened as he posted a note on his office door, canceling his classes. He couldn't stand the idea of facing the slack-jawed students while their obvious boredom burned a hole right through him.

Not today.

Walking home to his cozy neighborhood outside the small college town, Sam took a side street to avoid the main entrance to the school. The girl's blood would still be there.

What am I going to do? Sam thought, not for the first time.

As far as he could remember, the dead girl hadn't taken his mandatory Intro course, but the thousands of names and faces had blurred together over the years, so he couldn't be sure.

Actually, everything was a little blurry these days. Sam's shoving match with the cell phone voyeur felt like a distant memory of something he only witnessed. He didn't know what had come over him, but maybe it was a knee-jerk reaction to someone disrespecting the dying.

If that student had been there and photographed Julie's death, Sam probably wouldn't have stopped with a shove. But his wife had died alone, with no one to hold her hand and comfort her. Sam hadn't even known she was dead until an hour later.

Did Lauren Redman really say, *Sammy, we can't run anymore*, as she lay there dying on the pavement?

Those words disturbed Sam, but he didn't know why. The poor girl was dead. Why was he so bothered by her last words? She probably had a boyfriend named Sammy. Or a brother. It was a common name. Just because *he* was standing there didn't mean she was speaking to him. She probably had no idea where she was, let alone that she was dying.

The words didn't mean *anything*. It was just the last firing of synapses as what remained of her brain shut down. Some fragment of a memory, maybe.

This conclusion should have comforted Sam, but it didn't. He just kept hearing the words over and over in the dead girl's halting voice:

Sammy, we can't run anymore.

Sam started into the foyer of the house he had shared with his wife until her sudden death, but stopped in the doorway.

Like always, he vividly recalled every detail of the day he arrived home from a run and discovered he was a widower.

He closed his eyes and relived it again for the hundredth time. And why not? What else was he going to do tonight?

On the morning Julie died, Sam was soaked from head to toe in sweat, his feet ached, and his legs moved like they were made of marble as he paced the driveway to cool down and keep from tightening up. The winter air clung to his exposed flesh and steam rose from his clothes. Two hours of running never felt better than in these moments when the hurt and the joy were still fresh.

His mind was just starting to come down from his runner's high, the rush of endorphins that washed away all of the pains, distractions, and annoyances of the real world.

No matter how badly his legs hurt when he finished a run, his mind was always clear and ready to face new challenges. Julie had taught him this trick not long after they first met on a blind date. She called running her secret weapon for a happy life.

After Sam completed his cool-down routine in the driveway, he tried to open the front door, but something had been pushed up against it from the inside.

He had to shove the door open to discover Julie lying at the bottom of the steps, a tiny pool of blood next to her head. Her phone was still clutched in her hand like a talisman and her arms were twisted under her body, as if she had fallen down the steps.

She was dressed in her purple jogging suit with her top still zipped. That meant she hadn't made it out the door for *her* morning run, which usually started an hour after Sam's most Sundays. She ran for speed; her husband ran for distance.

Sam stared at his wife's motionless body for what felt like an eternity, not quite understanding how this could be happening. This wasn't right, this was all wrong. What exactly was he seeing? Time was moving so very slowly in the silence of the house.

Then he knelt and very gently touched her wrist.

"You love your melodramatic English Department bullcrap," Julie said to Sam one evening early in their marriage while she helped him out of his suit. This was a few months after they moved into the house and nothing was really unpacked yet.

Sam had just finished telling her about the latest crisis in his department. Was that the time the janitorial service cut back to only emptying the office trashcans every other day? It was hard to keep all of the bullshit straight, year after year, and he still couldn't believe how much bitching and moaning his well-paid colleagues could muster about such trivial matters and perceived slights. He would often think of the old saying about how inter-office battles on college campuses were so goddamned brutal because so little was at stake.

"What do you mean?" he asked.

"If everyone in your department weren't a little insane, you'd be bored to tears and you know it," Julie said, slipping her fingers into the elastic band around his waist.

Sam couldn't deny the truth in her statement, especially considering his underwear came off before he could reply and they spent the rest of the evening in the bedroom.

That was one of the many good times they had shared in their ten years of marriage, so many he couldn't even count them, but he didn't think it was fair those moments were done and gone forever.

Their ten years of marriage had been wonderful, but he had been promised a lifetime.

Upon finding his wife's dead body and touching her cool wrist, Sam whispered, "This isn't melodramatic English Department bullcrap" for reasons he still didn't understand.

Julie might have been able to explain it to him. She saw things differently than he did, after all, and that was what made them perfect for each other.

Then, with his hand still on Julie's wrist, Sam asked the quiet house: "What am I going to do?"

Every time Sam opened the front door, he expected Julie to be there, dead again, but of course she never was.

Julie was buried in the Haverton Community Cemetery on the far side of town and Sam walked to her grave three or four times a week during his lunch break to discuss the latest news and drama with her, just like the old days.

Today, Sam had wanted Julie's input on his big decision: whether to take a year's sabbatical and use it to pursue some other career.

Like always, he had sat on the ground and eaten the peanut butter and jelly sandwich he brought from home, leaning against her granite marker and picking at the grass around the base, keeping everything neat and tidy. The day was overcast and forlorn. Sometimes he felt like the funeral had never ended.

To his credit, Sam never actually heard Julie reply to any of his questions or observations, but he liked the idea that maybe she was out there somewhere, listening. He didn't really buy into the whole afterlife concept, but if it were possible for Julie to still exist on some other level of the universe, Sam would gladly change his beliefs in a heartbeat.

She probably would have the answers he needed, too. What to do with the rest of his life was a pressing decision for Sam. He had to request the sabbatical by Friday if the paperwork were to be approved in time for the fall schedule.

Sam understood he wasn't doing the students any good. He had cancelled more classes than he had attended this semester. At any other job he would have been fired, but he had tenure and the union wouldn't let anything happen to his position.

So Sam's livelihood wasn't in any danger. He could just put himself on cruise control and retire with full benefits at the age of sixty. Plenty of his colleagues were already on the thirty-and-out plan, after all. It was practically tradition.

But what would he do with all of the years to follow? Would he sit around the house writing reams of so-so poetry and watching television? Would he go to his desk and read old syllabi and pretend he missed his glory days? What kind of life would that be?

Besides, putzing along at work for a couple of decades without giving a crap wasn't how Sam wanted to live. He wanted to really be *alive*.

Of course, he also wanted Julie by his side to carry out their plans—the fixer-upper in the country, the beach house, the second honeymoon to Bermuda, the babies, all the beautiful babies—but that was an impossible dream he still clung to with a quiet desperation.

No one seemed to be holding Sam's inattentiveness at work against him, at least. Most people understood the depths of profound grief.

Really, who could blame him for not wanting to discuss Colonial Period American Literature while he was still attempting to comprehend how his beautiful bride, who was in better shape than him, could have been felled by an aneurysm while coming down the steps for her morning run, her brain shutting off before she even landed on the tile floor?

As far as Sam could tell, no one cared that his classes were falling so far behind, least of all the students.

Standing there in the foyer again, Sam thought of the second dead jogger to enter his life this year. He wondered if the parents of Lauren Redman had been notified yet.

They were probably driving across the state to visit her in the morgue, to confirm her identity.

Sam believed the only thing worse than finding your beloved dead on the foyer floor was getting that dreaded phone call and making that drive, wanting to believe it would just turn out to be a terrible misunderstanding.

Sam knew his wife was dead the moment he found her. No mistaken identity, no hoping for a miracle.

He guessed he should be grateful for that, but he wasn't. Julie was still dead, either way.

After Julie's death, Sam developed a condition that reminded him of a phenomenon he heard about all the time in his field. The symptoms snuck up on him out of nowhere and he was deep in the affliction before he realized what was happening. He blamed the grief.

Truman Capote, Ralph Ellison, Harper Lee, Gabriel Garcia Márquez, and Arthur Rimbaud all knew variations of the condition quite well, even if some of them suffered from it before the phrase was officially coined: writer's block.

Only Sam's problem wasn't with his writing. He continued to churn out poetry at his normal rate and he had updated his notes and syllabi for next semester without issue, just in case he felt a renewed vigor for teaching or simply couldn't pull the trigger on the sabbatical.

Sam didn't have *writer's* block. He had *runner's* block.

The last time he even tried to run—maybe a month after Julie's death, when he desperately needed to escape from the world—was so dreadful that he held no ambition to make another attempt.

Like most people with a mental block, Sam understood exactly what he wanted to do and how he used to do it, but his mind wouldn't let him get into the correct cerebral gear, which created a little cycle of hell for him to experience again and again. He needed to run so badly some days, but even the thought of wearing his running clothes could push him to tears.

The last time Sam had tried to go for a run, he sat on the edge of the bed and tied his running shoes, convinced this time would be different. He loved running. The act of getting out there and attacking the road was the only thing he had left that could truly make him feel good—and this time everything would be okay, he just knew it. Something had changed, something was different today.

Sam stood, stretched, and then headed down the stairs, his mind clear and his heart full of confidence, but he never even made it outside.

When he reached the last step, he tripped and fell, landing hard on the tile floor, sending a sharp blast of pain into his elbow and a dull ache echoing through his bones.

He found himself in a position strikingly similar to Julie's death pose, and he cried for over an hour, shaking uncontrollably.

He hadn't put on those shoes since.

Sam had never realized grief could run so deep and be so all-consuming, but these days he understood the misery of knowing you'd never be able to have the one thing you needed most to fill a gaping emptiness in your world.

The love of his life was gone, he couldn't run, and he didn't want to teach anymore...what was the point of riding the Earth around the sun year after year after year?

That was the question his mind got stuck on when the hopelessness became too much. He knew there was an answer, and the ease with which he sometimes contemplated that answer scared him badly.

As darkness settled across the land, ending yet another lonely day, Sam couldn't help but think of Lauren Redman's final words again: *Sammy, we can't run anymore.*

A few hours later, Sam dreamed that he was running, following the trail around campus.

His legs had never felt better and there was no pain. He could go a hundred miles if he wanted. Maybe more.

Sam was calm and collected as the campus rolled past him like a groovy Technicolor background. The sun was shining brightly through the trees and everything was incredibly vivid and alive. Birds were singing. A breeze cooled his sweaty skin.

Sam couldn't remember spring ever being this beautiful and he never wanted this run to end, but as he neared a small wooden bridge over a stream, he saw two women jogging in his direction.

This wasn't unusual considering how many students frequented the trail, except for one important detail: both of these women were dead.

They were running side by side and they were smiling, showing off their bloody teeth. Julie's hair was maroon from the small pool of blood she had died in. The top of Lauren's head was missing and bits of gray matter were speckled across her pink field hockey shirt.

Sam tripped and stumbled to his knees as all of the color drained from the dream.

Then he screamed.

The two dead women gaped at him, startled, and screamed back.

Their mouths were open so wide.

Their teeth were caked in dirt and blood...and then they shielded their faces with bruised and broken fingers.

They had clawed their way out of their graves.

Sam fell out of bed, soaked in sweat, his heart racing.

He crawled across the bedroom floor and into the master bathroom, where he lay sobbing.

He hadn't experienced a single bad dream since Julie's death, but this one was like a thunderbolt through his head.

Sleep had been the one place he could escape, but now that refuge had been stolen from him.

He was lonelier than he had ever felt in his entire life. He really wasn't prone to melodrama like some of the prima donnas in his department, but he was completely overwhelmed and exhausted and disoriented by the nightmare. Every moving shadow made him cringe in terror.

This was all too much.

What was he going to do?

He couldn't live with nightmares like that.

He simply couldn't.

He couldn't run, he couldn't sleep, and his wife was dead.

What am I going to do? Sam thought. *What am I going to do?*

What *could* he possibly do?

Sam closed his eyes and sobbed, hating the answer that came to mind yet again.

A few hours later, Sam opened his eyes.

Sunlight had slipped between the curtains and into his bedroom, washing over him where he lay on the bathroom floor.

Next to him were the running shoes he had given up when he realized his days of pounding the pavement were probably over.

He had no memory of retrieving them from the closet where he had once tossed them with a mixture of sadness and disgust.

Sam looked at the shoes, caked in dirt and grass-stained.

He heard the dying student whisper: *Sammy, we can't run anymore.*

Sam didn't believe in messages from beyond the grave, yet those dying words were true for both Julie and Lauren, weren't they?

Neither of them could run anymore ... but Sam could. What the hell was runner's block anyway? He hadn't run in almost six months, and why? Because his mind was somehow stopping him?

"What a load of melodramatic bullcrap," Sam whispered.

Getting to his feet, his body ached from the awkward position he had slept in, but he didn't give it a thought. He put on his running shorts, a gray t-shirt with the Havertown College logo, and his running socks with the extra padding on the heels. He laced up the shoes. They felt just right.

Sam took the stairs slowly, his hand on the railing the entire way, careful to avoid a repeat of what happened the last time.

When he reached the foyer, Sam opened the door without stopping to second-guess his decision.

A few minutes later, he was jogging toward town and he never looked back.

Sam understood where he was headed as soon as he made it out of the house: the trail around campus.

He passed by the entrance to the school where Lauren Redman died in a puddle of blood, probably not even aware that her run had come to a tragic end.

He locked his eyes on the road ahead of him and he ran even harder.

When Sam reached the start of the dirt trail, his heart was pounding, but he couldn't slow down, not yet.

His legs were thundering under him like he was charging into battle.

Sam certainly wasn't expecting to see Julie and Lauren crossing the bridge in the woods, but he had to run across the bridge for himself.

They wouldn't be there. He was certain of that. It simply wasn't possible.

When Sam reached the bridge, the dead women were nowhere to be seen, as he had expected.

And yet, for a man who didn't expect to see anyone, Sam was maybe a little too relieved.

Ten minutes later, Sam arrived at the bottom of the hill in the Haverton Community Cemetery. His clothing was soaked in sweat, his heart was pounding like a jackhammer, his lungs were tight, and he hadn't felt this good in forever. It was as if an enormous weight had been lifted from his shoulders.

The sun was blazing brightly above the mountains to the east and the world was more beautiful than Sam ever remembered it being, even in the early days of his marriage when *everything* was picturesque and perfect. Every blade of grass shimmered in the sunlight. Every birdcall was a love song.

Sam had never felt relief like this. The gloom smothering him had been stronger and deeper than he realized.

This experience was more than his usual runner's high that lifted him away from the pains and displeasures of the real world. This was the cure to end all cures.

Julie had been right, as always. Running really was the secret to a happy life.

Today, Sam wasn't running from despair and loneliness, he was running toward a bright and welcoming future.

But as he reached the hill where Julie was buried, Sam slowed to take in his surroundings. There was a change in the air. His vision and his senses were still clouded from the runner's high, but when he really concentrated, he could hear shoes pounding the pavement behind him.

He stopped, frozen by the sound. Those shoes were the only thing he could hear and they were suddenly so loud. No wind, no rustling of grasses, no birds in the sky.

Sam couldn't force himself to look back and see who might be coming. His newfound colorful world was being drained of light and he was terrified.

There were heavy, rapid-fire breaths behind Sam as the person got closer and closer. Only the breathing didn't sound human, it was more like an angry dog chasing down its prey. The impacts of the shoes echoed around Sam as if he were locked in a windowless vault.

Inside his ears, a voice whispered: *Sammy, we can't run anymore.*

Sam staggered in the direction of Julie's grave.

There was someone standing at the top of the hill, a silhouette against the gray sun. She raised her arms, reaching out toward Sam.

He ran, and the world grew bright again, full of colors and sounds that were wonderful and overwhelming.

Sam basked in the light and all of his agony melted away, returning him to that comfortable place, the place he never wanted to leave again.

He understood he had to keep running if he wanted this beautiful day to continue. He dug deep inside himself and ran even harder, the shadowy figure growing ever closer.

Sam prepared to embrace whatever he found at the top of the hill.

How the Wind Lies

DURING THE YEARS his family lived in the colonies, William Carver was firm but fair so long as his wife and children remembered his rules for good living: calloused hands do the work of God, defend thy honor only at the expense of thy humble heart, delay no task lest the load grow even heavier, and never speak a lie lest thy lie becometh the truth.

Yet life in the colonies felt like someone else's memories as William worked under the blazing sun on the flowered plains, tilling the land beyond their vegetable garden for additional planting to prepare a stockpile for the winter. The change in seasons was still months away, but the previous winter had nearly claimed their lives and he would take nothing for granted.

William turned the soil by hand with the hoe his father had made in the old country. That was fine. Difficult labor in the heat of the summer sun left him sweating and aching, a reminder that God rewarded His hardest workers. William was a bear of a man and he attacked his tasks with an almost religious fervor.

On a clear day, he could see for miles across the flatlands, and the grasses surrounding the homestead often danced and swayed in the gentle breeze. Since his family's arrival here, William had discovered the winds of these western plains spoke in a variety of voices, many he had never heard in the colonies. Sometimes the wind was enraged, pushing black clouds across the endless sky. Sometimes the wind whispered and soothed, cooling the sweat on his neck.

With the exception of the Indians, who had left them alone so far but could sometimes be heard in the distance, William felt like his family was living in total isolation. That certainly hadn't been the plan when they departed the town they had always called home, but at least they had escaped the danger back east. He thanked God for that every morning and every night.

There were three other homesteads nearby, abandoned and overgrown. William did not dwell on the dilapidated nature of the cabins he had once helped build. There was no time to memorialize the people who had lived within the homes for such a short time. Instead he focused on the future, for he only had so much energy to give each day and this land demanded everything from him.

William returned his full attention to his work. His eldest son George should have been with him, but Sarah had suggested the boy could use a day to play and explore, and William had eventually decided she was correct, as he so often did. His wife was wise and he took her counsel seriously.

Now, though, George came to his father from the fields to the west and said, "Something's killing the buffaloes."

William studied his boy. Young George Carver was thirteen and full of bluster and noise, but he had never told a lie as far as his father knew.

Sarah worked quietly out of earshot, scrubbing clothes in a wooden tub filled with water from the nearby stream. The young twins, Peter and John, played in the dirt by the cabin's door and they took no interest in the conversation.

"What do you mean?" William asked.

"Their fur is white and their eyes are milky and the stench is awful." George removed a handful of white fur from the pocket of the pants his mother had sewn for him. The tufts floated away on the breeze.

"Go to the creek and wash your hands, boy," William said. "I'll see to this."

"Yes, sir."

William walked into the fields of waving grasses that continued for miles in every direction.

He walked with a heavy heart.

He feared he knew what was killing the buffaloes.

William studied the horizon for any sign of the terrifying Indian tribes they had been warned about when they headed west. He rarely had time to reflect upon matters beyond the immediate needs of his wife and children, but as he ventured further from the homestead, he considered how they had come to live in this place. If what he feared were true, the journey had not put enough distance between them and the danger.

Ten families had set out across the country, fleeing the terror ravaging their community, but only four families reached the open plains. Some turned back when supplies ran low and some were claimed by the big river, drowning when the rapids flipped their rafts while the other helpless travelers watched in horror.

The four families who survived built their homesteads just in time for the first brutal winter, but that wasn't enough to protect them. Their numbers dwindled as the snowy days marched on, and by the time the warmth of spring awakened the land, the Carvers were the only ones left.

William had done his Christian duty and given those other men, women, and children a proper burial as they passed. Treat thy neighbor as you would treat thy kin, he always said, yet their names were already fading from his mind. They were with God and memories of those who had passed served no meaningful purpose to his daily tasks.

William was the only man left, and as such he carried a tremendous weight upon his shoulders. He rarely slept, spending his nights watching for Indians and other threats that might lurk beyond the safety of their homestead.

He was also waiting for something he didn't dare speak of.

There was a very specific sound, one he had only heard once before, back in the colonies when he suffered a very close call that could have ended with his demise.

The sound was a harsh whistling, like the cry of an animal stabbed by a hunter's knife, and yet it was both loud and soft as it rose and fell, beckoned and repelled.

If William heard that sound again, their journey had been for nothing and his entire family would almost certainly perish.

William found the dead buffaloes easily enough. Their death scent was carried to him by the wind. The odor was unmistakable. The buffaloes reeked as if they had been corpses for weeks, not the mere hours every other indication pointed toward. There were tacky drops of blood on the grass and the last terrified bowel movements hadn't solidified.

"My Lord," William whispered, covering his mouth with his hand.

He approached the nearest buffalo with trepidation, pulling back the bleached fur from the top of the head. He did not relish the thought of touching the animal, but he had to be certain his instincts were correct.

In a shredded patch of fur, he discovered what he had feared: two puncture wounds of equal size through which the buffalo had been drained completely of blood.

William did not linger at the massacre. He sprinted back through the tall grasses as the smell of death chased him on the wind.

In the distance, Sarah screamed and William ran even harder.

The screaming ceased before William reached the homestead, his heart pounding hard in his chest.

George and Peter were sobbing as they held onto their mother in the clearing by their cabin. Sarah cradled little John in her arms, rocking him as she had when he was a mere baby. He was dead, his skin as pale as chalk, his eyes milky white.

To William, the cause of death was unmistakable. Rage and revulsion and despair flooded through him. He dropped to his knees and grabbed the boy away from his wife. John's head rolled loosely on his tiny neck.

"Where was he?" William demanded.

"He and Peter were behind the other cabins," Sarah said through her tears. "I went for them to begin their chores and I came upon John in this state. I screamed and screamed."

William turned toward Peter. "Son, what did you see?"

"Nothing, Father," Peter said, tears pouring off his face like sweat. "He just fell dead in the grass."

"Did you see him fall?"

"No, I was watching the clouds."

"All of you, get inside."

His family didn't question his command. They hurried into the cabin and closed the door, leaving William with his dead son.

After fortifying his courage, William lifted John into his massive arms and hugged him like a ragdoll. The boy seemed to weigh nothing and was far too light for a corpse, which normally grew heavier in death.

William closed his eyes and ran his hand through John's thick hair, which was dry and brittle like aged straw. With a grimace, he used his fingernail to explore deep into his son's scalp. He discovered a wet mess encircling two wounds in the skull, just as he had expected and feared.

John was drained of blood.

William dug a grave for his son alongside the other crosses marking the resting places of their travel companions. His enormous hands ached from the digging, but the pain reminded him that he was a man with responsibilities to honor.

The stink emanating from the corpse was horrendous, another sign the boy had been killed by the beast they had hoped to escape. But how could that nightmare of a monster have known where to find them? It didn't seem possible, but William was not a man to deny the truth he witnessed with his own eyes. The beast was here and would need to be dealt with or their own lives would be taken from them.

William gently placed his son in the hole and spoke a short prayer. John's withered corpse lay small and helpless in the shallow grave.

William covered his boy with the freshly-turned soil.

Just as he had buried the others.

That night, as William lay awake in the darkness and listened to his wife and children quietly sobbing, he contemplated the myth of the Salem Vampyre: how it sucked the blood directly from the brains and how the odor of the corpse would become unbearable.

The Salem Vampyre's reign of terror was the reason the ten families had headed west. No one could determine where the Vampyre was hiding and, unlike the Vampyres of the old country, this one didn't seem to mind the light of day. He could be anywhere. He could be anyone.

Not only did the townspeople fear becoming the Salem Vampyre's latest victim, but some said if even a drop of the Vampyre's blood touched your flesh, you would become his servant and stalk your loved ones and neighbors.

Rumors ran rampant that others were already joining the Vampyre in his hunts. Neighbors turned against each other and there were no safe quarters to be found. No one could be trusted.

There was talk, so much talk, but one particular thought returned to William again and again.

In the old country, you would push a stake fashioned from wood through the heart of the Vampyre, causing the beast to burst into flames and die.

William spent the night considering this. He did not sleep.

"Are you certain you didn't see anything?" William asked his wife the next day. They sat at the table where they had eaten all of their meals, many of them very meager, especially during that first winter. Sarah's eyes were stained red from the force of her weeping.

"I'm certain. John and Peter were playing and when I went outside to remind them of their chores, John was lying in the grass. I thought he was fooling me until . . . until I saw his pale skin."

"Where was George?"

"He had gone to the creek, as you instructed. Do you really believe the Salem Vampyre has come?"

"Yes. Somehow the monster tracked us, but I will stop him once and for all."

William crouched inside the cabin, using his hunting blade to sharpen one end of a slat he had taken from his dead son's bed. Slivers of wood piled between his feet like shed skin.

His mind and body were exhausted, but while he worked, William remembered how he had nearly met the Salem Vampyre face to face back in the colonies. He had been making his way home late one night after drinking ale, and he had taken the long way so he could watch the moonlight dance on the narrow river racing to the nearby ocean.

The world was very calm, as if William were the last man in the colonies, until a harsh whistling from the woods broke the peace. The sound was unlike anything he had ever heard before. The whistling rose and fell, like a song carried on an unnatural wind, and the noise chilled him to his bones. This was both a calling and warning spoken in the same foreign voice, summoning him while also pushing him away.

William couldn't help himself; his feet moved without thought. He was several steps into the woods when the whistling stopped as quickly as it had started. The spell was broken and William stumbled back toward the path, horrified by his loss of control. He hurried home, and by the time he reached his own bed, he was convinced the sound was merely a lingering effect of the drink he had imbibed.

The next day the patriarch of the Smithee family was found near that very spot on the path, dead, the latest victim of the Vampyre. Had William persisted in investigating the noise, he might have joined Mr. Smithee in the hands of the Lord, leaving his poor family to fend without him. That had been a very close call indeed.

Not more than a week later, William and his family and the others had pooled their resources to purchase wagons and supplies. They headed west, where rumor had it you would be safe from the monster walking among them.

Yet here was William fashioning a stake from his dead son's bed while George and Peter played just outside the door, honoring his instructions not to wander. Off in the distance, Sarah washed in the creek. She was badly shaken by the sudden loss of their son after they had traveled so far to start this new life, and William had suggested a cool bath might calm her nerves.

He took great care as he carved the stake, knowing his calloused hands were doing the work of God, and he was nearly finished when Sarah screamed. The piercing wail was much closer than the creek. William bolted to the door then stopped dead in his tracks, unable to believe what awaited him in the bright sunlight.

Peter lay on the ground not far from the cabin, pale and bloodless and as dead as his twin brother. Sarah had fallen to her knees beside the withered boy. George stood nearby, his face blank.

William scanned the area. There was no one else to be seen for miles.

He stumbled out of the cabin on trembling legs and fell to his knees next to his wife. Together, they held their son.

George watched, his face expressionless.

In the scorching light of the unforgiving sun, William dug another grave.

The blazing heat and the pain deep in his heart left him shaking, but he did not stop until his work was done.

"I'm scared," Sarah whispered that night, holding their last son as he slept. Her eyes were drifting closed. She was exhausted from the terror of the last few days, but she didn't dare release little George from her grip.

William checked outside again, gazing into the darkness. The grasses swayed in the wind, but there was no one to be seen. Or heard. They were alone and his mind was ablaze with troubling thoughts.

George must be our Salem Vampyre. He has to be. He was the only one around both times. And he is the one who found the dead buffaloes. It has to be him. But Sarah doesn't know . . .

William slumped onto the wooden chair like a broken old man being crushed by the weight of the world. He watched his son sleeping in candlelight that sent shadows dancing across the room. Sarah held the boy tightly, as if she feared he might float away. Her eyes had closed.

A voice that sounded much like William's own whispered inside his head: *Kill him while you have the chance.*

No, I can't, William thought. *He's my boy.*

Who else must perish before you'll do what must be done? the voice asked. *Delay no task lest the load grow even heavier.*

The only sound in the cabin was the gentle calling of the wind sweeping across the plains, but George's eyes snapped open. The boy said nothing, but he turned his head toward his father. Their eyes locked. Staring at one another in the uneven glow of the candle, William spotted a glimmer in the boy's gaze. An unnatural light.

I must, William decided. *I must finish this before it's too late. He's not my son.*

Yes, the voice agreed. *Your work must be completed. It will be quick. Plunge the stake into his black heart and he shall burst into flames, ending the horror.*

William removed the stake from under the table where he had secured it with a bit of rope. He grabbed George from Sarah's arms with one rough tug and dragged the boy into the middle of the room.

Sarah's eyes opened and she looked around, confused and disoriented. She saw what was happening and she reached for her son, but she moved much too slowly.

"May the Lord forgive me," William whispered as he knelt over George and raised the stake above his head.

George's mouth opened and William drove the stake into his heart, cutting off any words he might have been preparing to speak. His high-pitched squeal of agony tapered into rough coughs and he convulsed, spitting blood. William fell backwards in his haste to avoid the fluid, lest he risk catching whatever had infected his boy.

George shuddered, his fingers clawing at the rough floor. Sarah crawled to her son and pulled him into her arms as blood poured from his mouth. The stake remained in his chest.

"Get away from him!" William demanded, but his wife either did not hear his order or she ignored him for the first time in their marriage.

"Mother," the boy whispered, his eyes locking on hers before he took one last, shuddering breath.

Moments passed, but George did not burst into flames as the Vampyre was rumored to do upon the arrival of his own death. Instead, Sarah held him and rocked him and cried his name.

"No," William whispered, pressing his hands against the sides of his head. "He didn't burn. It wasn't him."

Sarah stroked their dead son's hair as if in a trance. After a few minutes, she gently laid George on the floor and staggered to her feet. She studied her husband as if he were a stranger whom she had never met, a stranger with madness in his eyes.

"Why?" Her voice cracked and her hands trembled.

"I had to stop the Salem Vampyre," William said. "I thought it was the boy. It *had* to be him."

Sarah stood there, the candlelight flickering across her face. She seemed to be staring a great distance beyond the walls of the cabin. Her mouth opened and closed several times, but no words came.

When Sarah moved, she moved quickly, lunging across the room and swinging her fists at her husband. She landed blows with the fierceness of a woman pushed to the brink of insanity.

She had never done anything like this before in her entire life, and William recovered from his surprise and began easily deflecting her punches. He saw the unnatural light burst to life within her eyes. It was the hunger of the monster that had stalked them from the east.

William shoved his wife away, sending her flying like a ragdoll.

"This madness must *not* continue," he said, bending over and pulling the stake from George's limp body.

Sarah scrambled into a sitting position against the cabin wall. She tried to stand, but William was too big and too fast. He grabbed her foot and dragged her next to their dead son.

Sarah's eyes widened and she gasped as William raised the bloody stake and brought it down. He thought she might scream, but all of the breath flowed from her mouth in a wounded hissing noise. She winced and a trickle of blood escaped her lips. She blinked several times, slowly, and then the light left her eyes.

William backed away, waiting for his wife of so many years to burst into flames.

But she didn't burn either.

William stared at her body, unable to comprehend what this meant at first.

"Neither of them was the Vampyre? But there's no one left . . . "

The voice in his head replied: *You, William, you're the only one left. You killed your wife and sons.*

"I had to," William said.

You killed them. You killed them all.

"I had to stop the Vampyre!"

William . . . what Vampyre?

William flung the cabin's door open and walked out on legs that did not feel like his own. He fell to his knees below the watchful eye of the bright moon.

Memories collided, forming and breaking apart again. He saw people screaming, men and women and children alike, their faces round and pale. He had tried to forget who they were, but how could he forget his closest friends and neighbors who had traveled to this place with him based on his promise that they would be safe from the terror?

In these memories, William saw their horror as they raised their arms to block a blow or avoid an attack, but they were overpowered, each and every one. They were struck down by someone much bigger and stronger, their chests pierced by a sharpened stick. Blood sprayed from the wounds. No one burned. No one ever burned.

Disgust rose inside William as he realized who had wielded that stake. His stomach clenched and dropped in his gut.

All of the memories flooded back. He could remember the slick blood coating his face as he did what he thought he had to do, his own eyes wide and yet blinded by fear.

He had killed his friends and family in his hunt for the Vampyre. Yet, after each murder, his mind closed upon itself, blocking the memories and the truth. He told himself they had died of a sickness and he repeated this lie often enough that he truly believed it.

"What have I done?" he called into the night.

The voice whispered: *Never speak a lie lest thy lie becometh the truth, William.*

William crawled back through the open door and into the cabin. He continued across the floor to the bodies of his dead wife and son, dragging himself with bloody fingers.

He considered the terror of living on the plains all alone with the memory of what he had done. The endless view of nothing but the flowering grasses waving at him. The howl of the wind in the night as it shook the cabin. The bitter winter that at times seemed to be without end.

Defend thy honor only at the expense of thy humble heart, William.

He grabbed the stake, dripping with the blood of his wife and son. He aimed the point toward his own chest. It was time for his hands to truly do the work of God and put an end to the horror.

William whispered a prayer, but as he prepared to jerk the stake deep into his own chest, another voice whispered in the back of his mind.

This was the voice of Sarah, and hearing his dead wife speaking to him nearly stopped his heart.

She said: *William, my love, if there is no Vampyre, how do you explain the dead buffaloes drained of their blood? Or Peter and John?*

Sarah had always given him the wisest counsel, he realized, and tears formed in his eyes.

A noise outside the cabin seized William's attention, sending a shiver down his spine.

A whistling started deep in the grasses. The familiar sound rose and fell, growing shriller with each passing second, approaching the cabin. Closer and closer and closer still.

Just outside the doorway, the whistling stopped.

William stood, nearly collapsed, then steadied himself, the stake still gripped tightly and ready to be used.

He approached the door with heavy legs that fought his every movement. He didn't really want to learn what might or might not be waiting for him outside the cabin, but he also couldn't stop himself.

William opened the door.

He stood there for a moment, terrified beyond words.

Then William screamed, and his scream, like the screams of so many others, was carried away on the wind.

Perfect Little Snowflakes

E VEN IN THE DARK, the motel room was ugly.

Melissa was just sixteen, had never spent a night away from home, and this was not where she wanted to be.

Matthew pushed past her and into the bathroom, closing and locking the door. Melissa stood in the doorway, the winter wind blowing around her, cutting through her dress, biting into her flesh as if she wore nothing at all.

They had left the Black Hills Diner in such a hurry, Matthew practically dragging her by the arm, that she had forgotten her jacket in the booth. She wondered if someone would put it in the Lost and Found box at the front of the restaurant. She loved that jacket.

The walls of the motel room had been painted beige years ago and the popcorn ceiling was yellowed. This was the sort of place that didn't have a "no smoking" policy until the legislators in Harrisburg declared that particular vice to be against the law, at least when it came to restaurants and hotels.

There was a frayed wicker chair, a twin bed with two pillows tucked under the green covers, and a battered wooden dresser with an ancient television and a faded placard:

Welcome to the Black Rock Motel! Checkout is Noon. Sorry no smoking! Enjoy your stay!

There was a scuffed nightstand with a wind-up alarm clock and a Gideon Bible. The hands of the clock pointed at eight sharp, but Melissa knew it was closer to eleven. Her parents would be wondering where she was.

Melissa closed the door, leaned against the wall, and rubbed her temples. A dull headache had been building all week. Her forehead throbbed. Her thin lips were painfully chapped.

She took two steps and sat on the edge of the bed, the box spring screeching under the weight of her petite frame. She picked up the alarm clock and wound the metal key, not bothering to set the correct time. The minute hand slipped forward with an audible click.

Melissa wrapped her arms around her belly. It was still small. For now.

She hadn't told anyone other than Matthew—not her parents, not their friends—but everyone would learn her secret eventually. She and Matthew had two more years of high school left and they couldn't exactly hide a baby.

Maybe in the rest of the world this situation was acceptable these days, the sort of thing that might even get you a television show, but not in the small town of Black Hills, a place where people lived for the talk. The gossip. The community would whisper about how Melissa loved spreading her legs, would spread her legs for anyone, in fact. Gossip was king. It didn't matter that Matthew had been her first. The first boy to say he loved her and the first boy she kissed and the first boy she truly loved. They had taken things so much slower than most of their peers. None of that mattered.

Melissa considered herself a modern, independent woman, even if she were still just a little girl in her father's eyes, but this week had tested her. She had never understood how circumstances could change so quickly without any hint of trouble on the horizon. One day she was a teenage girl in love with her boyfriend, the next day she was a mother-to-be with no idea what to do.

The bathroom door remained closed. She loved Matthew, but he wasn't handling this as well as she had hoped. He had barely said a word since she shared her news with him earlier tonight. He had mumbled something about dinner and he drove them to the Diner where he said nothing, and then he had mumbled something about them needing to leave and they had left in a hurry, and then he had mumbled something about her staying in the truck when he stopped at his father's house on the outskirts of town.

Matthew had returned a few minutes later with a wad of cash he had probably stolen from his father's drinking stash and then he drove them to this motel. She waited in the truck while he paid for a room.

Melissa stood again and opened the curtains, revealing the smudged window. Falling snow painted the night sky white. There was a rocking chair outside the door, rocking in the winter wind. The flickering neon signs proclaimed BLACK ROCK MOTEL and VACANCY. It always said VACANCY these days.

Matthew's second-hand truck was the only vehicle in the parking lot. Beyond that was the road and beyond the road was the forest, thick with barren trees and dead underbrush. In the distance, deep in the valley, the lights along Main Street bisected the small town they called home.

Melissa wished everyone would just go away for a while so she could think. The world was a meaningless hum inside her head, a silent bombardment of the accusations and taunts she knew would be coming. She was weary, even with Matthew here. Maybe *because* Matthew was here. She had thought things would somehow get better once he knew the situation they were in, but she had been wrong.

"You okay?" she asked the locked bathroom door. Water splashed in the sink. No reply.

Melissa returned to the bed and she watched the falling snow and she thought about the growth inside her belly, the baby who couldn't be much bigger than a few clumped snowflakes.

When she was a little girl, her father had once drunkenly told her that all children were like perfect little snowflakes: each one was different and unique and flawless in conception, but you never knew where they would land once they hit the ground. She still didn't know what he had meant and, like most of his drunken sayings, he probably didn't either.

The bathroom door creaked open and Matthew emerged. His baggy pants hung around his hips. He had splashed water on his face and his hair was wet. There was a heaviness in the way he moved, as if he were the one who had been wrestling with a week of sleepless nights punctuated by nightmares and terror.

"How are you doing?" Melissa asked.

Matthew didn't reply. He sat in the wicker chair by the door. He stared at the floor.

"I've been better," he finally said, his voice low. "What are we going to do?"

"I don't know."

"We have options."

"I know."

There was silence. Melissa watched the snow. She thought about the baby and that word. *Options*. She understood what those options were. None of them appealed to her.

"You can't be pregnant," Matthew said.

"I'm sorry." It was all she could think to say.

"How did this happen?"

"I don't know."

Of course she knew. They both knew. It was a stupid question and a stupid answer.

A few minutes passed.

"I'm sorry," Matthew whispered. His hands were shaking. "Really, I'm sorry."

"Matthew, I love you."

He didn't reply. He stared at the carpet.

"Matthew, I love you," she repeated.

"I love you, too," he said, his voice distant.

"How are we going to tell our parents?"

Matthew watched the floor like a nervous little boy who had done something bad and was waiting for his punishment.

He said, "My father will kill me. And the shit at school. Do you have any idea what they'll say in school?"

Melissa flinched. Last night she had awakened on the floor of her bedroom, drenched in cold sweat from a nightmare. Kids in her biology class had been mocking her, scolding her, asking her if she did it for free or if you had to pay for her services. Her belly was huge in the dream and everyone took turns punching her and she screamed as the front of her dress turned red and the liquefied remains of her baby flowed from between her legs.

So yes, she had concerns about what would be said at school.

"Matthew, we can figure this out."

"We have options. It's really small, right? It doesn't even look like a person."

Melissa didn't reply. She considered what Matthew had said as the ancient alarm clock marked each minute. She was almost hypnotized by how slowly time seemed to be moving and how muddled the thoughts in her brain had become. So little sleep, so many emotions, and yet the Earth just kept spinning and spinning as if she didn't exist.

Melissa looked out the window again. The snow was falling faster. She thought of her baby. Their baby. The clump of cells like a snowflake. A snowflake growing inside of her. A perfect little snowflake that might land anywhere, do anything.

"I want to keep the baby," Melissa whispered. "We can do this together. I know we can."

For the first time since they left the Diner, Matthew raised his gaze to meet Melissa's hopeful eyes. His hands began to clench and unclench. Faster and faster.

Melissa felt a strange twinge of fear, but something else simmered deep inside her, too. A realization had been nagging at her for most of the night. Right now she didn't actually care what people would say, what people would think. Right now she just wanted Matthew to demonstrate that he loved her as much as he had when he was out of breath, gasping in her ear, promising her the world.

"Do you understand?" Matthew asked, as if he had been saying something she didn't hear. He stood and paced back and forth before the window. The snowy world outside was surprisingly bright behind him.

"Understand what?"

Matthew moved faster. Melissa had never seen him agitated like this before. They had known each other since the first grade and she couldn't remember his hands ever shaking this much.

"There's only one way," Matthew said. He removed his father's snub-nosed revolver from the pocket of his baggy pants. The gun was silver with a black grip.

"What are you doing?" Melissa hadn't realized how truly terrified she was until the words escaped her mouth. Her chapped lips burned.

"This is the only way," Matthew said. He stepped forward, extending his right arm.

Once again, Melissa was amazed at how circumstances could change so quickly with so little warning. That thought throbbed inside her head, directly behind her eyes, as if a sizzling piece of metal were poking her brain. She wanted to scream. This wasn't the boy she had fallen in love with. He was supposed to love her and support her and give her the world, just as he had promised.

Melissa reached out and her thin fingers grabbed the barrel of the gun, yanking the revolver from Matthew's hand. Surprise flashed in his eyes and he lunged forward, knocking her to the floor. They rolled against the wall and he wrapped one hand around the gun as he pried at her fingers.

They rolled again and suddenly Matthew was on top of her, his weight pushing her against the floor. Their fingers struggled for control of the trigger and then there was a roar, unexpected and impossibly loud.

A hole appeared in Matthew's hand at the end of the barrel. A matching hole exploded in the middle of his forehead. Blood and gray clumps splashed onto the wall.

Matthew remained frozen, looming above Melissa, his surprised eyes locked on hers. Then he rolled backwards, landing on the threadbare carpet, his eyes still open and staring at the yellowed popcorn ceiling.

The gun fell to the floor with a thud.

Melissa pushed herself away, crawling backwards to the other side of the room. Her heart raced and she didn't think she'd ever be able to slow it down. She couldn't focus on anything except the dead body as her mind screamed, *Get up, get up, get up!* and she didn't know if she meant Matthew or herself.

Time had been moving so fast for a few seconds there, but now it slowed again. The clock on the nightstand ticked away the minutes. Melissa soaked in the heavy silence of the motel room, which was deafening inside her head.

Finally, she stumbled to her feet. The beige walls and her frenzied thoughts spun. She opened the door to the outside. A frigid winter wind blew the falling snow through the doorway. The white flakes landed on the stained carpet.

A chill bit into Melissa. The wind whipped past her thin dress. The pick-up truck's windshield and hood were already white with snow. To her left and right were the other, unoccupied rooms. Dull lights burned along the overhang, creating an eerie chorus line.

Melissa sat on the rocking chair outside the door. Snow landed on her skin as the cold wind attacked her with a savage ferocity. A tear trickled down her face, transforming into a tiny diamond of ice by the time it reached the corner of her mouth.

She rocked and she watched the snow and she clutched her belly tighter. Before too long, the air stopped being so cold and a warmth spread throughout Melissa. The sensation was almost pleasant.

As she rocked, Melissa realized the person she had come here with couldn't have been the real Matthew. Whoever that had been, he acted nothing like the boy she loved so much. He must have been some kind of imposter.

Soon Melissa forgot about the dead body in the motel room and the heart-pounding terror of what had happened.

Instead, she remembered the promises the real Matthew had made her and she waited for him to return while the snow piled higher and higher, forming an ocean of perfect little snowflakes for as far as she could see.

The Plague of Sadness

THE WOMAN DOESN'T REMEMBER when the coldness began to fester inside her, but she's terrified.

Her hand trembles on the doorknob to her baby's nursery. The room is pink and yellow and full of stuffed animals and there are white lacy curtains on the windows. The woman can see the tiniest detail when she closes her eyes, and she tries with all of her might to back away.

There is darkness behind her eyes, but it won't stay still. The darkness moves and dances.

The woman opens the door and steps into the room.

In the corner is the white crib. Anne Marie is asleep, finally asleep, a gift from God that there's sleep after days of crying and fussing and sickness. She looks like a beautiful china doll.

No, no, no, the woman thinks as she reaches for her child. A tear trickles down her face.

Dispatcher (female): 911, what is the nature of your emergency?

Woman's Voice (barely audible): It's *so* cold here.

Dispatcher: Ma'am, you'll have to speak up. What's the nature of your emergency?

Woman's Voice (more clearly): *So cold.*

Dispatcher: Where are you, Ma'am?

Woman's Voice: I just drowned my baby girl.

Dispatcher: What? What happened to your baby?
Woman's Voice: The coldness just won't quit.

(Sound of a gun cocking is clearly audible.)

Dispatcher: Ma'am, I'm sending someone to your location, just hold on . . .

(A gunshot. Then two distinct thumps as the gun and the woman drop to the floor.)

Dispatcher: Oh my God. Ma'am, ma'am? Are you still there? Oh my God, someone get Harry, I think this lady just killed herself!

There is a great deal of paperwork after the call, but Sheila is numb as she provides the required answers. She's never had anyone die on her before. She's certainly had some close calls—like the man who cut off his thumb while trying to figure out his new circular saw—but nothing like this. Even that Darwin Award runner-up survived. But this woman—whose name she doesn't even know because nothing showed up on the call screen—hadn't reached out in time, and Sheila had merely been a witness to her death.

Sheila's boss, an older man named Harry Duncan, sits in the tiny break room with her in case she needs anything. He is kind and supportive. No one will blame her for how the call terminated. She responded quickly, she asked the right questions, she hadn't been drinking or sleeping on the job. The call was textbook, even if the outcome wasn't ideal. But the paperwork must be finished, just the same. All of the t's crossed and all of the i's dotted.

Sheila doesn't know whether she'll ever be able to sit at the command console again. She now understands why many dispatchers don't ever come back, not after something like this.

"You did everything you could," Harry tells his shell-shocked employee for the third time, as if reading her mind. "I'm not supposed to say this, but some people can't be saved."

Sheila winces. She thinks of her own baby at home, a baby whose father was ripped out of their lives by a drunk driver, the baby who is her last living connection to the man she had loved so completely.

How could you hold your struggling baby in the bathtub until her little face stopped crying and the bubbles ceased to rise from her tiny mouth?

Sheila's mind is spinning with questions that don't even feel like her own thoughts, and she wants to scream. She realizes she *hates* the dead woman. Sheila has never desired to hurt anyone this badly, not even the drunken Steelers fan who killed her husband. Somehow, she even forgave that selfish asshole who didn't even apologize to her in the courtroom. Yet Sheila wishes she could go back in time to yesterday and murder this woman to save the baby and she has no idea how to feel about *that* thought, which just won't leave her alone.

"Why would someone kill her kid?" Sheila is asking herself as much as she is asking Harry or the walls of the room. "How *could* she?"

"I don't know. I just try to bounce back the best I can because there will be more people to help tomorrow."

Sheila signs the last page. Her hands are shaking. "If it's okay, I think I need to leave."

"Do you want a lift?"

"No, I'd rather be alone for a while."

Six hours later, Sheila is rocking her sleeping baby in the living room of her pleasant little house on the edge of town. The curtains are pulled nearly shut and the room is dark, but a sliver of moonlight sneaks across the floor.

Outside there are sirens. More sirens than she's ever heard in her life, as if the world is coming to an end. Perhaps it is.

After the disastrous call, Sheila felt so much anger, but eventually that anger sunk deep inside of her, transforming into a coldness that now grips her like a vice.

Sheila doesn't know where the coldness came from yet, but she

The Last Beautiful Day

LOUIS STEPHENSON'S WORK BEGINS with a ringing phone in the middle of the night, but the bad news isn't for him.

This is not the first late night phone call he has received since he put his name on the volunteers list at the hospital. It seemed like a good idea at the time, as morbid as the work sounded, but these days he's having serious doubts about his decision.

Louis answers the call on the second ring, hoping Melissa wasn't disturbed in the other room. She hasn't been sleeping well these past few months, not since they lost the baby, and insomnia is only one of the symptoms troubling her.

Louis holds the phone but can't open his mouth to answer. His therapist suggested he volunteer for this job. She said it would help fill the growing void deep inside of him, the emptiness caused by his overwhelming grief, but Louis thinks maybe the last few months have been the result of God playing a cruel joke on him. First the dead baby inside his wife and now these phone calls.

"Hello," he finally answers. He can hear the sounds of the hospital in the background. Names being called over the PA system. A machine beeping. The clicking of a keyboard as someone updates a patient's chart.

"Mr. Stephenson?" the nurse asks.

"Yes, I'll be there soon," he replies, not needing her to make the official request. What else can he say? He has an obligation to fulfill.

Louis hangs up the phone, slides out of bed, and dresses. On his way to the stairs, he opens the door to the nursery, peeks inside.

Melissa is on the floor, her head rested on the tiny pillow her mother made last year. Her hands grip a matching yellow and green blanket that is much too small for her, holding it like the lovey it was meant to be. She stares at Louis, unblinking. The Winnie the Pooh nightlight brightens the room just enough to make the tears in her eyes sparkle like diamonds.

"I have to go," Louis whispers. Melissa does not approve of what he is doing and she does not respond. Before he closes the door, he says, "I love you."

Downstairs, Louis retrieves his black briefcase, which is stored next to the front door. The first time he received a call, he wasn't properly prepared and he forgot everything he needed in his nervous rush, in his fear of where he was headed and what he was expected to do, much like a first-time father fumbling to get his wife to the delivery room.

Returning home to try again made that first call even worse than he ever imagined it might be, but he learned from that mistake and will never repeat it.

Louis parks in a space labeled PHYSICIANS ONLY. He puts a laminated green pass on the dashboard and he sits there, his hands on the wheel, his eyes locked on the bushes next to the building but seeing nothing. He's not a doctor, but a nurse slipped him the pass when she heard why he was coming to the hospital so often. She cried when she spoke with him and he felt he had to accept her gift.

The nurse's name was Linda and she had been with Dr. Green when he brought Louis and Melissa the bad news three months earlier: their baby died in utero, so sorry.

Louis couldn't help but hate the man. He remembered the exact words of the doctor's attempt at comforting them: "Don't worry, you can always try again and have another baby."

Melissa had remained motionless in the hospital bed while Louis sat in the chair in the corner of the room and stared at the doctor in disbelief, as if everything around him were a bad dream. Nurse Linda took Melissa's hand when she realized Louis couldn't move to comfort his wife.

Then the doctor gave them more bad news: Melissa still needed to deliver their dead baby.

Melissa turned her head toward Dr. Green, the motion slow and deliberate, and quietly said, "Get out."

The doctor did as she asked, but Nurse Linda stayed, saying nothing when there was nothing to be said and answering the few questions they needed to ask.

After the delivery, Melissa remained quiet and distant, staring off into space. When the doctor asked if she'd like to hold the baby, she didn't respond. Louis thought this question was horrible, but he later learned it was standard procedure. Everyone reacts differently to discovering they've been harboring a corpse in their womb, his therapist explained, although those were Louis's words, not hers.

In the quiet delivery room, Nurse Linda cleaned the little baby boy, as if he were a real baby and not a lifeless husk. Then she offered the baby to Melissa again. This time Melissa nodded and the nurse carefully placed the tiny baby into her arms.

For the next half hour, Melissa cried and rocked their little boy while Louis sat in silence, wishing he could do something, anything. His wife cried, but their baby did not. His name was Kenneth.

Now Louis sits in his car and replays these events like he always does when he arrives at the hospital. The moon is full, lighting up the world with strange blue highlights. The city is an empty, lonely place this time of night.

His hand finds the key in the ignition. He could just leave, driving away before anyone knew he was even here, but what about the woman waiting for him inside the hospital? She needs him to do this thing that disgusts him. She's in her hour of need and she has called for him. He made a promise he must keep.

Louis gets out of the car, slams the door, and hurries inside, his black briefcase clutched tightly in his hand. He has to keep moving or he'll lose his nerve.

———————

A nurse leads Louis to the room, giving him the little bit of information he'll need. Her name is Heather and they've met before. She thinks why he is here tonight is ghoulish—it's a common reaction. Even Louis agrees.

He cannot get comfortable with the smell of the hospital, no matter how many times he visits. Nothing good has ever come from an encounter with that mix of bleach, disinfectant, and floor wax, but he always forgets how the smell will affect him until the moment he walks in and the emotions strike him in the stomach like a fist.

Nurse Heather knocks on the patient's door. Louis isn't surprised to see the room number. He's been here before.

"We're ready," a voice whispers from beyond the threshold.

"Mr. and Mrs. Jones, this is Mr. Stephenson," the nurse says, leading Louis into the room. Although this couple has never met him, he's become something of a celebrity at the hospital. "He's the gentleman you asked about."

Mrs. Jones is sitting in the bed and cradling her little girl in her arms.

Mr. Jones is sitting in the chair in the corner, his hands held tightly to his face.

"We can take as much time as you need," Louis says, following the script he created with his therapist's help to try to make this easier for everyone, including himself. It will make you more confident and put the woman at ease, she said. Louis does not feel confident. No one in this room is at ease.

Louis places the briefcase on the rolling cart by the door. Nurse Heather stands in the opposite corner of the room in case she is needed. This process doesn't always end well. People don't know how they'll react to what's about to happen, even though they asked for Louis by name.

"What's your little girl's name?" Louis asks while preparing his equipment.

"Annabelle," the mother replies, wiping her eyes.

Once he is ready, Louis just stands there, knowing what he has to do, but unable to move. An icy blade twists in his stomach. Mr. Jones looks up for the first time and Louis can see the anger in the man's bloodshot eyes. Is that rage meant for him? Or maybe for God? Louis has felt a lot of anger toward God this year.

"That's a pretty name," Nurse Heather says to fill the awkward silence. "Mr. Stephenson, are you ready?"

Louis nods and moves into position next to the bed, raising his camera and preparing to take the first and last family portraits of little Annabelle Jones and her mother.

To the unaware observer, the baby could merely be sleeping, but she will never open her eyes or coo or cry. She will never grow up and run the hundred-meter dash in gym class. She will never be asked to the prom. She will never have to make the tough decision of attending her first-choice college or the one her boyfriend has been accepted to instead. She will never be proposed to, she will never marry, she will never have babies of her own.

Little Annabelle's only destination is a tiny coffin the size of a shoebox.

Louis takes the first photo, then the next, and soon he's lost in his work.

Louis sits outside the hospital on a bench under a tree, watching the rising sun peek above the mountains to the east. The sky is angry and purple and beautiful with the light of a new day. The sun is millions of miles away and sometimes Louis wonders if the sunlight is disappointed when it arrives.

Louis tries to clear his head. He sees little Annabelle in her mother's arms, so very dead and so very small, and then he remembers the sight of Kenneth in his wife's arms. Every time he comes here to do this job, it's like Kenneth has died all over again. Kenneth, the little boy Louis never got a chance to know but who meant the world to him anyway.

He leans over and vomits. He wipes his mouth with his sleeve. He sits and he wonders what he's doing. Photographing dead babies only makes the void inside him bigger. The process does not make him feel remotely useful or helpful like his therapist suggested it would.

Louis is lost in his thoughts and he doesn't notice Nurse Linda approaching.

"What you're doing is wonderful, Mr. Stephenson," she says, stopping next to the bench.

Louis looks up. He thinks, for just a moment, that it's almost like she read his mind from across the parking lot.

"My wife and some of your coworkers don't agree."

"You're giving these families something special, Mr. Stephenson. They may not realize it today, but in six months, when the worst of the grief is over, they'll want to thank you. You've given them a memento more powerful than a stillborn birth certificate. You've given them proof that their love wasn't in vain. Don't you wish you had a photo of Kenneth?"

Louis nods and lowers his gaze, wishing her away. He has found it's easier to agree with people when he doesn't really know what to say. If he agrees, hopefully they'll leave him alone.

"Mr. Stephenson, you should go home and see Melissa. It's going to be a beautiful day."

Nurse Linda pats him on the shoulder and walks inside where she'll be working with all of the living babies today and tomorrow and the day after that.

Louis sits on the bench and watches people come and go. Eventually, he drives home to try to comfort his wife and convince her to go outside and sit in the sunlight with him, but as he goes through the motions, he can't help but wonder what Nurse Linda meant.

It may be a beautiful day in the world where she resides, the one where almost all of the babies survive, but he lives in a world where the babies always die.

It will never be a beautiful day for Louis, not as long as the phone keeps ringing at unexpected times and he keeps traveling to the hospital with his camera. Not as long as little Kenneth keeps dying again and again, every week, every month, every year for the rest of Louis's life.

He wants to ask what beauty can possibly be found in a world where the wonder of birth and the numbness of death are apparently the same thing, but he's afraid the answer might be none at all.

So he sits with his wife in silence because Kenneth is still dead and nothing has changed since yesterday and nothing is likely to change tomorrow.

The sun will rise, the sun will set, and there isn't anything they can do except wait for the phone to ring.

Story Notes

BRIAN JAMES FREEMAN

OR MOST OF YOU, this book is done. "The Last Beautiful Day" is where the fiction ends. All that follows are some of my thoughts on where these stories came from, insomuch as I actually have an answer to that question.

Many readers don't care for an author to pull back the curtain and share additional information at the conclusion of a story collection. That's a perfectly acceptable position to take, and if you're one of those readers, you can safely close the book now and know you're missing nothing.

But some readers *are* interested in story notes and this section exists for them. That said, stories *can* be spoiled if you dive into the notes first, so if you've arrived here before reading the rest of the book, please do kindly flip back to Bill Blatty's introduction without further ado. Thank you.

"RUNNING RAIN" was written when I was considerably younger and running *a lot*. Those days are long gone due to a degenerative disc in my back, which basically means it feels like someone is twisting a rusty pry bar into my spine throughout the day, gradually ratcheting up the pain with each passing hour. It is not particularly pleasant.

"Running Rain" arrived in two parts. In the fall of 2003, my wife and I had been married for a little over a year and we were living in a ground-level apartment in Forest Hill, Maryland, not far from my work. I was running like a demon back then, usually after sundown as I've always loved running at night, and the weather one particular evening was very much as described in the beginning of this story. For whatever reason, that memory stuck with me, even though nothing eventful happened.

Then, about six months later, the entire story just popped into my head from out of nowhere during another run. My short stories tend to arrive in a burst of unexpected inspiration and "Running Rain" arrived complete with the ending, which some readers loved and others didn't quite follow. (I've received more correspondence about this ending than any other story I've ever written.)

When I got home that night, I wrote the story as quickly as I could and I was really pleased with how it turned out. There's a rhythm to the language I enjoy, and even after all these years, I liked "Running Rain" enough to put it first in this collection. I tried to clarify the ending a bit, too.

"MAMA'S SLEEPING" is a previously unpublished story written in the spring of 2016. The inspiration was a news article I had read a few years earlier about a rent-a-furniture delivery person who discovered a young child and his dead mother in an apartment. Most of "Mama's Sleeping," from the opening lines to the nature of the ending, formed in my mind before I had even finished reading the article. I just didn't get around to putting it on paper for a while.

In real life, the delivery person was a good person who did the right thing for the child, but I tend to focus on the bad guys in this world, which I suspect feeds my muse a fairly unhealthy diet. "Mama's Sleeping" features the worst person I've ever written about, as far as I'm concerned, but hopefully the reader doesn't realize how bad he is until the end of the story. In real life, some of the most awful people seem perfectly okay until it's too late.

One other note: throughout the story there are hints about what's happening in the world outside, but I tried to keep them subtle enough that no one would really notice until the second read. I hope I was successful.

"**AN INSTANT ETERNITY**" might be my wife's favorite story of mine, and my favorite as well depending on the day and my mood, but it almost didn't make the cut for this collection. Not because my feelings for the story have changed over the years, but because deep down I know there's a novel wanting to grow out of this material.

I wrote the first draft of this story in college, more than sixteen years ago, and the novel is still only partially written, so here's the short story in the meantime.

The good news is, I'm writing the rest of the book as chapbook installments for my supporters on Patreon, which means I finally get to introduce readers to the untrustworthy pastor who offers his help in the old stone church down the road from the town, the abandoned amusement park kingdom of the ghoulish cult leader who calls himself The Blood King, and the people of the mountains who have been hiding from the rebels.

"**WHERE SUNLIGHT SLEEPS**" was inspired by a camping trip in the fall of 2008. Nothing particularly unpleasant happened to us that weekend, but a quick glimpse of a man walking hand-in-hand through the woods with his little boy resulted in this story. I'm sure that father and son had a wonderful weekend. I strongly doubt there was a murder in their shared past. Yet, thanks to a few seconds of watching them walk on a trail, I got this story, which I had a blast writing.

"**MARKING THE PASSAGE OF TIME**" was written early in my marriage in an apartment very much like the one in the story. I wish I could say the world has become a better place since then, but I'd hate to lie to you.

"**WALKING WITH THE GHOSTS OF PIER 13**" was written on June 12, 2002. Crazy that I know the date, right? But writing this story changed my approach to short fiction and without that the rest of this collection probably wouldn't exist.

Here's what happened: my soon-to-be bride and I went to Hershey Park for the day. Like many people, terrorism was a thought close at hand that year and something I saw got me wondering what would happen if gunmen seized the park. The entire story, from the opening line to closing line, was firmly planted in my brain between rides.

We spent the night at the home of my future in-laws and I wrote the story on their PC tucked away in the old garage turned family room. When I was done, I emailed the file to Richard Chizmar, who was in the process of hiring me to work at Cemetery Dance Publications, and he bought it the next day for the first *Shivers* volume. That turnaround time is insane for me. I usually don't let anything leave my desk without *many* rounds of rewrites and revisions. But like I said, this story changed my life.

"A Mother's Love" was born when someone asked me how far is too far to go to get someone you love the help they need. My own mother still hasn't read this one, but we'll see what she thinks when she does.

The entire story arc of "Pop-Pop" arrived like a tactical nuke while I was waiting in the drive-thru line for my breakfast sandwich at a fast food restaurant. The experience was like watching a short film inside my head: starting with the teenage twins and their mom standing in the living room, to the discovery in the attic, all the way to Gram-Gram's revelation at the end. Because I'm not a natural at writing, I messed up the execution on my first attempt and the story required a few dozen revisions to get right, but I love how the final draft came together.

"Answering the Call" is the third oldest story in this book (based on publication date, at least) and also one of my favorites. It was inspired by the memory of a family friend saving the family's answering machine tape (remember those?) because it had her recently deceased mother's outgoing message on it. She wanted to be able to hear her mom's voice again and that answering machine provided a way.

The cool thing about this story's publication history is it was the *second* story I submitted to Tom and Elizabeth Monteleone for

Borderlands 5. The first story wasn't working for them. I tried three or four drafts and it just wouldn't click.

But I wanted to sell a story to the *Borderlands* series, dammit, so in a fit of inspiration, I wrote "Answering the Call" instead and sent that. Tom and Elizabeth loved it and only asked for one change. The original title was "Answering the Call of the Dead" and, as they correctly pointed out, that title would have robbed the story of much of its power.

This story and "Walking With the Ghosts of Pier 13" represent the fewest number of drafts between being written and sold for any of the stories in this book. They're also two of the oldest stories in this book. I wonder what that means . . .

In the summer of 2000, I was home from my sophomore year of college and mowing the lawn when some guys drove by and threw a beer bottle at me. They missed; the story "THE FINAL LESSON" landed. Brian Keene bought this one for the old Horrorfind website, back when publishing fiction online was still a relatively new idea. The title then was "Bigger and Better," which I liked, but "The Final Lesson" fits the themes considerably better.

"LOVING ROGER" sparked the one face-to-face conversation I had with Richard Laymon. This was at Brian Keene's house while I was in college. I had no idea what to actually say to Dick, so I basically hid in the corner, like I usually do, and said nothing. Finally, I gathered the courage to speak with him, still unsure of what I should actually say, and I ended up talking about the first thing to pop into my head: a paper I had written for one of my journalism classes the previous semester.

The class was about writing feature news articles, but the final assignment was something kind of different. The professor told us to imagine a wife driving home with a surprise for her husband. We were to describe the drive and the surprise, using as many details as we could, "kind of like a short story."

I wrote "Loving Roger" based on the assignment prompt and I'm guessing it was unlike anything anyone else in the class came up with. I'm still not sure why I actually took the approach I did, given the subject matter and how old and conservative the professor was. The idea was just *there*, so I ran with it like I normally would when I had an idea for a story.

After I turned the paper in, it wasn't very long before I had second thoughts. Sure, my take on the topic was what came naturally to me, but had that *really* been a good idea for this particular class?

When I received my paper back, I immediately saw all of the red ink at the top of the first page and my heart dropped. Then I read what the professor had written:

"I don't understand what you've done here, but it's VERY creative. A+"

I passed the class.

So, not knowing what else to say, I told Richard Laymon this story there in Brian Keene's dining room and then I asked him: "Is that a good sign or a bad sign?"

He thought about it for a long moment and replied: "I think that's the *best* sign."

Everyone laughed, and I was relieved and thrilled to meet one of my heroes and not make too much of an ass of myself, even though in hindsight I have absolutely *no idea* what my question meant.

"AMONG US" would have appeared on a website I ran in 1999 and 2000 called Dueling Minds if I hadn't shut down the experiment before the next issue was due to be posted. The "webzine" featured work from some incredible authors and artists, and was a lot of fun to put together, but I simply ran out of time in my schedule to work on it.

Each issue featured four or five stories inspired by the same piece of artwork, giving readers the chance to glimpse how the imaginations of these different authors worked. (Later on, I'd use the same idea for an anthology called *Dueling Minds*, which was published in the Cemetery Dance Signature Series.)

I no longer have the artwork that served as the inspiration for "Among Us" but I clearly remember it involved a face inside a man's glowing chest. I think the story is fun, if pretty different from what I focus on these days.

Also, huge thanks go out to Allen K for giving this one a home in his *Inhuman* magazine, along with some great new artwork to boot.

"NOT WITHOUT REGRETS" started life as part of a novel and was published as a standalone chapbook by Cemetery Dance Publications in 2004 under the title "Pulled Into Darkness." Almost everything in the version of the story that appears in this collection is different, though. I slashed 4,000 words during the most recent edit and rewrite, changed the characters and their dynamics, and generally left nothing the same except for the overarching premise. But I like this approach better, so here we are.

The opening scenario in "WHAT THEY LEFT BEHIND" is fairly close to something that happened to me in real life. In the early 2000s, my father-in-law was moving his logistics business into an abandoned IBM office building. Not because his company was failing like the one in the story, but because business was booming and he needed more space. The only facility available that met his needs was this old office building, which required a ton of demolition work. We spent weeks gutting the offices and conference rooms to convert the structure into a proper warehouse, but before the demo work began, I gave myself a private tour of the abandoned hallways and offices, of course. It wasn't as creepy as the building in "What They Left Behind," but it certainly wasn't a place I'd want to spend the night.

"THE TEMPERAMENT OF AN ARTIST" is an extremely early story of mine, written in middle school and sent out on submission without any revisions because I was a young idiot back then who just couldn't wait to send out a new story to torture the editors I found in the *Novel & Short Story Writer's Market*. It ended up being the second story of mine to see print, published in a little paper zine in 1995 that doesn't even seem to have existed if you search the web for information now. I was surprised to like this story as much as I did when I opened the dreaded "old stuff" folder while considering the contents for this book. It's not great, but it's kind of fun, I think. Especially if you put yourself into the head of the wildly optimistic thirteen-year-old kid who wrote it while believing his work could set the world aflame.

"THE GORMAN GIG" is a rare story for me where the ending came first and I worked backwards, and I will freely admit that I was heavily inspired by an Ed Gorman short story I love. The ending of "The Gorman Gig" isn't exactly the same as Ed's story, but the general idea behind the twist sure is. I emailed Ed to ask if he'd mind me cribbing from his ending. He did not, which wasn't surprising given what a sweetheart he was, and I tipped my hat to him with the title. Ed's story, in case you haven't read it, is called "Beauty" and it's downright chilling.

"ONE WAY FLIGHT" is my nod to *The Twilight Zone*, which was an obsession of mine growing up. I'm not sure my dad and I ever missed one of those marathon runs of the show that appeared on certain holidays.

In September of 2012, Cemetery Dance Publications decided it would be a fine idea to publish thirteen Halloween stories as eBook Singles for Halloween the following month. Makes sense, right? I wrote "MONSTER NIGHT" for the occasion. I'm not one who has any original ideas for the black and orange holiday, but I tried my best to do something different.

"TOMORROW COULD BE EVEN BETTER" is another story that was originally written in college, but this one has never seen print anywhere. It's the story that almost made the cut (three times!) for *Borderlands 5*, but Tom and Elizabeth Monteleone didn't dig the ending of that version of the story. On my final attempt, I even tried a different ending that was actually worse than the original ending. They asked if I could try one more time, but I wrote "Answering the Call" instead and everyone went home happy.

This story lingered in my "Can I Fix This?" folder for many years after that and I thought about it often. One day, when I was thinking about nothing in particular, I finally realized who the mysterious customer had to be and everything fell into place. A few tweaks early in the story and then a brand new ending (everything in "Kathy's After Time") did the trick.

It's not the best story in this collection, but I like it as much for the way it turned out as for the struggle it was to write... and I'm glad it's finally finished.

Although "ONE MORE DAY" was first published in 2009, it was actually written many years before. I can't remember exactly when, probably when I was in college, but I do recall the moment the story sparked to life for me. I was looking into a mirror one night and I realized if I didn't blink for a while, my own face began to appear unfamiliar to me. Boom, like that, the story was off to the races.

"THE CHRISTMAS SPIRIT" was written in November 2016 and published for the holidays that same year. The idea of fascism taking over a country certainly isn't new territory for fiction (or non-fiction, unfortunately), but I wanted to hide that aspect of the story until as close to the end as possible to catch the reader off-guard. Some readers did not like the reveal very much at all. This one is definitely set in the same universe as "One More Day," which is why I've placed them together in this volume.

"SILENT ATTIC" and "DANNY DREAMS" are deleted chapters from an early draft of a novel called *The Suicide Diary*, which I wrote in a frenzy in January 2004. I'm not a novelist at heart and I think my experience with *The Suicide Diary* is what made me accept that truth once and for all.

In the years following that one-month writing whirlwind, I revised the book through several dozen drafts, trying the story from different angles and different approaches to make it hum, but it just never gelled in a way I liked.

Agents, though, absolutely loved the sales copy and pitch I wrote for the book. I queried 120 agents over the years and 63 of them asked for the manuscript. That's a stunningly high percentage, at least in my experience.

In the end, all but three of the agents passed on my strange little novel, yet somehow those three offers of representation arrived within days of each other. I ended up signing with one of the agents and she might have been even more excited about the book than I was.

I won't go into the sad history of what happened next, but *The Suicide Diary* hasn't seen print as of November 2017 when I'm writing this, so you can probably make some good guesses if you know the publishing business.

One hot August day in 2017, as my wife and I were herding the kids to the car after a visit with some extended family in Hanover, Pennsylvania, an ice-cream truck came rolling up the street with its music blaring. All of the children who lived in the neighborhood came pouring out of their houses to greet the ice cream man. "ICE COLD DAN THE ICE CREAM MAN" was born in that moment. A reader asked me if this story takes place in the same world as "Mama's Sleeping" and I think that is very likely indeed.

"LOSING EVERYTHING DEFINES YOU" was originally written for an anthology about family revenge stories. The book was never published, which is a shame because it had a beautiful cover painting by Alan M. Clark, if I recall correctly. I tried searching for the title of the anthology and Alan's name, though, and nothing came up, so either my memory is wrong or that happened on a slightly different Earth and I'm stuck with the false memory of it. This story was eventually published in *Shivers IV* as "Something to Be Said for the Waiting" way back in 2003, and even with many revisions over the years, I'm still not sure if the ending works the way I want, but that's the ending the story gave me, so here it is.

"AS SHE LAY THERE DYING" is another running story that came to me during a run, which probably isn't all that shocking. This time the run was on the campus of Shippensburg University when I was an undergraduate in the late 1990s, yet I never got around to writing the story until more than a decade later.

That's an eternity for a story to hang out in the back of my head, patiently waiting its turn, but I'm glad the time finally came to write this one. Not many readers catch the ending ahead of time, but when they do realize what the professor has done and why the story is concluding the way it is, they tend to get a jolt from that realization. I like that in a story.

Like "Running Rain," I do get questions from readers about this ending, but I decided not to revise the text of this one to make it one hundred percent clear-cut. I think the subtle nature of this particular story is important.

"HOW THE WIND LIES" was published in 2016 by Keith Minnion as a beautiful chapbook through his White Noise Press, but the first draft was written in college under the title "Isolation." This is a story where my first attempt didn't work out as well as I would have liked and I filed the story away for another day.

When Keith asked if I had anything he could publish, I thought of this one because I could immediately envision his artwork gracing it. I returned to work on the manuscript, found a few narrative elements that had been buried the first time around, and dragged them to the surface where they made all of the difference in the world. Time between drafts: approximately fifteen years.

"PERFECT LITTLE SNOWFLAKES" was originally written in the late 1990s and submitted to an anthology when I was in college. I was thrilled when the editors bought it. That anthology has not been published yet, but I really believe it might be someday. Hey, I'm an optimist at heart. That said, it was time to collect this story before too many more years passed.

"THE PLAGUE OF SADNESS" is a little slice of life piece and sometimes

I think it's the doorway into a novel I'd really like to write eventually, but who knows if that'll ever happen. Some readers don't quite get the point of the kettle on the stove at the end, but if you connect back to what the mother on the opening page did, the horror should become clear.

"THE LAST BEAUTIFUL DAY" is another story that was inspired by a real news story. Did you know that what Louis is called upon to do at the hospital is a real job? I didn't, but the moment I learned about it from a news article, this story demanded to be written. The idea lingered in the back of my head for years before I had a chance to write it down, yet it appears here almost word for word as I imagined it, which I think I've already mentioned is extremely rare for me.

As an aside, I didn't have kids when "The Last Beautiful Day" was written, but I do now, and one of them arrived via an extremely difficult and stressful pregnancy that seemed on the verge of ending badly at any moment. I'm extremely grateful for both my kids and their good health, but I worried every single day during the pregnancies that I had jinxed my family by writing this story.

Okay, now we've *really* reached the end of the book, I promise.

I hope William Peter Blatty was correct and some of these characters linger in your head or your heart after this volume is placed on your bookcase, traded in at your local used bookstore, or deleted from your e-reader.

Until next time, stay safe and watch out for your own ghosts hiding deep inside of you . . . You never know where they might want to take you.

Special Thanks For Patreon Supporters

The following people generously supported my Patreon page on October 1, 2017 and my deepest thanks goes out to them:

Vicki Liebowitz, K. Edwin Fritz, John Fahey, Roxane McLarnan Geggie, Lori Adams, Paula Francisco, Janice Hill, Lori Reynolds, Ron Reese, Matt Schwartz, Adam Harding-Jones, Jason Canny, Elena DeGarmo, Jason Sechrest, Doreen Acton, Joseph Cameli, Aaron Cohen, Anna DeHennis, Lisa A Toombs, Kris van der Sande, James Coniglio, Gary St. Clair Jr, Pamela Koch, Julie Hight Sullivan, Deanna Kubisty, Edward Roads, Pamela A. Abel, Rich DeMars, Stephen Bamberg, Kerry McKenna, David Kipp, Keejia M Houchin, Ann Waters, Rockie Suttle, William King, David Ray, Rose Milligan, Hunter Shea, Kim Meier-Carroll, Brian Keene, Veronica Ukas, Pamela Taylor, Darren Heil, Sue Wilson, Robert Mingee, Shannan Ross, David McClung, Sean Strange, Michael Fowler, Joel McCandless, Robin Trischmann, Paul Fry, Ross W Davidson, Brian Freeman, Patrick Bishop, Maegan Heil, Tami Kietzmann, Philip Wickstrand, Debra Torma, Daniel Zacharski, Scott W. Briggs, Thom Millman, Bill Standwill, Dan Newman, Harold Dean Cook, Ron Weekes, Twikie Simms, Alan Caldwell, Russell King, John Questore, Susan Gray, David Greenlaw, Louis Toth, Steven McDonald, Ronda Pennington, Bill Swaim, Richard Platt, Michael

Anderson, Todd Nesbitt, Michael John Pawly, Mary Grace Panebianco, Kevin F Wilson, Wanda Weldon, Gary Phillips, Roger Terry, Amy McDermott, David Pagan, Robert S. Righetti, Michael Sauers, Martin Garcia, Brian Nicola, Donald Shelton, Anderson Yee, Susan Jo Darling, Todd Houts, Kristy Lytle, Brandon Cockrell.

If you're new to my work and would like to learn more about the rewards I'm creating for my readers, please visit this page:

https://www.patreon.com/BrianJamesFreeman